MEGAN ALBANY is a proud First Nations woman of Kamilaroi and European heritage who has worked as an editor, scriptwriter, songwriter/composer and journalist. She has written for publications including *The Guardian* (UK), *Metro* (Ireland), *Irish Echo* and the *Koori Mail*. She was both a writer and editor for leading Indigenous magazine *Deadly Vibe*; the founding editor of *InVibe* magazine for Indigenous youth in custody; and was a researcher for *Can It Hurt Less?*, an SBS documentary into Australia's juvenile justice system. For five years she was part of the scriptwriting team for the Deadly Awards (the Deadlys), the National Aboriginal and Torres Strait Islander Music, Sport, Arts and Community Awards, which screened on SBS TV, and she was one of the founding concept developers for the NITV health programs *Living Strong* and *Move It Mob Style*.

Megan has a Master's in Creative Writing, has taught creative writing as part of the Disadvantaged Schools Program and has taught literacy on Pitjantjatjaran lands. *The Very Last List of Vivian Walker*, her first novel, was shortlisted for The Banjo Prize in 2020 and highly commended in the Australian Society of Authors 2020 Award Mentorship Program.

Megan lives with her thirteen-year-old son, her husband and their moodle in the Northern Rivers of NSW. Connect with her on Instagram @meganalbanywriter, on Twitter @Megan_Albany or on Facebook @meganalbanywriter, and learn more on her website, meganalbany.com, where you can find an original soundtrack Megan specially produced for *The Very Last List of Vivian Walker*.

The Very Last List of Vivian Walker

MEGAN ALBANY

The Very Last List of Vivian Walker

hachette
AUSTRALIA

Published in Australia and New Zealand in 2022
by Hachette Australia
(an imprint of Hachette Australia Pty Limited)
Gadigal Country, Level 17, 207 Kent Street, Sydney, NSW 2000
www.hachette.com.au

Hachette Australia acknowledges and pays our respects to the past, present and
future Traditional Owners and Custodians of Country throughout Australia
and recognises the continuation of cultural, spiritual and educational practices
of Aboriginal and Torres Strait Islander peoples. Our head office is located on
the lands of the Gadigal people of the Eora Nation.

A catalogue record for this
book is available from the
National Library of Australia

ISBN: 978 0 7336 4695 9 (paperback)

Cover design by Christabella Designs
Cover illustration (sneakers) by Ben Sanders; cover images courtesy of Stocksy and Shutterstock
Author photograph by Raffaella Dice
Typeset in 12.6/19 pt Dante MT Pro by Bookhouse
Printed and bound in Australia by McPherson's Printing Group

The paper this book is printed on is certified against the
Forest Stewardship Council® Standards. McPherson's Printing
Group holds FSC® chain of custody certification SA-COC-005379.
FSC® promotes environmentally responsible, socially beneficial
and economically viable management of the world's forests.

This book was conceived and written on Bundjalung Country. I acknowledge the Traditional Custodians on whose land I live, work and learn. I am proud of the pivotal role all First Nations people continue to play in our community as we continue to strive for excellence and equity. I pay respect to our Elders, past, present and emerging. Sovereignty was never ceded; Australia always was and always will be Aboriginal and Torres Strait Islander Land.

Dedicated to the many wonderful souls I have been privileged to travel with. Even though you have moved on, I know you didn't go very far as I feel you all every day.

To Rebecka Darling-Darren (nee Delforce) for showing me how to look at death differently and being hilarious to the end. To Daz for following Beck to the end of the earth. To Gavin Jones, my brother always, for being the deadliest of all and welcoming me back to Country. To Manfred, my favourite father-in-law, for loving me and giving me Marc. To Uncle Paddy for your dignity and hatred of puns. To Pling for how joyfully you lived and for photographing every house we ever lived in – big job! To Herbie for the love, respect, music and fashion advice. To Steve for everyone you ever stood up for, including your irrepressible Ulrike. To Lisa for being part of our family and travelling the road from Westfield Liverpool to Italy to Byron. To Kerrie for the music and the best answering machine message ever. To Glen for hero-worshipping Marc as much as I do. To Tania for the laugh I still hear to this day. To Poppa for your strength. To Nanna for your gentleness. To Gran for your pikelets!

Prologue

At first sight, some people think I look pregnant until they notice my stylish grey skin, then they look away. I am pregnant with death. The tumours are bloating my stomach but there's still so much to get done, and only a couple of months left to do it all. Unfinished business. I need to write a list.

<u>MY LIST</u>
- Clean the fridge
- Declutter the playroom
- Fill my script
- Get my tax up to date
- Choose songs for my funeral
- Restore Poppa's lowboy
- Clean out my wardrobe
- Sand the French doors into the bedroom

- Amend my will
- Write a letter to my son
- Delete my Tinder profile
- Give my husband a list

My husband, Clinton, is used to my lists. I make lists, prioritise lists, redo lists, fish lists out of pant pockets before washing them, follow up on lists and inspect the work once it has been done. But, out of the blue, Clint has not only written a list for himself, but he has also made me a list. What is he thinking? He must be emboldened by the fact I am dying. He thinks I am too weak to kill him. Men do not write lists for their wives. Surely, he knows this. I tell my girlfriends. Their mouths drop open and, for once, they cannot speak. This is akin to marital suicide. But I guess Clint figures our marriage is dead when I am, so he has nothing to lose.

CLINT'S LIST
- Have sex – which he has crossed out to read: Make love
- Go for long walks in the countryside
- Lie in each other's arms

CLINT'S LIST FOR ME
- Finish your novel
- Play with your son
- Take a hot bath
- Recuperate

Basically all the things I don't have time for because I am too busy with my everyday list. His utopian version will have to wait.

'Mum, Mum, can you play with me yet?' My eight-year-old son, Ethan, interrupts my train of thought, so I stop mid-synapse.

'Just a moment honey, I am working on my list.'

He rolls his eyes. He knows all about my lists.

Now that I've got cancer, I know I should be letting go and being in the moment with him, but seriously, what mother has got time to spend with their kids? I realise if Ethan is going to have a hope in hell of booking into any of my few remaining time-slots in the countdown to D-day, he had better have a list of his own. Turns out his list is simple.

ETHAN'S LIST
- Play handball with Mum
- Build a robot
- Have a sleepover

I optimistically decide to add to his list, even though my experience to date gives no indication my son will actually do these jobs:

- Tidy his room
- Cook us all dinner

CHAPTER 1

My list: Clean the fridge

When you open the door of our fridge, you get a history lesson. There are at least five meals my son wanted to 'save for later' that remain untouched and are now inedible. There are six or seven bottles of vitamins and herbal cures one of us started to take but never finished. The unspoken rule with these concoctions is if they are too expensive to throw away we just leave them in situ until they accidentally reach their expiry date. Only then can we justify binning the evidence of our failure to achieve yet another new year's health resolution. These days, I no longer feel guilty when I look at them. Four weeks ago, the doctors told me I was in an advanced stage of melanoma and gave me a three-month prognosis. I'm incurable.

Being incurable is quite a relief. I don't even have to pretend I am trying to get better. I can eat whatever I like, use toxic skin-care products, breathe polluted air – after all, what's it going to do, give me cancer? If I were to add up all the time and money I have spent on what I now realise are totally useless organic products over the years, I reckon I could have finished two university degrees and bought a sportscar. From here on in, I am putting myself on a liver-clogging diet.

I am staring aimlessly at the inside of the fridge, wondering where on earth to start, when Ethan comes in. Despite being eight, he recently rediscovered the joys and mess-making potential of playing in the sandpit. The fine sand is stuck between his toes, but it will only stay stuck until he reaches the house, then somehow, magically, it will unstick itself all over the floor. It generally waits until he reaches the lounge room before it dislodges on the rug. It's not what I would call a rug anymore: it's more of a rug-pit. When Ethan's friends visit, I should really just tell them to stay inside and play on the rug as I am sure there is more sand in here than in the actual sandpit.

I find my list and add – 'Clean the rug', then cross it out and write, 'Throw the rug out'.

I like the rug. I used to love the rug, but now it's one more thing I look at that makes me feel bad. There are still so many jobs to do. Aren't I meant to just be contemplating life, its meaning and everything? Mums don't die in peace apparently.

Of course, Clint and Ethan were amazing when they first heard about the cancer. I wasn't allowed to lift a finger for at least a week. But now, it's dragging on and, even though I do look like I'm dying, none of us really believe it. It's kind of surreal. We're all dying anyway, but, like the vitamins, I have a use-by date that we're trying to pretend is not there. We're also trying to pretend

I have lived some sort of incredible life, like I was supposed to, so we can make sense of why I was on the planet in the first place.

For Ethan, having a dying mother is the new normal. At first he let me milk my cancer for all I could get; now I'm lucky if he makes me a cup of tea.

I look at my gorgeous boy standing there caked in sand, stomping his sandy feet all over the rug, and can't believe I am going to leave him behind.

'For god's sake, Ethan, look at all the sand you've brought in,' I blurt out, defaulting to nagging mother mode. 'How many times do I have to tell you to wash your feet before you drag the whole of the outside in?'

He looks up at me, smiles, grabs some grapes, dropping a few on the floor, says, 'Sorry, Mum,' then skips out the door, scattering sand and grapes as he goes.

He seems unaffected by it all. Except at night. When it's dark, we both want to hold on to each other. He sleeps with me a lot these days, but last night I was so exhausted I banished him to his room. In the middle of the night, I heard him crying.

'Mama, Mama.'

It takes me longer these days to get out of bed and Clint, as usual, slept through the whole thing. When I reached Ethan's bed, he was still crying but by then it was in his sleep. I stroked his forehead and kissed his cheeks and finally he took a shuddering post-sob breath in, then seemed to settle. I put my forehead against his. His breath still smells like it did when he was a baby. I breathed it in; there is nothing more precious than this. When morning came, we went back to yelling at each other while I tried to hold back the king tide of mess that seems to be taking over our lives as I get sicker and less capable of being a supermum.

Now back to the fridge. When Clint and I were first married, it was always clean. We ate out a lot. The fridge contained the barest of essentials. Coffee, wine, chocolate, milk, expensive fruit that families can't afford like mangoes and raspberries, and leftovers from restaurant meals. Back then, nothing stuck to the shelves and nothing grew in the back in a bowl. There were no hardened, inexplicable objects that had gone beyond rotting to petrified. Nine years ago, cleaning the fridge just involved eating the chocolate.

Last week Clint did the shopping and 'helpfully' unpacked everything into the fridge, dumping new fruit and veg on top of last week's unused produce. He seems unaware that the compost bin and the fridge's vegetable tray are not one and the same. He thinks we bought the as yet uninvented new model with the in-fridge composting system.

When you are dying this shouldn't matter. You should savour every moment and not care about the trivial things in life. You should be able to focus on all the wonderful eccentricities of the people you love, stop being a control freak and be in awe and gratitude for every precious second you have together. But dying happens moment by moment, so there is still plenty of time to be irritated, provoked, frustrated, angry, resentful and really, really annoyed by the people who will miss you most when you are dead and gone.

The fridge door beeps at me. I have been holding it open and staring at it for too long. I am making it uncomfortable. I shut the door. Where are the gloves? I had a brand-new packet of them.

4

I check in the cupboard under the sink but rummaging makes my back sore, so I stand up and look out the window. My son and his friend Tyson are pretending to be roosters scratching in the sand with beautiful rooster combs on their heads. My gloves. I notice they have also destroyed the pile of neatly raked together clippings from the fresh-cut grass. Clint promised to put that in the green bin last night, just like he promised to bring in the washing that's been on the line for three days.

He's lucky he's at work today as I have already started fantasising about a food fight. Not a fun romantic one like when we were young, but one which involves me screaming like a banshee while holding up every piece of slimy vegetable for Clint to inspect before slapping them onto his bare scalp.

He used to have such beautiful hair. It was longer than mine and took hours to groom. It did look incredibly handsome, but I have to admit part of me was happy when it all fell out. I thought when he went bald he would lose the obsession with his own head, but he only got worse. He could see every blemish and freckle. Every time he went out in the sun, he put way too much effort into making sure his head tanned evenly. He even found products for his scalp. I'm not sure if they were supposed to make his head reflective or somehow make it water repellent. Either way he was determined to do whatever it took to make sure his bald scalp looked its best.

I am no closer to having a sparkling fridge so I grab a garbage bag and Clint's *Star Wars* cap he left lying on the kitchen bench, and open the fridge door. I use his new cap like a snowplough to push the contents of each shelf holus-bolus into the garbage bag. Tupperware, good fruit, dissolved vegetables, new leftovers, fossilised dinners, the lot. It feels amazingly satisfying not to care. I empty the entire contents of the fridge and freezer into the extra-strength bag and take it straight outside to the bin. I come back inside and open the fridge and freezer door. I take a deep breath in. The cold air opens my lungs like I am standing on a mountain in Austria. As I stare lovingly at the achingly beautiful sight of an empty cooler I want to sing about the hills being alive as if I am Maria in *The Sound of Music*. I have exceeded myself. I can tick 'Clean the fridge' off the list and give myself bonus points for also having cleaned the freezer.

Only then do I hear the key turn in the front door. Clint must be home early from his job buying toilet paper. He assures me the motel allows him to procure far more impressive items, which is apparently why his official title is Purchasing Officer as opposed to the less flattering moniker I prefer. He walks into the kitchen with his *I did something right* smile and a bunch of flowers.

'Let's go out for dinner,' he says, pulling me close.

'Great idea,' I answer enthusiastically, reaching behind me with one arm to push his now putrid *Star Wars* cap out of sight.

I know he's trying to work on the first thing on his list, but I am happy to steer him away from the kitchen for now.

'Look out the window,' I say, pointing my head in the direction of the little roosters. They have just finished covering themselves in grass clippings. I can see the beginning of a rash starting on Tyson's back.

'Oh, no.'

Before I have time to think I am running out the back via the medicine cupboard. Tyson, it appears, is allergic to grass.

I grab the antihistamines from the first-aid kit and race towards the sandpit. Luckily it is next to the pool, and despite my diminishing strength, I manage to pick Tyson up under one arm and dump him straight into the pool.

'Duck your head under,' I yell. I should have more accurately said, 'Rooster your head under,' but the undercurrent of humour is lost as I watch him start to welt.

I grab a pill from the packet and administer it to Tyson using pool water I have scooped up with a snorkel. By this time, Clint has finally clued on to the fact something is wrong and has strolled out to us. He is so relaxed. I used to love that about him. But now it drives me crazy. How on earth is he going to cope in an emergency without me?

I have netball reflexes. When Ethan was young, I could catch him a split second before his head hit the cement, or at least put a foot out to buffer his fall. Years of playing goal defence as a teenager had given me the ability to see things not only happening but about to happen. The nettie had also given me shocking knees, which hadn't been helped any by the Catholic Church's unpadded kneelers I'd used religiously every Sunday.

Tyson is now splashing about in the pool as if nothing happened. The pool is full of grass clippings, and the rubber glove is about to make its way into our filter system, so my arm automatically ricochets out to get it before it clogs up the newly repaired valve.

Clint seems to be moving in slow motion despite my rapid-fire instructions, 'Can you grab a towel and the calamine and my phone, so I can call Tyson's mum to let her know what's going on?'

I can talk faster than speed typists can type. Clint responds slower than a three-toed sloth. Luckily the antihistamine appears to be working, and Tyson's welts are visibly reducing. I feel myself breathe for the first time in about ten minutes. Killing your own child is one thing, but killing someone else's, well, that's just rude.

•

After Tyson's mum arrives, rescues her child, thanks me for the first aid and apologises for not letting me know about his grass sensitivity, I collapse exhausted onto the lawn. I have forgotten how quickly I get tired these days. I look down at my chest; it is rising and falling in quick little pants like a puppy on a hot day. There is no room in my belly for long, relaxing inhales, it is otherwise occupied – my metastasised tumours are not good at sharing their space. Sometimes I imagine a baby in my womb. I rub my hand proudly over my swollen belly, longing for it to kick, so I know there is life inside. The illusion doesn't last for more than a second as my fingers discover new random lumps disrupting the terrain. My skin isn't smooth and tight, and I don't exactly have that pregnant glow about me, but for a few seconds it takes me back to how soft and womanly I'd felt when Ethan was inside me, safe and secure.

Before I was pregnant, I always felt more masculine than feminine. Not that I looked in any way masculine, I was just, let's face it, a bit bossy. Clint was the first person who didn't want to squash the bossiness out of me, but even he didn't *really* love me until I was carrying his child. While I was expecting he looked at me differently and took on a kind of protective air. I'd missed that after Ethan was born.

But now, here's that look, back again. Every so often, I catch him out of the corner of my eye staring at me mistily. When I was pregnant, my hormones helped me reciprocate his mushiness; now they just bring out the lunatic in me. I should be feeling loving towards him but my intolerance for his failings is growing with my tumours, which only serves to make me feel guilty and angry.

Lying out in our back garden behind our house on the hill, I look across to the little portable building that was supposed to be my meditation room. It faces the town in the valley below. I call it my little red caboose. It was meant to be the place I would go to each morning to journey into gratitude before spreading peace and love throughout my home upon my return. At least that's what I convinced myself I would use it for when I bought it on impulse from eBay. Instead, it has become yet another guilt-inducing purchase, having only ever been used once, when I was desperate for two minutes to myself. Even then, I failed to meditate, preferring to read trashy magazines about people living lives I was never destined for. But now, when I know I should be making the most of every moment I have left to spend with my family, I want to run into my caboose and close the door tightly on my husband, my child and my list. Nothingness is calling me. I should be scared. Instead, I am almost looking forward to the freedom of having nothing left to do and knowing 'the answer' before anyone else does.

I don't want to leave my family, but sitting in my caboose, I feel myself rest in peace.

CHAPTER 2

Clint's list: ~~Have sex~~ Make love

It's our first date in months. Ethan is at home with my mother, Isabelle, who, according to Vivian, has one purpose and one purpose only: babysitting. Mum is no doubt brainwashing our son and reprogramming him with her preferred values as we speak.

The waitress takes a deep breath and I look up at her apologetically. These days I find it hard to make decisions. I can feel Viv getting frustrated next to me. She rolls her eyes at the waitress and tells her to come back in a minute.

We came to this restaurant in town on our first date ten years ago. Back then, Viv thought I was funny and good-looking. Now I just piss her off. It's been that way since Ethan was born. It started with him not sleeping through the night, and her irritation grew little by little. The less he slept, the less I could do right. These days she only has to look at me to get fired up. I can't do anything properly, and now she's dying.

I was meant to be her rescuer and carry her off on a white horse to somewhere we'd live happily ever after. She had so many walls up when we first met, and I slashed through them like they were the thorns surrounding Rapunzel's castle, but somewhere along the way I must have cut into her. I thought I was healing her wounds, but I'm worried I might have been responsible for them. I can't escape the feeling I am the cause of what's been eating her up inside. I knew she didn't love me the way she thought she was supposed to love someone. It wasn't like the movies. She was always complaining the house was a mess and that she wasn't the kind of mother she'd wanted to be, and then I lost my hair. Viv had been in love with me when I had hair. She'd run her fingers through it at night and stare into my eyes. Now there is no hair, no stares and no love. I want to remind her of what we once had. But everything I try seems to agitate her more.

The waitress has returned, and I still haven't read a word on the menu.

'What are you having, honey?' I ask.

'Duck,' she says curtly, 'I am having the duck.'

I know I should order something different as she likes to share meals; instead, I just say, 'Great, I'll have the same please.'

When the waitress walks away, Viv gives me that look. It's not indifference, it's not frustration, she just hates everything about me right now. If we weren't in a public place, I would be bracing myself for the onslaught. Instead, she tightens her mouth, gets out her phone and puts her headphones into her ears. I know she is listening to Tony Robbins. He will calm her down and stop her wanting to blame me for everything that's ever gone wrong in her life. It usually takes about fifteen minutes. She wishes she was married to him instead of me, every woman does, but I can't hate him because he saves my skin every time.

I look out the window while I wait for her anger to pass. Outside, rain is washing away the day, the dirt and the dust. I feel tears well up in my eyes. That happens a lot these days. That's why I got a table by the window. I look away, so no one can see me. A woman is crossing the road with a trolley. She runs towards the awning outside the restaurant to get out of the rain. She starts to squeeze the rain out of her hair but pauses when she sees the tears running down my face, and my wife's still hardened expression. She smiles at me, a mixture of pity and embarrassment. There is no attraction there. Women don't look at me like that anymore. I am middle-aged, bald and invisible. All they see is a boss, a door opener, or a dad at a P&C meeting.

I've become ordinary. My guitar is in the closet. My motorbike is somewhere in the back of the garage, inaccessible behind all the things we've accumulated in our ten years together. Before we were married, when we were child-free, we weren't each other's ball and chain, but now we're both tied down and too exhausted to pull the weight anywhere, so we just stay put. We'd grown used to the indifference, the lack of lust and the quiet desperation until Viv got her diagnosis. Now it's all meant to change, but it's just getting worse, and I know I'm not helping matters.

I glance away from the woman and see Viv's mouth softening. She's always had the most beautiful mouth, even when she's angry. I quickly look back out the window as I remember I haven't wiped my tears away. She mostly hates it when I cry. She says she doesn't have time for that luxury. The woman is still there outside, looking in at me. I realise she is homeless and possibly a little mad. Now she's trying to say something through the glass.

Oh shit, I think, *she's asking for money.*

I hate these moments where you're torn between guilt and a sense of righteousness. You don't want to give someone money to spend on alcohol or drugs, but I guess if I lived on the streets, I would turn to the bottle. I mean, shit, I'm not even homeless and I could happily use a drink for comfort. Then I realise her hand isn't out for money. She is holding something and gesturing for me to come out and get it.

Great, my wife will love this, I think to myself.

But I can't ignore this woman. Something about her eyes is compelling me.

I look across at Viv; she's in her own world, hanging out with Tony who is once again coming up trumps. I kiss her on the forehead as I get up from the table. She will think I am going to the bathroom.

I head to the door and, behind Viv's head, I gesture to the woman. She walks away from the window, pushing her trolley in front of her. Outside the restaurant, the cold air hits my face, and I take a sharp breath in. I hadn't noticed I'd been holding my breath. I do that a lot. I inhale a mix of patchouli, unwashed dread-locks and a slight undercurrent of urine. But there is no smell of alcohol. The woman smiles at me. She has remarkably good teeth. She pushes something cold and hard into the palm of my hand.

'Rose quartz,' she says. 'Pink is love energy and heals a broken heart.'

She fishes around in a pile of rocks in the trolley and pulls out a black stone.

'Black onyx for your wife. It will help.'

I look down at the rocks and then pull out my wallet.

'No, no. These are a gift. I don't need money, everything I need is provided by the universe.' She looks up at the sky as it continues to bucket down rain.

'You're drenched,' I say.

She laughs and walks out onto the road. Ignoring the oncoming cars, she starts singing loudly in the rain before running back under the awning. Her face is lit up with joy. *She's mad*, I think to myself, *only crazy people are that happy*.

'Thanks for the rocks,' I mumble, slipping them into my pocket.

'Crystals,' she corrects me. 'Healing crystals.'

'Yeah, thanks,' I say and walk back inside.

Viv hasn't noticed I've been gone and now I actually *do* need to go to the bathroom, so I make a detour.

'Are you all right?' she asks when I finally return to the table. I've been gone for much longer than my usual bathroom break. When you have been together as long as we have, you start to be able to time each other's ablutions. That's what happens with romance over the years. You get to know each other down to the un-finest detail.

'Bit of a funny tummy,' I reply. She nods, satisfied with the answer but unsatisfied with what she has just visualised. We see each other through domesticated, raw lenses and, more often than not, don't like what we see.

The waitress returns with our two ducks.

'I wonder if they were related?' I say out loud.

'Who?' asks Viv.

'The ducks,' I answer.

She shakes her head. Our romantic night is off to a flying start.

This is one of those restaurants where they rearrange the duck to actually look like a duck. I prefer my meat to be anonymous lumps. I lean over the plate and sniff it suspiciously. My wife hates it when I do this. She says I look like a wild animal, and not in a good way. It's something I've done ever since my dad shouted me food poisoning, courtesy of a dodgy rider at one of his unpaid gigs. Viv rolls her eyes but says nothing. She is great at saying nothing, but I am not so good at interpreting what her silence means.

I look over her shoulder, trying to avoid her gaze, which is not what I would call the look of love, but then my luck changes. In the corner of the room, an overweight man with a dishevelled shirt is dining alone. Well, not exactly dining, he is shovelling his main meal in with a dessert spoon and chewing loudly with his mouth open. As he chews, he continues to try to push even more food in, despite it being obvious there is no more room left in his gob. What doesn't fit is spilling out the sides of his mouth and back onto his plate. Disgusting and perfect!

I lean over and whisper conspiratorially into Viv's ear, 'Pig at a trough, over your right shoulder.' She hardly eats these days and has been distractedly pushing her meal around her plate, but now she stops and puts down her fork. She loves this game and 'accidentally' drops her spoon onto the floor. When she picks it up, she turns to look at him. She sits back up and leans in towards me. It is the closest we have been for months.

I feel her hot breath on my ear as she whispers, 'I wonder why he's dining alone?' She raises one eyebrow, relaxes back into her chair and starts to giggle like a little girl who knows she should be behaving.

I haven't heard her laugh for weeks and that, combined with her closeness, starts to make my jeans feel one size too small.

She takes off her shoe and rubs my leg under the table. It's been so long since we've even pecked each other on the cheek, let alone touched. She is now scanning the room, looking for our next target.

'Feral Lisa by the door,' she whispers.

I pretend to cough so I can turn inconspicuously away from the table in the direction of Viv's gaze. It's the woman with the crystals. The maître d' spots her at the same time and starts officiously heading towards her.

What the hell is she doing in here? I think to myself as I watch her scanning the restaurant for me.

A waiter reaches her ahead of the maître d' and bars her from entering any further. I can see her arguing with him and then notice she is showing him something in her hand. *Oh no.* It's my phone; I must have dropped it outside.

'I wonder if she has a booking.' Viv laughs. I try to laugh along.

'Doesn't look like it,' I say, hating myself the minute the words come out of my mouth.

The maître d' and the waiter are starting to manhandle her towards the door. I want to stand up for her, but I am still sitting.

She takes one more desperate look over her shoulder and, as they jostle her outside, she sees me. I try not to meet her eyes, but she notices the expression on my face. She looks down at her hand then deftly drops the phone into a pot plant next to the front door, giving me a quiet smile. She walks back out into the rain.

Viv flicks her hair out of her face and looks at me, her eyes sparkling for the first time in months. I squeeze her hand and call for the dessert menu.

CHAPTER 3

Ethan's list: Play handball

I am watching the steam rise from my cup of tea. There is a chip on the mug, but I can't throw it out. It was a gift from my colleagues when I finished work to start my death journey. It is decorated with daisies with a black trim around them. They obviously didn't put too much thought into the fact I would soon be pushing up the same flowers adorning my mug. Or perhaps they did. People are always weird around death. There are a few camps they fall into: the ones who change the subject, the ones who look at you with pity, the ones who try to talk to you about God and, worst of all, the ones who are really into it. They're the worst type, they are not scared of death at all because they are 'spiritual'. They call it a transition and want to celebrate your life rather than bawl their eyes out at your funeral.

I personally want everyone to be completely and utterly devastated when I go. I've even contemplated hiring wailers just to enhance the sense of the horrendous loss of me. I will be no longer, and while it hasn't made me spiritual, it has made me incredibly mindful of everything, even how cute my son can look when I catch him with his finger up his nose mid-pick. When he notices me watching, he quickly pulls the offending digit out and wipes it on his shirt. I smile at him, and he grins with that guilty 'but I know you adore me, Mama' look only he can get away with.

'Are you finished your cuppa yet?' he asks for the tenth time.

'Yes, all right,' I say, skolling the last mouthful. 'I'm done.'

I owe him about six hundred games of handball. It is his currency, and I take full advantage of it whenever I need to bribe him to do something. I bribe him a lot. Last week at a playdate, a friend's son told us that mothers shouldn't bribe their children. His mother and I had looked at each other in horror. If we didn't have bribes and we could no longer dish out the threat of corporal punishment, what on earth were we left with?

These days playing handball hurts and I want to avoid looking in pain around my son as much as possible. So this morning, in preparation for the big handball cash-in I knew was coming, I upped my morphine. I love pain meds, and I love my palliative care nurse for telling me that, at this stage of life, every drug is a good drug. Since I got my diagnosis I've had more drugs than Janis Joplin at Woodstock. Prior to that, I'd been a drug virgin.

Like most things in my life, I like to blame my mother for that. After all, thanks to her many ongoing issues, she brought us up as if we were part of a fundamentalist religious sect that didn't allow the use of any western medicine at all. If we had a fever, we were put in a cold bath; if we caught a cold from being left in a cold bath for hours, she gave us garlic and lemon juice; if we broke our arm well, luckily that never happened as I am sure she would have just given us a sprig of comfrey and hoped for the best. I'm not sure she even believed in these remedies or if she was just too poor to go to the chemist. Her habit of scattering piles of food scraps outside because she couldn't be bothered walking to the garbage bin meant there was always plenty of random plants sprouting up to choose from. Even if she'd been rich or hadn't been an accidental early adopter of composting, she probably still wouldn't have given us any drugs, as she was highly suspicious of institutions, especially those involving the medical profession.

When I left home, I rebelled against much of my upbringing, but hadn't been able to shake off all her influences, so I'd avoided doctors and pharmaceuticals like the plague. Obviously, that didn't really work out for me, as apparently if the doctor had picked up on the melanoma earlier it wouldn't have metastasised and they might have been able to do more than just help me live terminally ever after.

At first, I put the headaches down to detoxing, and my increasingly agonising back to having fallen off my on-again-off-again yoga wagon. But when the pain finally got too much, I went to a local masseuse, who took one look at me and sent me straight to the doctor's, where I was introduced to the joy of painkillers and began my love affair with morphine. Since my diagnosis, I have been in less pain than I've been in for months. I love that now I am dying, suffering is out of the question and I don't have to worry about the long-term side-effects of any drug I binge on. I up my meds whenever I can, and revel in whatever relief I can get.

Not that the drugs have left me totally pain free, but they do allow me to play handball with my son without focusing on anything other than my overwhelming desire to win at all costs.

We have, of course, slightly altered the rules to make it easier for me. We play in the garage with the roller door closed so the ball never goes too far. We play half-court and have a special rule: no low balls, nothing below my knees, as bending over is too painful even with the drugs. This has the advantage of severely handicapping my son, who has made a recess career out of getting down and dirty in the handball stakes by returning the ball as low to the ground as possible. When we first instigated this rule, Ethan had complained bitterly about how unfair it was. I resisted the 'You think that's unfair, try having cancer' retort, as tempting as it was. I generally manage to avoid the C-word with Ethan, but use it to my full advantage when it comes to Clint.

For the first few weeks of the new handball rule, I had reigned supreme. There is no 'taking it easy on the kid' in my world. No, he had to step up if he wanted to beat the mother of all handball champions. Unfortunately, he has now started to adjust, and I can see that beating Ethan is not going to be as easy as it used to be. So many small joys are being taken away from me.

The ball bounces past me, and Ethan starts doing his bum-wiggle celebration dance and jumping around yelling, 'Match point, match point!'

'I'm tired,' I say. 'Maybe we should finish this game later.'

I love doing this and waiting for his reaction – 'That's not fair, Mum, you can't quit now!' – but instead, for the first time ever, he stops jumping around, looks at me and says, 'That's okay, we don't have to finish the game.'

I feel tears well up in my eyes. Not pity from my son, that's just too much. I look deep into his eyes and say, 'What's the matter, are you chicken Mama's gonna beat you?'

The game is back on.

CHAPTER 4

My list: Declutter the playroom

Ethan has kept everything he has ever been given, found or made. He will grow up one day to either run a museum or a library. His playroom has the wrong name. It is a storage facility. There is no room for playing. There is no room for friends to stay. There is no room to move, no room to vacuum, no room to dust and no way of knowing where on earth to begin. It is a room full of all my failed attempts to organise my son's growing mountain of stuff.

Unfortunately, not only is Ethan the most sentimental of all children but he also has a photographic memory. This means I can't throw out a thing. So where to begin? The door can only partly open, so I decide to start by clearing a path behind it, so it can at least swing on its hinges once again.

Behind the door is failure number one. A pile of at least twelve crates I was going to use to organise the playroom last time.

Some are full, some are empty, and some are now cracked and broken. Over the top of them is a bright 1970s quilt cover that was supposed to disguise/decorate the pile and make it look presentable, like I meant it to be that way. I tug at the quilt to try and dislodge it, but it isn't going to shift easily. I put one foot up against the crates and tug again, knowing when it finally comes free that, even though I will very probably tumble backwards, I can't possibly hurt myself as there is no room for me to fall over.

After an enormous heave, the quilt dislodges, but unfortunately so do the top two crates it was attached to. I am now wedged between piles of memories with a quilt over my head. Luckily, the fallen crates are both half empty and land on my head rather than my stomach full of tumours. I can hear my poppa saying, 'I hope that knocked some sense into you,' but it's too late for that.

If I had any sense, I would simply close the door and leave the room as it is, to be cleaned up after I am dead. I admit it's tempting to leave the mess as payback for all the years I had to be the responsible parent, cleaning and nagging while Clint got to be the fun one who said, 'Come on, your mum's in a cleaning frenzy, let's go outside and play.'

Instead I manage to roll unceremoniously out of my predicament and flick the lid off the crate nearest to me. This was meant to be a box for puzzles, but it only has one in it. It's a 2000-piece puzzle with tiny parts that a childless relative with no idea bought for Ethan when he was four. It was opened once but never attempted. I look at the cover; it only has two colours with slight shade variations, which, of course, makes it even more difficult. It isn't even a nice picture; the tree is bare, black against the orange sky and looks like a teenager drew it in a particularly hormonal moment. There would be no satisfaction in completing it. I open the box. That is my first mistake.

Four hours later I have only put together thirty pieces and half my day is gone. What was I thinking? Is this how I want to spend my time? I should be making every minute count; instead, I am sitting in filth, still in my pyjamas, attempting to do an impossible, ugly puzzle. I am a disgrace. Where is my existential bliss? Where are my deep 'Aha!' moments? Where are my Facebook friends holding on to every boring moment with me?

I guess they are busy with their own lists. Life hasn't stopped for them. Of course, they all messaged when they first heard the news. They offered their services, 'If there is anything I can do . . .' and then logged out before giving me a chance to answer. What was their rush? It wasn't like they were going to have to put up with me for that much longer anyway. But I could see the relief on their Facebooks when they got to go back to their lives.

I think that's why I got off socials soon after I got my diagnosis. I knew if I saw one more of my friends' delicious meals or smiling, Insta-filtered faces I was going to go mad. Call me anti-social but I'd rather see photos of women losing it with their kids and crying while they wash up, or YouTube clips of slamming doors, depression, overdue bills and cancer, goddamn it.

I think I should start my own YouTube channel. Here's me throwing up this morning after my delicious meal at the café. Here's me, half an hour before you arrive, shoving all my mess into the pantry, linen cupboard and playroom. Here's me, making sure those doors remain firmly locked. Here's me, giving clever retorts to your insensitive comments, five minutes after you left and pecked me on both cheeks with a 'Ciao, ciao'.

I think I'll add 'Finish the puzzle' to my list. I like the honesty of its black, bare tree. This is the deepest thought I have had in a long time. Perhaps dying is making me wise after all. If it is, let's hope there is some sort of after-life. After all, what's the point of getting wise a month or two before becoming worm food? But who knows? Maybe the world needs wiser worms. Perhaps if we used worm wee from wise worms on our gardens, then humanity would evolve and get smarter. Perhaps worms are the key to the next great unfolding or perhaps it's time to get out of my pyjamas, have a cup of tea, get out of my head and get myself the hell out of the house.

•

There is a local café right near us that backs onto a creek; well, a pretend creek – it's manmade but beautiful. The sound of running water always makes me feel serene, provided there is a toilet nearby. I decide to walk to the café and feel much better as soon as I am out of the house. It's sunny and there's a light breeze. It's one of those days that makes you feel like nothing matters, and life is all okay. It's funny how quickly moods can change, from depression to enjoying a breeze blowing in your hair. I've always felt better outdoors. Inside walls my thoughts can close in on me, but outside they are pulled to something else. Nature calms me but even people-watching can make me feel better. I like imagining other people's worlds, especially because most people are pretty screwed up, so it generally makes me feel better about myself. The café isn't like that for me, though. I have come to know and even love all the regulars. They smile and call each other 'mate', 'love' and 'darlin''.

Today, my favourite waitress is here, she always calls me Sweets and, even though she's a young goth, she makes me feel like a kindy kid who has done something right and is waiting for her gold star to be put up on the star chart.

I watch as she runs up the stairs with an armful of dirty plates and spies me heading for my regular corner chair. 'I'll be with you in a minute, Sweets,' she calls over her shoulder.

I sink into the chair, tired yet again. It's an old armchair they probably got from Vinnies, but it's comfy and reminds me of my nan's house. There's a crocheted blanket on the side which I have used on more than one occasion, but today it's warm enough to stretch my legs out in the dappled sun. I pull my skirt up slightly to try and catch some vitamin D. It's always a shock when I see my body. My legs are blotchy, and my muscles are losing their tone. I used to love my legs. My feet are still pretty though. I've always prided myself on having pretty feet; it's not a very common trait. I figure I may not be a model, but some models have very ugly feet. I decide to add 'Get a pedicure' to my list. If you've got it, flaunt it, and, anyway, my toenails need clipping, and it's been ages since I put any nail polish on.

The waitress comes over with a chai and a chocolate brownie.

'Figured you were having your usual.' She smiles.

I want to reach up and kiss her. She knows me, she notices me, she serves me. I should have married her.

'You're the best! A waitress and a mind-reader, thanks so much,' I say, breathing in the scent of the chai.

She puts a hand on my shoulder, 'Welcome, Sweets,' and then, after giving my table a quick wipe, walks away.

Tracy Chapman is playing on the stereo and talking about some long-lost revolution. I used to talk about revolutions. I was engaged to an angry peace activist in my early twenties and we protested against everything. Steve, my fiancé, was a musician. He rarely washed, rarely made any money and rarely cooked or shopped, but I was smitten. He smoked roll your owns, drank Coopers to excess, indulged in the odd joint and called me Babe. I thought he was the coolest thing ever. We made love at least once a day, if not more, on his mattress on the floor. The angrier he was at the world, the more we seemed to make love. I had constant urinary tract infections, but that didn't matter to him, all that mattered was that we expressed our love for each other daily. When we weren't in bed or in battle with the powers that be, we spent our time breaking up on a regular basis. At the time I thought it was over ideological differences, but after seven years I finally figured out it was so he could get a bit of variety in his diet. He, of course, denied it but eventually I caught him eating out and left him, my ideals and a broken heart behind.

I take a sip of my chai and wonder where Steve is now. I know he is probably a fat, boring, cheating banker but I can't help holding a flicker of hope that he at least became a homeless musician and is ranting madly at passers-by about peace and pacifism. It would be nice to think one of us stuck to our political ideals instead of selling out for Sheridan sheets and a chiropractic-approved bedding ensemble.

Looking back, I can't believe how or why I loved him, and yet there is part of me that would throw in every skerrick of domesticity I have to return to those heady days where nothing mattered except ideals and sex. With time not on my side, I've still had the odd moment when I've considered stuffing everything into a backpack and walking down the road with my thumb out to see where life might take me for my final chapter. If it wasn't for Ethan, I imagine I would steal a Lonely Planet guide from the local library and, just for anarchy's sake, set off around the globe, ticking off a bucket list and reaching enlightenment before shuffling off this mortal coil.

Instead, I am enjoying a chai and a chocolate brownie on a sunny day. As I take another sip and inhale the aroma of cinnamon and cloves, I feel how much I am really, really enjoying it. It's the small things they say, and today, for once, they are right.

CHAPTER 5

Clint's list: Go for long walks in the countryside

Ethan spends far too long on the computer these days. He's escaping into a virtual world, and it's not healthy. I've been trying to bring him back to what boys should be doing at his age: hiking, biking, climbing trees and kicking balls. He needs a project to keep him off the screens, so I suggested we build a cubby together, but it hasn't been going quite the way I wanted it to. For a start, I can't believe one boy can whinge so much. Everything's too boring or too hard, or it's too hot to be outside or too cold. Like today, we'd hardly even put one nail into a board before he started up. And he's not just a whinger, he's a worrier. It drives me crazy. I want him to be strong and decisive, a go-getter who doesn't take crap from anyone. Yeah, I know, pretty much all the things I'm not, so what hope has he got, poor kid.

I asked him to go and get my tools and some supplies from the shed and ten minutes later I had to go and find him. He was sitting on the ground, muttering to himself as usual. He worried at a nail that was bent, as if worrying would straighten it up. He doesn't like mess or chaos; it unnerves him. Unless of course, it's a mess he created, then it's almost invisible to his eye.

I promised Viv we'd go for long walks in the countryside when we got married, so once I've finished screwing up as a dad, I've organised to take her on a surprise picnic. Long walks are kind of off limits these days, so I've found a place we can drive up to that has a beautiful lake perfect for short strolls, with benches all the way along to rest and watch the scenery. There's a place nearby that does picnic hampers, which is great, because if I cooked that would end the romance before it even started. I know I've left my run a bit late, but I'm trying to make up for lost time, and there have been a lot of what she calls 'broken promises' since we got married. I never meant to break them; I was just busy.

I spent a lot of time working so we could try and get ahead. Viv reckons too much time, but what was I meant to do? We'd just get some money in the bank then something would happen, a broken water pipe, a smashed car or that bloody storm damage to the roof. We never seemed to get to the place we were supposedly heading to. Somewhere along the way, we kept moving forward but in different directions, away from each other. Now I'm in a mad panic to try and set things straight and let her know I was only ever leaving her *for* her. I know my long hours left her feeling deserted, but I just wanted to take the pressure off. I wanted to give her the fairytale life I always meant to give her. I wanted to be Richard Gere in *An Officer and a Gentleman* and carry her off the factory floor, away from the hard slog to somewhere where life is like it is in the magazines she likes to read. Instead, we've barely managed to pay our bills on time and survive.

She doesn't know about the picnic. I've always been good at surprises and keeping secrets. She's never once guessed, or even half guessed, when I've been up to something. She really loves surprises; it's the one thing I get right.

Viv's been having a morning nap. She does that these days. It started with afternoon naps, but now it's mornings as well. She'll wake up soon and then we'll head off. I've told her I'm going to drive her to the pharmacy so she can pick up a script for her nausea and pain meds. She's always liked driving; driving and shopping and cities and cafés. I'm more of a nature boy myself. I'd rather spend time outdoors in the bush, under the stars, fishing and listening to the wind blow through the gumtrees. That's my idea of heaven. It bores her after a while, and something always manages to bite Ethan, a tick or a green ant or just a stack of mozzies. He has a big reaction to bites that usually leads to a trip to the doctor's, so that's always taken the fun out of outdoor family adventures. Before he was born, we used to at least go to parks because Viv prefers her nature manicured and organised. She likes botanical gardens where everything is labelled and there are cafés where you can sit and look at nature from a comfortable couch. She likes paths and lighting and mowed grass. I like somewhere I need a machete to get through, but today's all about her so the lake will be perfect.

Viv's finally woken up and Ethan, who has given up on the cubby, is taking her in a cup of tea. She can't get out of bed or even really open her eyes before she takes her first sip. She's always been that way. It's like a religion. Her nanna introduced her to the unproven fact that tea is an essential nutrient and a cure for everything life throws at you. She has collections of not just every sort of tea ever invented, but teacups, teapots, teaspoons and tea paraphernalia I never knew existed. I drink coffee, and don't know what the hell I am going to do with all this tea stuff when she's gone. I hate it when that thought pops randomly into my head. *When she's gone.* It's like this guillotine hanging above my neck. I honestly don't know if I'll cope. All I can do is try not to think about it, but that's getting harder as she is starting to look sicker and sleep longer and longer.

She's always worn make-up and so, for the first few weeks, she didn't look sick. I guess she was like a corpse done up; you couldn't actually see the colour of her skin. But now she's stopped wearing it. The first time she appeared without make-up in the morning was a shock, not just because she was sick and her skin was an odd yellowish-grey, but because her eyelashes seemed thinner, her cheeks were less rosy, and there wasn't the usual slash of red for her lips. I'd always told her she looked beautiful without make-up but, to be honest, these days I long for her to go back to her old habit and disguise herself. For some reason though she's decided now, when she looks like death itself, is the time to stop covering up what is really going on.

We've always worked best pretending. Pretending we're madly in love, pretending we're well, pretending we've got money and aren't racking up the credit cards, pretending we've got our shit together. I guess I'm partly to blame. I've always put her off every time she wanted to 'talk' or do more than just skim across the surface.

I was a champion rock skimmer when I was a kid. I wasn't good at much, but I could do that. My record was twenty skips across the lake near our house. No other kid even came close to that. The average was about three, some got up to ten, but I was legend status. I remember telling Viv about it on our first date. I'd thought it would impress her.

She'd laughed and said, 'Have you ever been asked how many rocks you can skip at a job interview?'

I hadn't realised just how few skills I had until I met her. She was older than me and seemed to have so much of her life together. She taught me to change a tyre, to cook and to dance (badly) but she never managed to teach me to do hospital corners on our bed or balance our budget. She also never taught me how to stop bragging about my rock-skimming abilities at parties. She would just cringe and walk away as soon as she heard any mention of large expanses of water.

While Viv is finishing her tea and waiting for the babysitter to arrive, I go outside, hunt through my rock collection and pocket my best skimming stone.

•

The lake is beautiful today. I'm not a poetic man, but if I was, I reckon I could say something that would make me sound brilliant and sensitive right now. Instead, I'm opting to keep my mouth shut and not ruin the moment. Viv has this serene look on her face that makes me want to not breathe in case I push her buttons.

From our bench I spot some plovers arguing with each other about where the most stupid place is to build their nest. The male is walking around, neck out, yelling at the world, right next to the site where the trucks pull in to empty the rubbish. The female looks like she is trying to find a 'safe' home for their young right in the middle of the footpath. They are terminator parents. I guess when you're a bird it's the quick or the dead. They're like those dads who cross the road playing chicken with the baby stroller. Now they are yelling at each other, arguing about where the best place is to birth the next generation of kamikaze birds.

Like most parents these days, we have done the opposite with our kid. From the time Ethan was born, Viv tried to protect him from everything. She played him classical music in the womb, fed him organic pesticide-free food, feng shui-ed his bedroom and free-ranged him instead of just laying down the rules. The one thing she hasn't managed to protect him from is death, although she bloody well tried. She protected him from the religious upbringing we both had. No reading about gruesome martyr deaths or filling him with guilt about every little sin he ever committed. But he's ended up too soft. She's left him exposed instead of slapping on some weatherproof paint to shield him from the elements. The very least we could have done was have him help us bury a few pets to get his head around the idea that death happens. Even my mum doesn't look like a grandmother should, wrinkly, decaying and smelling of Oil of Ulan. She's too busy at the spa, with the rest of the ageless generation, to have time to sit around knitting and contemplating her pending demise. While I'm not the biggest fan of Viv's lack of make-up these days, at least she's introducing some honesty into our boy's world. But it's only skin-deep. She's still trying to protect him from the knowledge that, at any time now, he'll be without a mother for the rest of his life.

The plovers have decided on the footpath, so they are attacking all the joggers and mums with prams who dare to walk near their nest. Viv looks over at me.

'I'm getting stiff, let's walk down to the lake.'

'Sure, honey,' I reply, instantly jumping up and grabbing her things. These days she doesn't protest when I carry her things. Not like when we first met, two years before Ethan was born. She was fiercely independent then, like a baby plover. I could tell she was completely vulnerable, but she couldn't. She would squawk at everything that came near her, including me. I loved her fiery nature and, luckily, she was way smarter than those dumb birds. She had a brain like a whip; it could cut through anything, including me. If you accidentally got in the way it would slice through your outer skin like butter. She'd been a challenge, that's for sure, but all my girlfriends before her had been compliant, not wanting to make any decisions on their own and always wanting me to lead the way. When I met Viv, I'd had to learn to follow. She sure as hell wasn't going to follow me anywhere. Even now, when she should be the slow one, she's already halfway down to the lake before I finish gathering her belongings. She'll be sore tomorrow, but she loves to move. I don't think she'll be able to rest in peace. She wants to be cremated, and that makes sense to me. She'll be able to blow around in the wind and follow the breeze wherever it takes her.

A little girl has run up to her and grabbed her leg; she's mistaken her for her mum. Viv looks down at her and laughs. She's always loved little ones. She looks so young when she laughs. The little girl has recognised her mistake and starts backing away, stumbling and falling on a nappy-padded bottom. Viv bends down and talks to her, pointing to her mother, who is now on the way. She blows raspberries and manages to distract the toddler from crying, despite the child's bottom lip being poised and ready. Viv is now sitting on the ground smiling and waving as the mother picks up her daughter and carries her away.

She won't be able to get up, so I rush to her side. I put my arms under both her armpits and lift her to her feet; she's light as a feather. She looks up at me gratefully, and there is something so fragile about her, I want to squawk at all the passers-by to keep them at bay. I want to yell at the world to leave her alone for once. Instead, I take her hand, and we walk the last few steps to the lake where a seat and a performance by a champion rock skimmer are waiting for her.

CHAPTER 6

My list: Delete my Tinder profile

At nineteen I had my first, very unsatisfying, one-night stand with a man whose name I never bothered to discover. Yet, when I woke up the next morning after our mutually abject failure, I still expected a romantic morning after. When he opened his eyes as I was gently stroking his hair, I had smiled and whispered, 'Good morning,' softly into his ear, to which he replied in disgust, 'Your breath *stinks!*' We had spent much of the previous night eating garlic bread and scoffing red wine, so I have absolutely no idea why he would have expected me to smell minty fresh, but his comment still managed to cut me to the core.

I didn't stay long enough to compare my breath with his, which I am sure would have vindicated me, but instead jumped out of bed in horror never to return again. I swore then that I would never tell anyone their morning breath smelt and I have vigilantly stuck to my word, which has meant every morning for the past ten years, I have silently had to endure Clint's less than perfect breath. I have also made sure, the second my eyes are open, to thoroughly clean my teeth, as I apparently need to maintain the upper hand in all things, even the breath department.

At least Clint never claimed fresh breath to be one of his assets. His Tinder profile read, 'Good head of hair, good provider, happy to have kids and pretty sure I am fertile, which makes me cheaper than IVF lol.'

My best friend, Marsha, set up a Tinder profile for me as a way of trying to change the topic of my drunken conversations to something other than my long-lost engagement to Steve. Having wasted my optimum early breeding years on that cheating yet self-proclaimed feminist, I'd been feeling my biological clock ticking loudly. Sometimes at night it even woke me up on the hour, every hour, and I worried I was steamrolling downhill towards an early menopause. I tried to ignore Marsha's constant shoving of profiles in my face, but one night, after we had both consumed a bottle of red each, I swiped right instead of left on 'pretty sure I am fertile' and, before I knew it, I was dating Clint.

Marsha is my larger than life, supersized and totally wicked friend. Growing up she'd been taunted about being part of the Brady Bunch, but she was as far from a goody-two-shoes as one could imagine. With her low, warm voice and ample bosoms, she could very easily have been a porn star. Instead, she had spent her life working a string of call-centre and customer-service jobs that left her jaded and poorer than a life on the small wet screen, but she is still hilariously funny.

Of course, after setting me up on my first lunch date with Clint, she'd expected to be given the full debrief and was waiting for me outside the front of my studio apartment when I arrived home. Before I even made it through the gate, she came bounding towards me like an oversized puppy.

'So, how'd it go? How did it go, go, go? I want words, I want pictures, I want touch, should there have been any,' she said, running her hand up and down my arm suggestively. 'But if there were any smells, you can keep them to yourself.'

I shook my head and laughed. 'You should have just gone on the date yourself, then you would know.'

'Ooooh, testy! Does that mean it was good?'

'I don't know.' I paused, unsure how to describe the easy, familiar, not bad but not good feeling I had on the date. 'He was polite.'

'Read boring,' she quipped as she followed me inside.

'I don't know,' I repeated. 'He was just different.'

'Different to Steve – extra big points for that.'

'He has great hair.'

'Well that's what he said on Tinder, so that makes him honest. That would be new for you,' she said, raising an eyebrow and pulling out a pen and paper. 'Not a liar, liar, pants on fire,' she scribed, 'unlike he who shall not be castrated, because for some reason you won't let me. Continue.'

'He works for his mum.'

'Oh good, that's good. Working relationship with his mother,' she continued writing.

'He paid for the meal.'

'Great. Cash is always great.' She nodded approvingly.

'He laughed at my jokes and told one or two of his own, but I'm not sure if they were only funny because of how much alcohol we consumed.'

'Possibly funny,' she said, continuing to take notes. 'Look, I think this is off to a very good start. And the fertility?'

'I didn't get a sperm sample.' I rolled my eyes.

'For goodness sake, woman, do I have to do everything for you?'

I put on the kettle.

'But seriously, bub, what did you think about him?' Marsha was never serious, and still isn't.

'I don't know. He's not Steve, he doesn't have any of that fire or those ideals.'

'Oh yes, those ideals! Like cheating on you.'

'This guy wouldn't cheat on me, I can tell that already.'

'No man in their right mind would,' she said firmly but gently.

'Yeah, thanks,' I replied then paused, serious for a second. 'I don't know why but I think I can trust him.'

My faith in Clint started at that very first date when the waitress gave me the once-over and decided she was far too good to be serving the likes of me, and then completely ignored our table. Clint showed the good sense to join the party when, in my defence, I went on the attack. As I loudly pointed out that being a waitress required zero skills and was not exactly a career move, instead of judging me, he'd picked sides – my side – and even quipped, 'I like you; you're a scoundrel. And there just aren't enough of those in my life.' I didn't catch on at the time that he was repurposing a Han Solo *Star Wars* quote. Years later when Clint took me to a *Star Wars* marathon at our local cinema, I also ID-ed other poetic but out-of-character lines he'd used to swing my affections further his way, including Padme's silver-tongued words to Anakin that her love for him was a puzzle she had no answers for, and Clint's version of General Organa's monologue about how he hated watching me leave after every one of our pointless fights. Little did I know back then that our romance only blossomed thanks to Clint's ability to use the force to channel Cyrano de Bergerac.

'Okay, so he won't cheat, he's got a good head of hair, he can give you that kid you've been banging on about and he still has some kind of relationship with his mother. What's not to like?' continued Marsha. 'Look, you don't have to fall head over heels for him, that always falls apart anyway. He just needs to be something near decent.' She started to bang her hands on the table. 'Drumroll puh-lease . . . I think we have a winner!'

While I still hadn't been totally convinced, I'd had Han Solo's words ringing in my ears and had to admit Clint was good, safe company who, compared with everyone else I was swiping at on Tinder at the time, was the pick of the bunch. He was happy to love me with my walls still very firmly in place and, before I knew it, I found myself starting to let him see through the cracks. He was also a surprisingly good kisser and the pathetic part of me melted in his arms, even while the jilted part of me tried to run, run as fast as I could.

Over the next few months, the Tinder inquiries began to drop off, mostly because Marsha had decided Clint was the one for me and secretly paused my account. I think she'd also liked that there was no way he would ever compete with her in the personality department. After that, it hadn't taken long until Clint started picking me up every Friday night to go to our favourite restaurant where we'd order our usual, judge the other customers as foreplay and then head home for our now routine, intoxicated sex. Before we knew it, we were well and truly used to each other. He was the only other person who seemed to be able to accept, and even love, the parts of me that previously only a Marsha could love.

When I open the app to erase my long-forgotten, paused Tinder account, I see the younger version of myself staring back at me with no wrinkles or frown lines acquired from keeping Clint on task or staying up late worrying about Ethan. I press delete, trying not to wonder what would have happened if Marsha and Han Solo had not pushed me into Clint's fertile arms.

CHAPTER 7

My list: Sand the French doors into the bedroom

This morning I am auditing all three of our lists in bed. So far, I've crossed off a grand total of one job on my own list – I have successfully cleaned the fridge. I have also completed one item on Ethan's list (playing handball) and one thing from Clint's list (going for a walk in the countryside). I appreciate Clint's optimistic inclusion of 'Have sex' as a list item, but I am not sure why he expects that to be bumped up as a priority now, when it has been coming after 'washing up' and 'mowing the lawn' for years. As for making love, I don't think we'd even know where to start, considering the last time we had sex Clint still needed instructions.

'Not there, Clint.'

'Not so hard, you're not a DJ trying to spin a record.'

In the end it was easier to get on with it and do the job myself, so for the past two years we've been living a self-sufficient lifestyle. Clint seems to think that now I'm dying and in pain it's the perfect time to revive our sex life. While I am in no way up for that game, I conceded to foreplay when he took me out to dinner and am planning to set him up to succeed with his future partner-to-be by writing an instruction manual.

While sex with Clint has never been earth shattering, the good thing for any woman willing to take him on is he's an enthusiastic pupil with plenty of room for improvement. Unfortunately, he can never seem to remember bedroom tips from one episode to the next, but that's a bonus really as then every time is like the first.

I still remember our debut. I'd never been one for putting off the inevitable but I drew a line between jumping into bed on the first night and waiting until I got to know prospective lovers so well that the idea of sex felt as exciting as going out for milk. With Clint I waited until our fourth date, which was one date too many as we were already starting to run out of things to say, especially Clint, who by then had told me all three of the funny stories he knew. As he pressed repeat on story number one I decided, *Tonight's the night.*

It wasn't a question of your place or mine as he was still living with his mother. My studio was so small you could cook your dinner and take a shower at the same time. We raced up the stairs without puffing, as we were both still young and relatively fit, pulling off our clothes as we went. Clint was behind me and managed to drop his pants but couldn't get them off his feet, so he kangaroo hopped his way across the threshold. What started off like a scene from a rom com ended like an instructional video for the *Rocky Horror* 'Time Warp' dance.

'Just a bit to the left, oh no, maybe the right. Get your hands off my hips, and bring your thighs in tight.'

Then Clint tried to get creative just as he was starting to do something vaguely arousing . . .

'Let's do that first bit again.'

It wasn't the best premiere night, but it did reassure me knowing my future husband didn't appear to mind being bossed around, either in bed or out. I was impressed by his ability to obey instructions then, and still am to this day.

I think I will divide his instruction manual into chapters in case the future Mrs Clint is not as good at giving clear, concise directions in the heat of the moment as I am. Chapter one: how to remove a woman's clothing with your teeth or hands, without getting either tangled up or ripping something. Footnote for Clint – ripping something is okay on your first date, after that you'd better go shopping and replace it. Chapter two: why getting drunk is not foreplay. Chapter three: how to tell the difference between groans of pleasure and groans which mean 'How much longer is this going to take?'

As I move on to the next item on Clint's agenda, I can tell it is going to be a whole lot easier to get through Ethan's list than either mine or Clint's. I will definitely not be completing my husband's dumb idea that I should write a novel. I haven't had the heart to tell him that the one line he loves so much, and thinks should be the opening to my book, is actually a prompt sentence we were given in a writing course I enrolled in, which of course I never finished.

I've always been better at helping others finish things than completing anything myself, which is probably why I haven't lived the life either Oprah or Dr Phil prescribe. I tried harder when I was a kid, but even then I wasn't exactly aiming for the moon or stars. I'd wanted to breed a rescue pup. Unfortunately, she wasn't interested in male dogs but preferred the legs of human visitors. Neither the moon nor stars were worth the embarrassment, so I'd happily fallen back into a life of mediocrity. With 'giving up' as my only real talent, I don't know why I should be surprised that in the end I will not be enlightened, famous, ground-breaking, saintly or even just nice.

Perhaps that's what I should put on the epitaph for my plaque. I'm going to be cremated, so instead of a headstone, there will be an engraved plate in the cemetery garden where I will be scattered. People can come and breathe in bits of me as they smell the roses. I've always liked the idea of coming up with my own after-death marketing slogan and getting one last shot at standing out from the crowd. I doubt, however, that I will win first prize for the most spiritual message left behind by a dead person as unfortunately, when I try to be spiritual, I end up cynical. I'm nothing if not consistent which is why I've decided I'm going to die the way I lived and plagiarise a dead person's last words to sum up my life. My favourite is, of course, Spike Milligan's 'I told you I was sick', but that's been done to death, so I'm leaning towards using lesser-known but just as funny quotes from dead nobodies. I was tempted to use 'Reincarnating, I'll be right back, don't touch my stuff' but in the end, after much research, I've decided to immortalise myself with this unforgettable piece of modern poetry: 'Died from not sending that text message to ten people'.

Next on my list, apart from getting out of bed, is sanding the French doors that were supposed to be the entrance to our parents' retreat slash boudoir. They were a second-hand bargain, painted black with graffiti scratched into them, to add to the public urinal aesthetic we were apparently going for. After we picked them up, Clint was supposed to have sanded them back to their original glory before they were hung, but at the time we had no doors, so they went up as they were and have stayed that way for nearly five years. At least now they are starting to serve a romantic purpose, as there is so much crap in front of them that, in order to prevent me falling, Clint has to carry me across the threshold every time we go to bed. It should make it like a honeymoon every night, but even though I currently weigh less than a diet-obsessed fourteen-year-old, he still complains about it. Most of the stuff is Clint's. I could, of course, just put all the things he's left in front of the door away, but I am making a point; a point that seems to have gone entirely unnoticed. He hasn't even questioned why he is carrying me to bed every night. It's another habit that's crept in unnoticed, like tolerating being kissed before teeth get brushed in the morning.

When I lie in bed awake at night, I read the graffiti. I know it by heart so even when the lights are out I can chant it over and over like a prisoner doing mantras. There is one funny line that I don't think I will paint over, 'Beware of the dog he's very sarcastic', but most of it was spray-painted by untethered teens whose idea of literary genius was to write a list of every swear-word ever invented. So, we have a lot of fucks and cunts in our bedroom despite our conjugal indifference.

Now as I stare at the doors, I feel like there is far too much black in my world. Unfortunately, I'm not exactly match fit right now, so I opt out of sanding and head out to the shed to grab the only can of paint I can still open with my aching hands. The lid is only partially on, and the hardening paint is full of lumps. I grab a dirty stick out of the garden to stir it with. As I mix it, I realise this is the hot pink paint Clint accidentally bought without bothering to check the colour because he was so excited it was on special. I can't be bothered looking for a different colour and frankly I don't really care as I'm not the one who's going to be looking at it for years to come. I go back inside with a paintbrush in one hand and try to push the pile of compacted clothes mixed with building materials away from the doors with the other. My strength is not what it used to be so I move what I can and leave the rest. Two hours later, the doors start to look passable, as does the pink-splattered sculpture sitting proudly beneath them.

I head back out to the shed to put away my painting supplies. I've got a headache from paint fumes and spending too much time inside. The sun warms my hair and jasmine takes me back to my happy place. I can breathe again. I take off my shoes, feel the thick grass underfoot and sense something that resembles relaxation. Five minutes later, I am bored. I decide to bring the laptop outside and get on to something I'd forgotten to add to my list: culling Clint's inbox.

Clint has 7549 emails, half of which are unopened subscriptions he signed up for. They are like a personal history lesson and evolve randomly from one era to the next. If he were Picasso, they would have artistic names like the Blue Period or the Cubist Period; instead, there is the Hair Regrowth Period, the Failed Handyman Period, the Fitness Equipment Period and, most recently, the Miracle Cancer Cure Period. I am pleased to know I am not the only person in the marriage who has been a complete failure at everything we set our minds to. No wonder he can never find anything.

Eight years ago, I asked Clint if he could please organise for me to take over all the bills and have them sent to my email address after he managed to miss five reminder notices for our rates. Even after the sheriff turned up on our doorstep and our house was almost repossessed, he still never managed to get around to changing the bills into my name.

I still remember that day, and the sheriff. He wasn't the kind of law enforcement officer you'd be hoping for when you are a bored, sexually unsatisfied housewife with post-natal depression and a screaming baby. Instead, he was a short man with greasy hair plastered down on his acne-scarred, stubble-covered face. His clothes looked like they were allergic to ironing, and his eyes couldn't focus on one spot for more than a minute. When he showed me his badge, I thought he was a homeless man trying to scam for money. He left me with a grubby piece of paper from the council, and it wasn't until I double-checked the number and then phoned it to make sure it was legit that I confirmed this was no joke. My husband on the other hand was.

At that time, Clint was working for a larger motel chain and was away more often than not, leaving me alone with a crying, colicky baby and a rapidly building sleep debt. Unfortunately for him, he made the mistake of actually coming home that day.

'We could be losing our house and all because you are too lazy to check your goddamn emails!' I screamed when he walked in the door, shaking the repossession notice two inches away from his face.

'It takes five minutes, that's all, five minutes a day for you to open a couple of emails, but nooooo, oh noooo, that's too much hard work for you to do. So instead –' I yelled with the veins in my neck bulging and my hair turning into snakes, 'your wife and your three-month-old baby might end up having to sleep on the streets. Oh yes, that would be easier, wouldn't it, than just opening your fucking emails.'

I threw the paper at him, and he picked it up, trying to read it while checking there were no knives within reach of me. By that stage, I was a completely crazy woman, and Clint knew it. He had witnessed certifiable craziness in my mother when we first told her we were pregnant, and he and I both knew I was a hair's breadth and a hormone surge away from it. My chest heaved, and I was breathing so hard I thought I might have been having a heart attack.

Clint finished reading and said, 'Oh, this is just bullying; they don't mean it.'

He waved the red flag, and I became the bull, running at him and slapping and slapping until he was able to grab my hands and restrain me. I tried to free myself, but I was exhausted by all the drama, and when he felt my internal collapse, he pulled me into his arms and I started to sob.

'I'm so sorry,' he whispered, kissing my head, 'I'm so sorry.'

That wasn't the first, or the last, time I would hear those words, but at the time I believed them, and he made a pact that he'd stay on top of things and never let it get that bad again. Not long after, the electricity was disconnected, followed by the re-issuing of the pact. Then the phone was disconnected, followed by another heartfelt apology. Then finally, after the mortgage went into default, I decided to take on checking his emails.

Since the cancer diagnosis, I've become slack at checking his inbox. I usually like to cull it whenever it reaches the five hundred messages mark. It's an adrenaline rush every time as the anger rises and I press delete like I am working in a vasectomy clinic. But this time feels different. When you first fall in love, you are celebrating firsts: your first kiss, your first date, your first anniversary. Now I am celebrating lasts, and this is the last time I will ever have to unsubscribe, file or delete any of Clint's emails.

CHAPTER 8

Ethan's list: Build a robot

The nurse with the syringe is coming closer. Clint winces and looks away. He hates needles. I smile. My regular blood tests to check my med levels and whether I am dying on schedule are made so much easier by watching him squirm. My hero turns a shade of green as the blood rushes from his face, and he breathes deeply, trying to ensure he has enough oxygen and doesn't swoon with a touch of the vapours. Ethan, on the other hand, is fascinated. He's inherited my sense of the macabre. He watches as the blood slowly fills the syringe.

'Cool,' he says, louder than he meant to. 'Mum, when we build my robot do you think we could make it have blood?'

And then he is off. His projects are always bigger than Ben-Hur. The robot phase started when I bought him a cheap Lego robot kit to entertain him around the time my journey of sitting around doctor's surgeries began. Now it has evolved into him wanting to make a life-size model capable of doing all his chores around the house.

'I don't think that's legal, Ethan,' I say.

'Not real blood, Mum.' He rolls his eyes at how incredibly stupid I am.

'I could get some clear plastic tubes, and then I can get some tomato juice and pump it around.' His voice is getting higher and faster as he bounces up and down in the chair. 'Hey, Mum, Mum, I just remembered, haven't we got a pump already, remember that one Dad bought to use on the water feature?'

Ah yes, I remember that one, I think, *job number 475* – something else Clint hasn't got around to.

'Yeah, yeah, I can use that one, is that okay, Mum, is that okay, I'll pay you for it.'

I laugh, paying me for things is his latest and cutest trait. Whenever he wants something and I say no, his reply is, 'It's okay, Mum, I'll pay for it.'

Lately, it has become sweeter because if I'm looking at something in the shops and then put it back on the shelf, he says, 'I'll buy it for you, Mum, do you want it, it's okay, I've got lots of money.' Generally followed by, 'Oh . . . I forgot to bring my money, but you get it, Mum, and I'll give you the money when I get home.'

His maths needs a little work. To date, I think he has spent the twenty dollars in his piggy bank twenty times over, and he still has cash left to burn. I wish I had his money box; it's like the magic pudding, it doesn't matter how many times it gets eaten there's still more to chew over.

Ethan is still bouncing up and down on his chair.

'Can I, Mum, can I?' he smiles at me with his head to one side. He is milking his cuteness.

'Yes, that's okay, you can use the pump. I highly doubt it's ever going to be used otherwise.'

'Thanks, Mum, thank you, thank you.' He is now dancing around the doctor's surgery, singing loudly. 'I'm going to have a robot with blood in it; I'm going to have a robot with blood in it.'

Good grief, it's so easy to be happy when you are a kid. It's also super easy to be angry, throw tantrums, think the world is going to end and believe in Santa, magic and the Easter Bunny.

The nurse tells me I can stop pressing down on the cotton-wool now and goes to put a band-aid where the needle was. But I haven't finished bleeding yet, and there's still plenty more where that came from. This male nurse is new to the practice and hasn't been told what a bleeder I am. He steps back away from the spurt of life still flowing in my veins, a look of horror on his face. How on earth is he going to survive in this profession? I look back over at Clint who, now that the needles have been put away, has returned to his normal colour. I nudge my head in the direction of the nurse who is hurrying out the door with vials of my blood. Clint smiles at me. Despite his needle phobia, my hubby is bizarrely good with blood – he associates it with the tomato sauce he used while playing doctors as a kid. He tries to use the nurse's hasty retreat to rescue some of his masculinity by grabbing a tissue and starting to clean my depleted platelets off the floor.

'Lucky you're okay with blood. Apparently our son is replacing me with a robot with see-through veins.'

'I heard.' He smiles at Ethan. 'And apparently someone promised him my pump.' He looks at me and shakes his head. 'How am I going to get any of those jobs you want done finished if you keep giving away all my supplies?'

'I just thought they might as well go to someone who will actually use them,' I say, laughing. 'Anyway, what jobs did you have in mind to finish?'

'I'll have to check my list.' He smiles.

'Okay, let's go,' I say, standing up and checking the cottonwool is still clamped on my arm. 'This isn't going to stop for a while, so we may as well head home. If you're lucky, Ethan, I might still be bleeding by the time we get there, and you can see if you can put some of it into one of your robot's veins.'

There are sentences you think you will never say as a mother and 'You can use my blood for your robot's veins' is one of them. 'Don't fart on your father' is another one, as is 'Don't eat the chewing gum off the supermarket floor', or 'For god's sake, who put mud in the freezer?' and 'Why are there rocks in my bed?'

Ethan is hopping from leg to leg with excitement.

'Real blood, I am going to get to use real blood. Hey, Dad, can you ask the nurse if he could give me a needle that I can use at home? Then you could donate some blood to the robot too.'

Clint instantly looks squeamish. I smile, and Ethan glances at me, grinning a wicked grin. We give each other a high five, laughing as we watch the colour drain once again from his father's face. Yep, there's something about that kid that just makes it impossible not to love him.

CHAPTER 9

Always on the list: Clean the bathroom

I think today is Wednesday but I'm really not sure as every school day seems to merge into the next. They all start with a moving feast, where I carry my breakfast around while looking for lost shoes and picking up dirty clothes with my toes. This is followed by trying to pack something vaguely nutritious for school lunch in under two minutes while double-checking if it's library day or not. Then there's the rush out the door to catch the bus while trying not to forget the lunch, library books, sports shoes, jumper, signed permission note and obligatory goodbye kiss and 'I love you', in case my frustratingly distracted child steps out in front of a truck. I don't want the last thing he hears from me to be, 'For god's sake, Ethan, how many times do I have to tell you to brush your teeth?'

Thankfully Clint has the morning off so he has volunteered to do bus duty today. This does however mean the combined nagging, whingeing and arguing volume will reach well above regulatory pollution levels, especially if Ethan needs an emergency toilet visit just as the bus arrives. The walls in our house are so thin that you can hear everything from grunting to wind breaking, so my planned sleep-in is interrupted by listening to Ethan let go of all his worldly cares.

Now that I am awake, I am busting so when Ethan finally emerges, I must reluctantly enter the bathroom as we only have one working toilet in the house and no working pelvic floor.

Despite Ethan's extended encore, he has not quite completed his performance, so I have to flush before taking my seat in the theatre that is now rich with eau de small boy. I reach up for the lavender spray and attempt to drown out the evidence. I had thought my job would be done when he was toilet trained, but Clint's mother probably thought that too and yet her son's record of flushing is also not as on point as one would have hoped.

Still, the toilet is my quiet place, my boutique retreat centre. All it takes is a few sprays of whatever strong essential oil I have on hand and I can feel nurtured while sitting amongst other people's waste, trying not to feel like I've wasted my life. Maybe that's what inspired the trend of mothers placing motivational sayings on the back of toilet doors. 'We are family, we love and respect each other and smile often,' which should continue on to say, '. . . however that respect unfortunately doesn't extend to the basic ability to not leave our shit for other people to deal with.'

Unlike the men in our family, for most of my life I've made a policy of taking care of my own business, although I did see a psychotherapist once. She wanted me to learn how to be assertive instead of aggressive. She told me I had put up walls to stop the rest of the world getting too close. *How close do you want me to let them all get?* I'd thought to myself as I sat in her perfectly renovated, clean, child-free haven.

Looking back, I can see how selecting this particular health professional solely based on her being the first to come up on my Google search was a little sloppy. But I'd been desperate. Ethan was two at the time and I'd just picked him up out of his cot after what felt like two days of constant screaming and tantrums. Even though I knew he was sick, running a fever and teething, I wanted to shake him until he was silent. I don't know what stopped me but I managed to put him back down in his room and then back safely away. My homicidal thoughts scared me enough to finally think about getting some help.

At my first appointment, I rationally explained how it was all Clint's fault and how little he was helping, and how Ethan was still not sleeping the night through and how sleep deprivation had been used as a form of torture during the war. She smiled back at me with her 29-year-old childless carefree smile and, with her pelvic floor held tightly in place, suggested perhaps it was actually me who was the problem. I was so beaten down, I refrained from telling her that once she married her perfect boyfriend, whose picture was on her desk, the dinners and flowers would stop and his hair would most likely fall out. Instead, I took a deep breath, thought of my baby boy and decided to do whatever it took.

She asked me to close my eyes, relax and take a deep breath. My chest shook with the effort of opening and I tried again while clenching and unclenching my fists to see if that would help.

'Okay, good, that's good,' she said in a surprisingly soothing voice.

'Now I want you to go back to a time when you felt loved and safe. A time when you were a little child, and all was good in your world. A time when you had no responsibilities.'

I tried to keep breathing but the more she talked, the tighter my chest became.

'Good, that's good,' she continued.

My 'everything's okay' mask was obviously on and reassuring her that she was indeed a very good therapist. I am not sure what age I learnt to put that mask on, but while I have never quite managed to go to my happy place, I have at least learnt to put on a happy face so I can convince other people not to dig too deep.

'Now, imagine you are looking into the eyes of this little child. I want you to tell me what you would like to say to them. What would you say if you really wanted them to know they are loved?'

These days I would say, 'Pick your clothes up off the floor' and 'If I have to ask you to flush the toilet one more time I am going to explode,' but back then I just nodded and tried not to say anything that would result in Ethan being taken into foster care while the therapist locked me safely away in a mental health clinic.

'Now that you are there in that safe, warm and comfortable place, I want you to take another three deep breaths and know you can always come back to this happy place any time you want to.'

I don't know why people always want you to go back to your childhood to feel safe. That's where I felt most helpless and at the mercy of the seemingly unpredictable moods of every adult around me. If she really wanted me to feel safe, she should have sent me to her clean, sanitised, child-free bathroom. But what she really wanted me to do was to let all my defences down, in front of her, even though I'd known her for less than an hour. If she wanted my trust, she was going to have to wait a hell of a lot longer than that.

The lavender smell is fading, so before I am once again overwhelmed by the smell of the boy I used to love to sniff as a baby, I give the room another three quick, sharp sprays. I like the closeness of the four walls in here. There is only one entry and it is locked. Even as I feel the wave of pain that accompanies my expulsions these days, this is still my happy place.

When I came home from the psychotherapist my walls had crashed down around me. The babysitter closed the door behind her and I lay grief stricken on the floor over the childhood I never had, while the sadistic part of me dug deeper and deeper into my wounds. I would have been lost forever in the cloying darkness of my thoughts and the physical pain racking my body if Ethan had not, once again, started to cry. Crawling on hands and knees to his room and seeing him standing up with his arms reaching out to me brought me back from the brink. Navel-gazing was not going to help me feed and dress my child or get him back to the doctor's. Nor would it help me deal with the pile of wet laundry in the washing machine or the festering dishes in the sink.

I realised then my emotional evolution would have to wait until after Ethan had grown up. I hadn't factored in my life getting cut short; like most mums I was planning on completing every-thing after my child left home. I guess I'll just be half-finished. At least I'll match our home.

I hear the door slam and it shakes the whole house.

'Bye, Mum. Have a good day, I love you!' yells my odorously wonderful boy, who has finally been ushered out the door by his father. The smile returns to my face at the sound of my little therapist's voice. Two minutes later I hear the school bus drive off, followed by Clint reversing his car out of the driveway. Peace at last. I undress and step into the shower. The water pressure still hasn't been fixed and I feel like I am attempting to crack a safe as I try to get the temperature right. When the water hits my shoulders, they drop away from my ears and I let out a big sigh. I breathe in steam and stand motionless under the hot water. I can see a tree outside the bathroom window and a willy wagtail is hopping from one branch to the next. The spirit bird is here, ready and waiting for me. He lightly hops and waggles his tail as if to say, 'Glad to see you got my message, won't be long, it's all just a bit of fun. You'll hop from this branch to another branch.'

He is probably a male bird so it's easy for him to flit from life to death. He has a mate at home feathering the nest, keeping the eggs warm and thinking about where the next meal is coming from.

I reach up for the shampoo and notice the grout. It hasn't been cleaned and is blackening. The scourer is still where I left it weeks ago as a hint for Clint. Despite the hint being followed up by an extensive nagging campaign, it remains unused. I pick it up and start to scrub furiously, which is the only way to scrub. If I had my time again, I'd start a therapy business of my own. No one cleans better than a frustrated woman. Instead of spending money on counsellors we could all just clean each other's bathrooms and wipe our slate floors clean.

But today, despite having a full tank of exasperation, I quickly run out of steam. I don't have the endurance I used to. I turn off the shower. While I am drying myself, I look in the mirror. My face surprises me. It always does. Despite my diagnosis I still look like someone who doesn't need anything from anyone. Not even a happy childhood. What I do need, however, is some Windex, so the next time I look in the mirror I won't see a reflection covered with smudged fingerprints and spattered toothpaste.

CHAPTER 10

My list: Get my tax up to date

My accountant's office is not exactly an office. It's a shipping container he dumped on his property, intending to build an office. It has one window and a door you need to slam three or four times before it closes. There are more than a hundred piles of files scattered all over the floor, and he has not vacuumed or dusted since the container was plonked there, yet he seems remarkably organised. He is actually the best accountant I have ever had. He gets me a tax refund every year and makes tea in a teapot with real leaves and unhomogenised milk that leaves a deliciously oily layer floating on the surface. He even serves it in a proper cup and saucer. I think it is the quality of the tea that has kept me coming back. It is certainly not the ambience.

I generally don't make a fuss when I come here for my annual visit, but today I feel like I can't breathe in any more dust or musty air. I thank him for the tea and ask if he wouldn't mind letting some air in as, despite its age and shoddily installed window and door, the container seems remarkably airtight. He tries to open the window, but it is jammed shut, so I attempt to concentrate on my tea instead of the hundreds of tiny dust particles I am breathing in, all lit up by the streaming sun. He sits down opposite me on a chair that looks like it belongs to Miss Havisham and a cloud of dust puffs softly into the air, enfolding us both in soft focus, like a cheap photography session. He is an old-school philanthropist, and apart from making fabulous tea, is great at the art of discreet donations via undercharging me for his services. Since my cancer diagnosis, he has refused to charge me at all.

That's the great thing about cancer, all the freebies. If I had known how many things you could get for free by being sick I would have saved myself a lot of money on gym memberships, naturopaths and vitamin and mineral supplements. It can be a bit weird taking charity from business owners I already know, so I prefer random freebies and am always on the lookout for opportunities to bring my death sentence into the conversation. If someone asks, 'Can I help you?' I simply answer, 'No, no one can help me, I have cancer,' and that's all that's needed to get a free box of chocolates, flowers, or even, on one recent occasion, my whole fruit and veg for the week.

It's a good idea to shop around because people's discomfort and subsequent generosity can wear off after a while. Perfect strangers are far more generous than family and friends who, after the first wave of attention, start to take your dying in their stride, saving their energy, money, tears and donations for later when they think you will need it most. I'd prefer it now while I can enjoy it, not when I'm in a morphine stupor, and the drugs are taking over while visitors eat my chocolates. It's a bit like leaving your travel plans until you are too old to make the most of them and too tired to even contemplate a holiday fling.

I look across at my accountant. He is one of those men who has grown old but is still surprisingly good-looking, in that men's catalogue, one-size-fits-all kind of way that has always left me unmoved. Unfortunately, I have always been far more attracted to imperfection and chaos than the steady, boredom of dating someone that mentally stable and financially reliable. I watch as he paws disapprovingly through my shoebox full of receipts. He looks up, catching my eye, and then quickly looks away again, politely trying to hide his displeasure.

'You've done a lot better this year with keeping everything,' he says.

I smile to myself and sip my tea. You can simply do no wrong when you have cancer.

I look out the window and notice his pet peacock is shitting all over the makeshift deck but putting on a spectacular display. The sun catches the brilliant blues and turquoise on its tail feathers and chest, and I am entranced by its beauty. Then it lets out the most god-awful screech, does another massive shit and flies up into the gumtree. Note to self, don't walk under the gumtree when you leave.

•

I have had friends tell me, on the odd occasion, that it is good luck to get pooed on by a bird. Those friends are the same ones who have dropped off since I got cancer as they only want to talk about all the good things in life. They love using words like gratitude, acceptance, destiny and the universe. Their other three favourite words are me, myself and I. I know I shouldn't be judgemental, as god knows I am one of the most selfish people I have ever had the misfortune to meet, but seriously, if you are going to be selfish at least don't disguise it as spirituality. I think the reason these kinds of people annoy me so much, apart from the fact that being annoyed appears to be my favourite pastime, is because for me spirituality is more of a smorgasbord than a set menu. I've always liked to pick and choose the best bits and leave the wilting lettuce for those who turn up late.

For instance, I am a big fan of Catholic ritual. I love a bit of frankincense and myrrh and those fabulous old incense dispensers they use to waft smoke over coffins at funerals. I also like their impressive candle holders, and don't mind a bit of confession – wipe yourself clean and off you go – either. The local church used to put on a very good after-mass tea, although unfortunately this tradition seems to be on its way out. While I enjoy a bit of gospel singing, especially if it's done by proper singers as opposed to old ladies with out-of-control vibrato, I'm not a fan of the actual gospel – too thick a book for my liking and not exactly a page-turner. I'm also not such a fan of the guilt, but am a *big* fan of Monty Python's take on all walks of Christianity.

But, please, don't try to make Christianity groovy. Give me musty antiques over God glitzy and well marketed any day. Nothing says there's no one even vaguely resembling cool in here than a Jesus slogan out the front of a church. Slogans like

'Jesus is my rock and that's how I roll', or 'Jesus said I'll be back way before Arnold did', or 'I may not be perfect, but Jesus thinks I'm to die for' really put the 'for Christ's sake' in Christianity. Though the best weird-arse slogan I've ever seen, which is apparently aimed at ensuring young Christian ladies remain that way, is 'Girls only kneel for Jesus'.

When it comes to eastern religions, I love all the intricate artwork, and who doesn't like a decorative buddha and a yummy veggo dish? However, as orange isn't exactly my favourite colour, I'll probably never be a monk, and as far as quieting the mind goes – have you met me?

Religious smorgasbords are never fully complete without a bit of New Age. I admit it's not an all-you-can-pray-for religion but it does make for great shopping, and I often spend my spiritual dollar on tarot cards, crystals, salt lamps and essential oils. I must also confess to having watched more than my healthy share of Oprah and Doctor Phil. Yet somehow my inner cynic still outguns my accepting, peace-loving side. I have had the odd occasion where I managed to feel grateful, but unfortunately they're often interrupted when I notice how Clint didn't bloody bring the washing in like I asked him to. Even my love for Ethan can vanish if I trip on his skateboard while repeating my 'I love my family' mantra.

When I got cancer, I knew I should be diving headfirst into anything that offered some sort of understanding of life, the universe and everything. Instead, I plunged headfirst into tubs of Ben and Jerry's, boxes of chocolates, reality TV shows starring people more messed up than me and attempting to clean my uncleanable house. I found myself starting to hum 'The Impossible Dream' only to change the lyrics and start singing, 'To clean the uncleanable house, to fight the untrainable husband, to go where the brave dare not shop'. I was turning into cancer's answer to 'Weird Al' Yankovic.

•

My accountant appears to be finishing up. He now has some questions to ask me. This is the part where he tries to get me to remember things about money I spent six months ago. This is also the part where I fail miserably. The most embarrassing questions are about larger amounts, such as who was B. Smith I transferred $1200 to months ago? You would think I could remember who I sent that much money to, but it's a big fat blank. I know Clint didn't do it because I handle all the money, so I do what I do every year. I take out a pen and paper and write down all my account-ant's queries to take home so I can try to backtrack through my diary and figure out what the hell I did with all our money. Most of the time I just make up something vaguely plausible because I can't remember what I spent last week let alone almost a year ago. I have a faint memory Mr Smith could have been a tradie I hired at the last minute after getting sick of waiting for Clint to finish something on his list. I normally google business names to try to jog my memory, but there are too many B. Smiths out there, so I make a note to only hire tradies with more exotic surnames in future.

Every year I make a resolution that next year I will stay on top of my tax and do my accounts regularly. I remind myself it only takes five minutes a week to track our budget. I always start out great, but within three months it's game over, and I know the final nail is in the coffin when I start saying, 'Why should I be the only one in the house who ever gives a shit where our money goes?' This year I decided to do my tax just before my birthday as I wanted to celebrate my guaranteed last year ever of doing bookwork. Yeeeeehah! Best present ever.

There's nothing guaranteed but death and taxes, and next year I can guarantee Clint will have to do our tax. Who says I can't get him to do anything on my list!

CHAPTER 11

List? What list?

Today is a blah day. I rip yesterday's page off my daily calendar to see what I have in store and read, 'Do not let all the things that are out of your control interfere with all the things *you can* control.' If my friend Sally hadn't bought it for me, I would have well and truly binned all 365 stupid inspirational sayings by now. I feel like shit today and can't even get motivated to look at the only thing I've ever controlled in my life: my list. The beds aren't made, the washing-up is stacked like a leaning tower in the dishrack and my house is telling me, loudly and clearly, I am a failure. The silence of my phone is also mocking me, telling me nobody likes me, everybody hates me and to go and eat worms.

I check my phone credit. I am still cashed up and connected, but not to anyone who cares, apparently. If I was putting on a New Year's Eve party every man and their dog would be here yelling, ten, nine, eight, seven, six . . . but no one wants to join this particular countdown. They will no doubt rally around for the dying highlights – the obligatory first visit to hospital, followed by the farewell visit and, even though they'd rather have a tooth pulled, they will duly inconvenience themselves by taking a day off work for my funeral. But when that's over and done with they will all just get back on with their lives and their own lists of things to do. For the first year they will remember my birthday, think of me at Christmas and, with a little effort, might even remember the day I die, but by year two, I will be a photo in an album that gets looked at occasionally and they will tut-tut and say, 'She died too young,' and then turn the page to happier snaps.

I know Ethan and Clint will remember me and miss me for a bit longer than the hangers-on, but, really, Clint's not going to survive for long on his own and, realistically, by the time Ethan is a teenager, I will be a distant memory he uses to get the sympathy vote when he's trying to pick up a girl. I can't exactly blame him. I don't remember much at all from when I was his age. I can picture my school backpack, the house we lived in and the 1970s wallpaper in my bedroom. I remember Mum, but only badly. Vicious words and letdowns get remembered for a lot longer than the endless, thankless tasks of mothering. I know my mum, in her better moments, must have spent hours neglecting herself so she could tend to my sister, Catherine, and me, but I have no recollection of her sleepless nights rocking me to sleep as a teething toddler or of her ironing school shirts or helping with homework. I do, however, remember every time she lost the plot and ranted like a mad woman, and every single unkind word she ever said.

On days like today I could easily drown in feeling particularly sorry for myself, so I am grateful when my phone rings with the theme song from *The Brady Bunch* about a lovely lady. I reach for it like I used to reach for a double scotch.

'Marsha?' I answer, my voice sounding shakier than I'd like. She doesn't hear me as she's too busy singing about bringing up three very lovely girls.

'Are you dead yet?' she asks cheerfully.

'Working on it,' I reply. This has become our standard greeting.

'How's the law of distraction going?' Marsha has been away for work, helping staff a new call centre, so I've been missing our regular shenanigans. But she's promised she'll be back in time for me to literally die laughing with her by my side. In the meantime, she calls me often and never fails to put a smile on my dial.

'It's not.'

'Why not?'

'I don't know. Feeling blah.'

'You? Never!'

'Just a little bit . . .' I say, taking in a big loud shaky breath. 'But big girls don't cry.'

'You're not the big girl, I am,' she corrects me.

'Yeah, well, I don't feel like a big girl today,' I confess, letting her get cosy under my skin because I know she'll laugh me out of it.

'Hang in there, baby girl,' she says using her deep, porn star voice to its full, soothing effect. 'I'll be back soon, in the meantime you just have a big cry on Aunty Sugar's mobile phone shoulder.'

'Will not.'

'Come on, cry for Aunty Sugar, you know I love feeling more together than you.'

'Get your kicks somewhere else.'

She starts singing 'Route 66', then continues to poke me.

'Well at least have a big cry when I get there so I can lick the tears off your face.'

'You are not a butterfly,' I say sternly.

Marsha heard somewhere about butterflies that drink the tears off turtles' faces in Ecuador, so because she is flamboyant and colourful, she's decided she is the butterfly. Apparently, I am the turtle because I take so long to get her jokes. I've told her I'm not slow, it's just that her jokes are not funny.

'I've told you before, there is no way you are the butterfly,' I continue, 'I am, and anyway, they don't come in your size.'

'You are mean,' she says sulkily. 'I wish you were dead. Oh wait, ha, ha, you will be soon.'

'Did you just ring up to taunt me?'

'Yes.'

I sigh.

'Feeling better?'

'Yes.'

'Great, job done. I will ring or text again on the hour every hour.'

'Please don't.'

'Oh, I will, you know I will,' she says, hanging up in my ear. Now that's love.

CHAPTER 12

Clint's list: Lie in each other's arms

The envelope slid under the door. We were poised and waiting. This was more than likely Viv's last birthday, so Ethan and I had been planning an extra special one, we hoped, for weeks. I had tried not to make too big a deal of it for Ethan, but he wasn't dumb, he got it, and he'd really put his heart and soul into it. He's such a good kid. I know I get tough on him sometimes, but underneath all that exhausting boy energy he's a sensitive little bugger.

We heard Viv wake up and we knew she'd be doing her usual stretching in the morning, which involves looking at her exercise chart on the back of the door, so we hoped that meant she wouldn't miss seeing the envelope slide under it. We heard her slippers padding towards us, so quickly, but not quite as stealthily as I would have liked as Ethan was giggling his little head off, we retreated to the kitchen. When Viv arrives a few minutes later, smiling and waving the envelope at us, we're sitting at the table eating our cereal as if we've been here all along.

'What's this?' she asks.

'What's what, Mum?' says Ethan, doing the worst bit of acting I have seen since *Rambo VIII.*

'Okay, okay,' she says. 'I'll play along. Hmm, I wonder where this came from?' She opens the envelope and is immediately covered in glitter, just as Ethan planned. He literally falls off the chair laughing and Viv smiles down at him. He so easily lights her up. She's never looked at me like that, not even in the early days. If he'd been another man, I would have punched his lights out by now, but, instead, I find myself looking at him the same way. He's the glue that's kept us together.

Viv reads out loud. 'Follow the arrows that start at the front deck.' It's been raining so some of our markings are a little washed away. As Viv follows the signs, Ethan jumps around her like a monkey.

'Hurry up, Mum, hurry up,' he urges.

'Why? Is the surprise going to run away? Hang on a minute, is it a horse?' She laughs.

'No, Mum.' Ethan rolls his eyes. 'But it would be cool if it was . . . maybe we can get a horse for your next birthday.'

I freeze and hold up my hand to try to stop him talking, but Viv just pulls him close into a warm hug and gives him a huge smile.

'Sure, honey, next birthday would be lovely.'

She is getting closer now. She follows the arrows behind the shade cloth to the spot that, until last week, was my designated hiding place for unfinished jobs and junk. When Viv sees the spa there instead, she opens her mouth, but no words come out. She looks at the two of us, then starts to sob.

'It's okay, Mum, it's okay,' says Ethan.

She looks up at me.

'Come on, love, let me help you,' I say, helping her out of her pyjamas and into the cossies draped across the stairs. I support her arm to keep her steady, and the look of relaxation that comes across her face as she sits in the steaming hot spa water is too much for me. I turn away so they don't see me wipe my eyes. I take off my dressing-gown. Ethan follows suit.

Viv notices our board shorts and laughs. 'Did you sleep in those?'

For a brief moment, there is silence while we sink into the heat. It dissolves all the anticipation of the morning and a little of the stress we have all been under. Viv looks at me.

'This wasn't even on my list,' she says, so softly it's barely a whisper.

But I hear it and melt even further into the water. Peace. Then Ethan dives under, comes up and spurts water out of his mouth and into both our faces.

'Ah so relaxing.' I laugh. 'Come on, mate, let's get your mum some breakfast and let her enjoy the spa for a minute.'

'I am enjoying it.' She laughs and spurts water back into Ethan's face.

Viv's birthday brekkie isn't as exciting as I would have liked, as with the nausea she's able to eat less and less, so I've kept it simple. Vegemite toast and English Breakfast tea. She told me that's all she used to have growing up, and for ages she couldn't face either of them, but since her diagnosis it's become her go-to meal. The nostalgia of it is comforting I guess.

Ethan's off to his mate's house for the day. They are planning to build a whole city of Lego in his room. His mate has been collecting the stuff for years, and the other day when his parents were planning a garage sale, his mum told him it had to go because he hadn't played with it for months. She sorted it into boxes only to have him suddenly develop a passion for it again. That's the way it is with kids, tell them they can't have something, or they've outgrown it, and suddenly they want it more than ever.

I guess it's the same with adults too. Now that Viv and I know it's not forever anymore and that the ''til death do us part' bit of our vows is almost past its due date, we've started to cling to each other. I'm noticing so many things about her I'd forgotten. Things that might have shitted me before, but now seem endearing. Like how she drinks her tea. She has a ritual. It has to be in a pot. It has to be leaf tea. The pot has to be warmed first and then, once the tea and water are in, it has to be turned three times. I never understood why you couldn't just stir it with a spoon, but anyway. Then you've got to wait a minimum of three minutes before it's poured. The milk must go in first, and then, before she drinks it, she lets the steam drift to her nostrils and warms her hands around the cup. By the time she's taken her first sip, I've already downed my first coffee. But this morning, as she comes back inside to make her obligatory second cup of tea, instead of wishing she didn't have so many bloody rules about everything, I watch her as the sun streams in the window. Her skin is flushed from the warmth of the spa, and she has a misleadingly healthy glow about her.

In his rush to get ready for Lego land, Ethan has left his breakfast things everywhere. Viv puts down her teacup and starts clearing the dining table, even though I know it hurts her. I don't say anything. Lately she's been wanting to be just left alone so she can get on with her jobs. She pauses on the way to the dishwasher, stopping midway and wincing, but then perseveres. She's a tough one. I sit back while she carries on cleaning, glad to have got this birthday morning right, but then when I go to take another gulp of my coffee, I let out a yelp.

'Bloody TMJ.'

She looks back at me, the spell broken.

'Your jaw?' she questions, clenching her own.

'Yeah, yeah, it's okay.' I try to downplay it while massaging my jawbone to stop it locking up.

A sharp pain shoots up the side of my face and, without meaning to, I grimace and moan again.

'You okay?' she asks, her eyebrow raised in disgust.

'Yeah, yeah, it just hurts a bit.'

'Try cancer,' she mumbles and starts packing the dishwasher furiously. She refuses to believe my jaw hurts as much as I say it does. She is silent for a moment, then the tirade starts.

'I thought you said you were going to see someone about your temporary mandy jaw thingy or whatever the hell it's called?'

I shrug, hoping to not add to her mood.

She shrugs back. 'What the hell's that supposed to mean. Do I have to organise everything for you?'

My plan today had been the birthday surprise, then a bit of brekkie, then to just lie in each other's arms and read a book on the front porch. We don't get much downtime these days between doctor's appointments, and I wanted her to have a normal day for her birthday, but lately with Viv the look of love can turn to the look of anger in an instant. Sometimes even just my walking through the door can remind her of every time I've ever done something wrong. It's not hard to trigger her when she keeps her weapons locked and loaded with every bit of historical ammunition that's ever made it through her armour. Her friends don't help either, talking about how pathetic men are with pain and how we're always getting man flu. Although this time I'm not sure what's bothering her most: my agony, or that she can't pronounce temporomandibular joint dysfunction.

I look over at her and she is crying as she does the dishes. Every time she slams another plate down, she flinches.

'Viv.' She ignores me. 'Viv, come on, love, let me do that, I can see you're in pain.'

'Yes, yes, I am in pain, and I'm being a bitch I know, and you did such a beautiful thing for my birthday, but I can't help it, I just hate you.' Her face contorts into the angry but fragile little-girl face I love.

'I just hate you and I hate the bloody cancer,' she tries to yell as she starts to sob.

I rush over to hold her and feel her sink into my arms, her tiny body shaking with sobs.

'I hate the bloody cancer too, love.'

•

That afternoon when we picked up Ethan, he was bouncing off the walls. He and his little mate had apparently only spent the first five minutes working on the famed Lego metropolis before they got bored. In the end, instead of creating a plastic city, they had spent their day learning magic tricks and eating copious amounts of sugar-laden food that he never gets to eat at home.

'Dad, Dad, Mum, Mum, can I show you a trick, it's awesome, it's totally awesome. Look, look, see, are you looking, so . . . Aw, come on, Dad, are you looking?'

'Yes, Ethan, I'm looking.'

'Mum, are you looking?'

Viv laughs. 'Yes, I'm looking, Dad's looking, the next-door neighbour's dog's looking, we're all looking.'

'Okay, okay, so watch closely. I am holding in my hand an ordinary toothbrush. Here, put out your hand and you can check it,' he says, handing it to me. 'Can you confirm that's just an ordinary toothbrush?'

'Yes, I can confirm that.'

'Good, good. Now I am going to wrap it up in this tea towel.'

'Oh no, not the tea towel, I'll have to wash that now,' moans Viv.

'It's okay, Mum, it's just a toothbrush.'

'Yes, but you've had it in your mouth. I can't very well use the tea towel on our good clean dishes now, can I?'

'Sorry, Mum.'

Viv takes a breath. 'It's okay, Ethan, it's just a tea towel. All right, show me your trick.'

'Okay, okay, so it's just an ordinary toothbrush, you're sure of that?'

'Yes, Ethan, it's just an ordinary toothbrush,' says Viv, smiling. 'And you're about to wrap it up in my ordinarily clean tea towel,' she says with a smile she reserves for Ethan when he's cheeky.

'Correct.' Ethan laughs, happy his mum is now along for the ride.

'So, I wrap it up in Mum's extraordinarily clean tea towel, and I say the magic words, abracadabra, bibbity boo, disappear little toothbrush while I do a poo.'

Viv rolls her eyes. Everything rhymes with poo when you're eight. Ethan shakes the tea towel with a flourish and, to our amazement, he has made the toothbrush disappear. He looks delightedly at our faces.

'See, see, I told you I could do it.'

'How in the heck did you do that?' I ask, seriously impressed.

'Do you want me to tell you, it's easy see –' starts Ethan before Viv claps her hand over his mouth.

'No, no, a magician never reveals his secrets.'

She starts walking him around the lounge room in a semi-headlock. He is wriggling and trying to talk through her hand.

'Dad doesn't want to know, do you, Clint?'

'Apparently not.' I laugh.

CHAPTER 13

Not on my list: Join a multi-level marketing scheme

When Ethan started going to daycare, I was still at the stage where you give a damn about what all the other mothers are doing, so I'd decided I'd better get a job to try to keep up with the supermums. The only trouble was I had absolutely no skills, having always been a starter but not a finisher. Growing Ethan was the only job I'd ever seen through to completion. And if I could have stopped halfway through the pregnancy and changed my mind, I probably would have. I definitely would have quit mid-birth, had that been an option. My motivation to join the ranks of working mums was boosted by the fact Clint's salary was crap and I had an undiagnosed addiction to op-shopping. It's amazing how much you can spend five dollars at a time.

Instead of diving straight in and applying for jobs, I decided to do what I'd always done and start yet another community college course, a two-day barista short study. Luckily it wasn't a three-day program, as by day two I was well and truly ready to quit, but when I tried to escape during the morning tea break, it was raining so heavily I realised I'd rather listen to one more lecture on milk froth than drown. Thanks to bad weather, I ruined my track record and actually completed something. Lucky I did though, as otherwise I would never have met Sally on the first and only day I ever worked as a caffeine-pusher before graduating to the far less aromatic world of insurance sales.

I was employed in a little pop-up coffee cart at a conference centre an hour's drive from home. I enjoyed being in the big smoke until morning tea came and I was overwhelmed by hyped-up participants taking a break from a Tony Robbins seminar. By the look on their faces, and the way they jumped around all over the place, high-fiving each other like there was no tomorrow, the last thing they needed was caffeine. Still, that didn't stop them from putting in what seemed like literally thousands of orders for double shot skinny lattes. Just as I was about to pour hot beverages over their enthusiastic little heads, the bell rang and they all charged back into the conference room, now even more charged up on coffee. As soon as they left, Sally, who had been politely waiting on the side, came up to the counter.

'I know this is a coffee van, but I don't suppose you have any chai tea?' she asked, smiling her thousand-watt smile, which at the time I thought was a result of too much Tony but have since realised is just her.

'We have chai powder,' I replied, trying to hide my disgust that anyone would even consider drinking that muck.

'Oh no, that's okay,' she said politely. 'I prefer chai tea made with leaves. Thanks anyway.'

She turned to walk away but I stopped her, immediately recognising a kindred spirit.

'I think I might have a couple of emergency chai teabags left in my handbag. I can make you a chai latte with one of them if that's any use to you?' I offered.

She beamed at me. 'Oh my goodness, that would be fabulous.'

We'd been unlikely friends ever since, especially after I came to realise her enthusiasm for life was genuine and not just the post–Tony Robbins manic attack it had appeared to be. That day she insisted on giving me a recording by Mr Robbins which, despite my cynical nature, went on to become my go-to happy place, because it reminded me of her. Later, she even managed to drag me along to a couple of his seminars, but, unfortunately, while I secretly lusted after Tony, I just couldn't bring myself to join the happy high-five brigade. Before I met Sally, I don't think I'd ever actually met anyone who was genuinely happy or who could look that exhilarated without needing meds, so I was still highly suspicious of joy in all its forms.

We've been friends for over five years now and while Sally is still super-big into Tony, she has also branched out into party plans and MLMs. Despite her new obsession with marketing on multi-levels, she remains my favourite little ray of sunshine and is always a perfect antidote to anything and anyone, so the timing of her visit couldn't be better.

Sally's journey into the world of party plans started with Tupperware, then expanded into selling scented candles before she went to the top of the food chain and began selling Thermomixes, or is that Thermomixi? Now I have cancer, she is super excited as her latest venture is a cure-all herbal remedy. If she can put me in remission and save my life, her business will go gangbusters. I have agreed to her coming around to give me her sales spiel. That's how desperate for entertainment I am.

Dying is not the exciting thing it's cracked up to be in the movies. On the big screen, it happens much faster and with a much bigger cast than in real life. On my set, I spend hours sitting around trying to distract myself, and there's far less weeping and wailing, as there's only so much grieving I can do before I get hungry, need to go to the toilet or get plain old bored with my own self-pity.

At times like this – or anytime for that matter – I would normally find glass half-full people, who are always trying to make the most of every situation, mind-bogglingly irritating. But with Sally it's different. Maybe that's because she's been a lecturer at the school of hard knocks. What she hasn't been through isn't worth mentioning. She's also the one who taught me about the power of distraction. As a baby, I wasn't easily diverted. My nanna used to say, once I had my mind set on something no amount of rattles or shiny things would get my mind off the problem at hand. But now, thanks to Sally, I am starting to discover distraction can be a salve for both body and mind.

Sally, as always, is exactly six minutes early. I don't know when or why I started timing her arrivals, but it's one of those habits that just became a thing, and now I love knowing I can time her to the second. She always does the friendly knock.

Knock-knockety-knock-knock (and a pause) knock-knock, and calls out, 'Viv, it's Sally.' She doesn't like surprises or visitors popping in unannounced as she, like me, has an over-the-top startle response. If you accidentally catch her off guard, she yells, jumps and looks like she is having a mini heart attack before she realises it's just a friend saying hi. After spending her childhood in foster care, it's hardly surprising she has quirks like that. Not that, according to Sally, her childhood didn't have its benefits. She says it's how her career in sales began – trying to convince multiple foster parents she was the gal for them. While she never did find a permanent home, she did hone her sales skills considerably.

'Hello, most wonderful woman and friend in the world,' she croons to me.

Her greeting lights me up every time and, even though I've heard her use the same line on everyone from her aunty to the local checkout chick, it still makes me feel special.

'Hey, Sal, come on in.'

'How are you feeling?' she asks.

'Like crap but that's why you're here, right?'

I am all up for this game.

'Oh, Viv, yes. I am super excited to share this with you.'

'Well don't just stand there, come on in.'

Sal is loaded up, which is also a big part of why I am always willing to be a guinea pig for whatever her latest money-making scheme is. She always arrives like Little Red Riding Hood, with a basket full of goodies, because, even though everyone she knows has already bought or refused to buy a Thermomix from her, she can't kick her habit of weekly cooking demonstrations. I pour boiling water into the teapot as she unpacks a table-load of food with everything from raw vegan cakes through to baked potatoes. It looks fantastic, but then my stomach turns and I realise I have momentarily forgotten about my nausea, dagnabbit. I pour some tea, happy to have an excuse to break out my fancy cups.

'Choose a colour,' I say, showing her my selection of vintage teacups.

'Oooh, I'll have yellow please,' she says with just the right amount of enthusiasm to satisfy me.

I pick up a piece of raw cake and put it on my plate to be polite, hoping she won't notice me not eating.

'So, Viv, I know you are fairly far along on your cancer journey and that your doctors have probably told you it is hopeless.'

'Correct,' I chime in, happy to have someone talking about my impending doom rather than avoiding the C-word for a change.

'Look, obviously I can't make any promises, but this product, well . . .' she shakes her hands in front of her eyes. 'I'm sorry I get very emotional about it, but, well . . . it's changing lives.' Sal is always this emotional in her sales pitches whether she's selling a vacuum cleaner, a timeshare or a cup of coffee. She only ever sells something she truly believes in, and Sal, god love her, believes in everything. That's one of the reasons I love her. Despite one failed relationship after another, Sal refuses to give up on hope or love. She's a dreamer through and through, and there's not a cynical bone in her body. Every time she visits, I feel like I get to go on vacation from myself, and today is no different. I allow myself to get swept along by her wave of enthusiasm. For a moment I start to think, *What if the stupid doctors are wrong? They've been wrong before, and I've never been that big a fan of western medicine. What harm is it going to do if I try this? It's not going to kill me.*

I feel hope lodging its foot in the door and trying to keep it open. I've already slammed hope's fingers in the door so many times I am surprised it would even bother trying to gain entry again, but it does feel nice to think I could live just a little bit longer. Maybe I'd write a different list. I tune back into Sal just as she starts showing me videos of people who have turned around all sorts of life-threatening illnesses after using her magic herbs.

'Now, of course, none of these people had terminal cancer, so I don't want to get your hopes up . . . but imagine if it worked, Viv! Oh just imagine if I could actually help you,' she says, her eyes misting with tears.

She has a 1950s Mouseketeer look about her that makes you believe that Lassie will find a way, and all is not lost no matter how bleak things get. It's how she's survived, and I wish I had even a tenth of her belief in the world. She's like an anti-venom to myself, and I relax into a world of fairytale endings and dreams coming true.

'Now – and don't argue with me, Viv – I am going to leave you a month's supply for free. If it does what I think it will do, we can talk about you signing up once you are out of the worst of it,' she says.

Now I find my own eyes welling with tears. Sal never gives anything away for free, she must be worried about me.

'Thanks, Sal,' I say, hugging her and trying to let myself be comforted by the MLM equivalent of Marie Curie.

But her generous act sends my mood spiralling downwards as I slowly begin to grasp that even Sally is scared I won't make it. She is never not positive. I find myself sobbing in her arms. This is real. I don't think I've ever totally understood that before. All this time, I've been going through the motions, taking the drugs, going to my weekly GP appointments to assess and adjust my meds, listening to the palliative care nurse tell me what to expect next and trying to get prepared. I've been keeping myself so busy because there was still part of me that somehow believed I might be one of the people who beat it. If I'm honest, that's why I wanted Sal to come here to offer me hope in a monthly subscription bottle. I have been waiting for remission and to be featured on *A Current Affair* as the woman who survives against the odds. I cannot make sense of my mortality; surely death didn't mean to include me? I am here, living in this body, and I cannot fathom how I can, in the blink of an eye, cease to exist.

I have lived averagely, loved tepidly and managed to sometimes get the washing on the line before it started to smell from having been forgotten in the machine. These are not major achievements, yet I am attached to all of them. I even like whingeing about my aches and pains. I love bitching about politicians and rising prices. I like getting a particularly good bargain online, only to decide to sell my purchase on Gumtree for less than half of what I paid for it two months later. I am not ready to give up. Not even on Clint. I've only just gotten used to all the things about him that really irritate me. He's familiar, and he's become family. We've gone from a few months of wine-assisted copulation to ten years of sobering company. I can rely on him to be annoyingly himself, to always need nagging for the smallest of tasks and to never even contemplate leaving me. But now I can't even depend on us being stuck together anymore. I'm going whether I like it or not.

By now, I am racked with deep sobs. Sal is struggling to hold me up as I collapse convulsively into her arms. She manages to get us both to the floor and then rocks me in her arms like a baby. When I finally stop crying, I look up at her, and she has this serene, peaceful smile on her face.

'Feel better?' she asks.

'Yes, thanks, Sal.'

The phone rings, and, without thinking, I quickly blow my nose and jump up to answer it like one of Pavlov's dogs. It is a telemarketer. I roll my eyes and mouth 'Sorry' to Sal. She smiles, and while I am on the phone, puts on the kettle, packs a box of her herbal remedies away in my pantry and pours me a cup of tea.

CHAPTER 14

My list: Restore Poppa's lowboy

This week had been full of surprises. Clint scored a new job as a purchasing manager at a new boutique motel, I got a spa and Ethan has a head full of nits. Not all great surprises, but Clint's new job does take the pressure off somewhat, especially as his new boss is an old mate. With a friend in the right place, he's managed to negotiate a contract that includes working from home a few days a fortnight. I am using his newfound time to try and make a bit more of a dent in my list which, so far, hasn't been going that well.

Next up is restoring Poppa's lowboy. I'm not sure if in my state I can bring it back to its former glory, but I can at least buy supplies for the job. First stop, as with most things on my list, is Bunnings.

When Poppa was alive there was no such thing as Bunnings, lattes or mobile phones, but miraculously he still managed to live, until he didn't. Poppa was the patriarch of our family and was one of those people who you never really expected would die. He'd survived the war, he'd survived life as a taxi driver, and he'd survived drinking International Roast coffee, so what could possibly kill him? He went on to survive a stroke, kidney failure and blowing a major artery in his heart. It wasn't until one of his children told him he wouldn't be going home from the hospital but was destined for a nursing home that he decided to check out. There had been a tag team of visitors from the moment he became ill. He wasn't going to be left in the hospital to die alone, not in this family. But, of course, in true Poppa style, he waited until someone ducked out to the bathroom to slip away without a fuss. Although, he had made sure there was a cute nurse on hand for one last flirt before he departed dearly.

When Poppa died, he left a hole in the family, and in my heart, where a strong man had been. He was irreplaceable, and no one was ever going to live up to him. He had been as tough, racist, simple, sexist and uncomplicated as most men of his generation. He was unapologetically himself, and yet when his grandkids and great-grandkids had taken issue with some of his world views, most of which had formed out of unimaginable trauma during the war, he proved you *can* teach an old dog new tricks. He opened his heart and mind at an age when most people aren't even able to open tight jam jar lids.

I lived with Poppa after he lost Nanna. They had married young and had been each other's everything. To the day she died, Nanna would still go out to the front of their house to wave him off to work and then hurry out into the backyard to where she could see him drive around the corner, so she could wave again. She died early and suddenly in her sleep of an undiagnosed heart condition. He woke up next to her and tried to cover her up with a blanket because she felt so cold. When he finally comprehended she was gone, he handled everything himself before calling the family to let them know Nanna had died on Mother's Day.

Her death left him lost and bewildered. He had never bought groceries and didn't even know how he took his own tea, as she had always made it for him. One month after losing her he lost his job and himself. My strong, six-foot-tall grandfather was no longer upright and no longer able to cope. I grieved silently with him and felt the weight of his loss for years.

He eventually found comfort in another woman's arms. They had been long-term friends and when she lost her husband it was only natural they would turn to each other. While Nanna and Poppa had been complete opposites, Poppa's new girlfriend was like his twin. They never married, but he stayed alive for her longer than he ever would have tried to alone. I still thank her for saving his life and giving me extra time to understand why I loved him so much.

After Nanna died, we cleaned the house from top to bottom. Nanna was an incredibly loving, tidy woman who always put things away. The fact she was putting them away into a cupboard that was slowly filling up with dust, or where a mouse had died so long ago it had turned into a mouse skeleton, escaped her attention. Hers was a house filled with love and little things like cleaning didn't matter to her. There were no rules or chores for children in Nanna's house, except that you snuggled her regularly and didn't tell your parents about the lollies she kept hidden in her bag just for you.

When Poppa died, I dreamt I was walking through their house kissing the stained walls and furniture, inhaling all their stability and kindness. I gave my sister, Catherine, everything she'd wanted from their estate in exchange for inheriting Poppa's lowboy, which smells like their house. When you open the door to the cupboard that used to store Nanna's sewing things, there is still a whiff of mustiness, dust and camphor.

For the past eight years, it's been on my list to restore, but I have been worried that when I scrape off the old paint to reveal the beautiful wood underneath, I will lose Nanna and Poppa's scent and won't be able to find my way back to them again.

When I was first diagnosed, I climbed into the lowboy like I used to when I was a little girl playing hide and seek and closed the door behind me. I smelt the darkness and yearned for them. It was then I understood I was going home. I was either going into nothing-ness or I was going to see Nanna and Poppa.

Wandering the aisles at Bunnings my heart flutters like a fluorescent light trying to come on. They were my everything but I've been pushing them out of my mind, getting busy with too many chores and too few lollies. I almost forgot how, even in their cigarette-filled home, they helped me to breathe.

CHAPTER 15

Ethan's list: Untidy his room

The moon slides slowly behind the mountains as the yoga instructor easily bends his leg up behind his head and gives a peaceful smile. This is not quite the easy yoga practice I had in mind, and the sound of games being played in Ethan's room isn't helping. He is meant to be tidying his room.

I hate yoga teachers. I hate how they don't have any wrinkles on their foreheads as if they don't have a worry in the world. It's not natural. They ease themselves in and out of unnatural contortions like they are made of rubber and never, ever fart while they are instructing. How is that possible, when every other person in the class is trying to disguise or mute their inevitable embarrassment? The instructors surely eat more lentils than their pupils, and yet, despite their incredibly relaxed state, their sphincter control remains impeccable. That's why I prefer doing yoga online. I also prefer it because I can yell at the teachers.

I am trying out a new instructor today who is already doing a good job of giving me the shits. While his asanas are obviously not designed for those of us who are terminating, I still think he might be the teacher for me as there are just so many things he does that I can criticise. Let's start with his smile, for example. Is that a genuine smile? No, it most certainly is not. It's a smug smile that says, 'I am superior to you on every level, both physically and spiritually, but even though I am superior, if you are under twenty-five I will still deign to sleep with you because I am in a committed "open relationship".' It's an open relationship because he has managed to convince his partner, who is in awe of his spirituality, that sleeping around is the process of an enlightened being. How we went from the complete celibacy of Buddhist monks to sleazy yoga instructors is anybody's guess, but that's twenty-first-century champagne Buddhism for you. With a bit of marketing buzz, even blue food colouring can become good for you.

The instructor has now begun doing mindful push-ups while in a full headstand pose. This is his beginners' yoga class. He has an alternative pose which involves kneeling and placing your head on the ground to prepare yourself for the full inverted posture. He is also demonstrating how you can still watch the video through your legs while doing this, so you don't have to take your eyes off him. This leaves your hands free to wipe the drool from your mouth as you ogle his impressive biceps. I am starting to love this video – there is nothing more invigorating than using your highly evolved yelling muscles to defend all that is flabby on your own body by yanking wanker tall-poppies down from where their pedestal has been straddling mother earth. I am sure, like all mothers, the planet has had enough organic bullshit piled on top of her for one enlightened lifetime. Ahh, I am feeling more relaxed already.

'Mum, Mum, there's a dead mouse in my room!'

There goes my Zen state.

'Where's your father?'

'He went out to get some hot chips.'

Clint has always had impeccably convenient timing when it comes to cleaning up anything, whether it's vomit, poo, wee or dead things.

'Okay, I'm coming,' I say, wondering if I could just wait until Clint comes home. After all, the mouse is dead so it's not going anywhere.

The yoga instructor has come down into a cobra position to show off his pecs. I think I'd prefer to deal with the dead mouse, so while he continues to try and turn on his online audience, I turn him off.

Luckily for me, my sense of smell is becoming as insensitive as I like to think the yoga instructor is. So, while my highly smell-sensitive child is holding his nose and pulling faces, I am able to effortlessly pick up the poor withered little mouse by the tail without so much as a gag. I look at its tiny body, and for a moment I feel sad for it and its cute little mouse family until I see all the shit they have managed to produce behind the toy boxes in my son's room. How can such small creatures manage to poo so much? I take the mouse outside and just manage to find the energy to throw it over my neighbour's fence. She won't notice, she never mows the grass, which I am sure is full of snakes, one of which will make an instant meal out of it. My neighbour is also blind, so I don't have to worry about her catching sight of me flinging dead rodents over her fence. I used to feel guilty about things like that, but now it just feels natural to use the resources you have. Why would I bother digging a tiny grave, even if I was strong enough, when the resident snakes can just eat mouseflakes for breakfast instead?

Cancer does get you out of lots of situations. I am not sure where I stand on the sympathy list when it comes to disabilities; still, I hold back from my urge to yell out as the mouse goes flying through the air: 'I see your blindness and raise you my cancer.' I wonder if anyone has ever done a study on that. Surely someone has received funding in a regional university somewhere to complete a PhD on who deserves more sympathy, assistance and government grants. Are you better off deaf, blind, paralysed, disfigured or dying when it comes to the community rallying around you? Cancer doesn't seem to be that great at eliciting support, not long term anyway. Dying is still a bit distasteful to most people. It puts them off their food and can be too much in their faces, but I kind of like that.

I've always enjoyed making people feel uncomfortable. Maybe it was growing up in a rough neighbourhood where the only thing you had to help you stand out from the crowd was shock value. Doing something Nobel prize–worthy, on the other hand, was the most dangerous thing you could do. It was like a neon sign that said you were no longer the same as everyone else. Even getting too posh a jacket or too good a job, or even just a job, could result in you being tried and found guilty of judging everyone around you. Not because you were, mind you, but because you were now a mirror that reflected all their insecurities right back at them, so they wanted to smash you to pieces or scratch your surface so you were no longer shiny. If you were smart, you would cover your mirror over whenever anyone was looking. I was never that clever, which is why, when I decided I deserved a better life free from my mother, I had to leave.

When Catherine and I first moved away from home, it was seen as a betrayal, even though we'd originally only been planning to take a break for the winter. Back then we'd gotten on better, and with no kids or husbands in tow, we thought we would stick to a bad thing and move in together. We left our dysfunctional childhood behind and, for a while, managed to play nice. We'd been Mum's carers since we were little, so it was a relief when one of Mum's siblings finally stepped up to the plate. It didn't last long though. The minute Mum lost the plot, Aunty Joan packed her bags, headed back to Sydney and offloaded caring once again. Unfortunately, Catherine's never fallen too far from the family tree, so I was left to pick up the torn pieces while my sister placed an ad for a new housemate.

After months of staring down the depressing barrel of a future with my mother, I eventually managed to navigate my way through mountains of red tape to get Mum into supported living so I could carve out some sort of a life. Not that I did much with my freedom other than attempt to rebrand 'running away' as 'travel adventures'. Despite packing the aptly named Lonely Planet guide and pocket-sized board games replete with loaded dice, I always seemed to end up on the road to nowhere and never managed to land on 'Go' or collect two hundred dollars. Finally, after one too many shared amenities blocks, I abandoned my dream of ever leaving this shit of a town for good. When I met Clint years later, it soon became apparent that staying put suited him to a tee. Before I knew it I'd given up on Mayfair and settled into the cheapest suburb on the board, right back where I started.

While Catherine's always been able to bolt pretty quickly, Dad makes her look like a non-starter. He left even earlier than the aunts and uncles. He was ahead of his time, having been a sperm donor before IVF was even thought of. He'd donated enough sperm to father myself and Catherine before heading off to service every woman in the district with his milk of human kindness. My mother had deluded herself into believing he loved her more than the others, which I guess in some ways he did, because he at least knew her name and had liked her enough to donate more than once. While I don't have any memories of him, I would still like to meet him, if only so I know which screwed-up parts of my personality to blame on my mother and which bits to blame on dear old Dad. It might also be nice to try and track down any possible half-siblings I have scattered in the least illustrious of places. Unfortunately, I appear to have run out of time to do any investigation into whether I have any siblings-in-sin, which is just as well, as I always thought blended families would get stuck in my teeth.

Unlike most children who don't know their dads, I have no fantasies about mine. Not that it would have been hard to be a better babysitter than my mother, but at least she was hanging around for the final credits.

CHAPTER 16

My list: Fill my script

I am juggling too many things at the moment, not just jobs on my list, but my phone, my handbag, a takeaway tea and a bag of shopping. The customer in front of me has finished being served, so I manage to put my tea on the counter, just as my mobile rings. The pharmacist says, 'Next,' and holds out her hand for my script. I answer the phone with my cheek, and she gives me a dirty look before snatching the prescription for my nausea, anxiety and pain meds out from where I am juggling it between my thumb and my mobile.

I am becoming quite the drug addict and have increased my regular MS Contin pain relief to both morning and night as well as taking Endone when I need a little extra kick. My nausea meds sound like my son's transformer toys, Maxolon and Ondansetron, and have indeed transformed me, along with good old Valium, which apparently can be used as something other than a post-party drug. Who knew? I am also now on the oh-so glamorously and appropriately named anti-constipation drug, Movicol, to help me move it, move it and counter the effects of everything else. My phone falls to the ground, and I accidentally hang up on Telstra after having waited for a call back from them for a week. I can't bloody believe it. I want to yell at the pharmacist, but sometimes these days, embarrassingly, I cry. I wish I had an umbrella, so I could put it up when I feel tears coming in public or, better still, use it to poke the pharmacist in the nose. I hate crying, it's messy and unnecessary, like rain when it's flooding – whoever decided that was a good idea?

•

When I finally got Mum into supported living, I escaped home for the second time and ran away to the desert. I loved how impolite life was in the red centre and how all my bodily fluids dried up. There was no rain and no room for unnecessary, water-wasting emotions.

The train journey to the outback had been monotonous and painstakingly slow, interrupted only by a long-awaited downpour that washed fifteen years of drought off the carriage windows. When the train pulled into what couldn't even be called a station, my weather-beaten uncle welcomed me to nowhere. I'd planned to spend a year with him, but my timeframe was promptly shortened when I realised he lived in a shed.

When I stepped out of his battered ute it was like walking into a whorehouse of death. He lived off whatever he could kill. For him, life was simple. You lived, you shot things, you survived and then you went six feet under. He said very little to me, but I still remember the few sentences he uttered because he repeated them at least five times a day for the whole time I lived with him.

'What are you worrying about all that for? There's only two things that make a difference: if the sun's up or the sun's down.'

I never made the mistake of reading any great philosophical undercurrent into his words as he made it clear to me he had no need for over-thinking, or even thinking.

He hated organised religion and instead prayed to the stars, the bush, the red dirt and, occasionally, during the outback camel races, the god of all gamblers. Every day, just before dinner, he talked about how good it felt to skin a kangaroo and throw it onto the campfire. Up until then I had loved the idea of a simple life in tune with land and Country, but the animal slaughtering, coupled with mind-numbing boredom, helped me realise I was destined for a life of much more important things. After three months, I headed back to town to waste my youth on relationship dramas, flatmate complications and, eventually, long lists of non-life-changing chores. Looking back, I realise even if I'd been older when I went to the desert, I still wouldn't have lasted. I wasn't born with a go-slow setting and, having no doubt multitasked my way through multiple incarnations, I wasn't about to change the habit of my lifetimes.

•

'Vivian Walker.'

The pharmacist calls out my name and hands me my script to sign. Just as I put my mobile on the counter, it starts to ring. I try to answer in case, against all odds, it's Telstra calling back, but instead I hang up again and spill my tea all over the counter. The pharmacist shoves a paper bag with my meds towards me and storms off.

CHAPTER 17

Not on my list: Attend someone else's funeral

When you are dying, you are often struck off the guest list for other people's funerals, but I have decided to gate-crash one regardless. A workmate from the insurance company passed away a few days ago, and I only found out about it when I saw her death notice in the local paper. I'm not sure if I wasn't informed because I am terminal or because my job was terminated. My previous boss JJ (which I always said stood for double jerk) had 'let me go' after he got wind of my illness. He managed to pull a swift manoeuvre whereby he not only got me off the books and avoided paying sickness benefits but also seemed to do it with a clear conscience.

After I left work, most of my co-workers breathed a sigh of relief that they didn't have to watch my demise. To be honest, if it had happened to someone else, I would have been the first to find a way to amuse myself until it was time for sandwiches at the wake. But as usual, someone beat me to the punch.

Sophie had been the company's receptionist and she talked to everyone the same way she answered the phone: bright, polite and professional. Unlike me she was popular and no wonder – she'd had the good grace to die suddenly so both customers and staff could get the formalities over and done with, and get promptly back to the job at hand. At only twenty-three, she was untarnished by life whereas I needed all the Brasso I could get and, even then, good luck finding the shiny happy person underneath.

I was looking forward to seeing the looks on my ex-colleagues faces when I rocked up on death's door. I was also hoping to pick up a few tips about things I may have forgotten to put on my funeral shopping list.

The death notice had requested people not send flowers but donate to a bicycle safety charity instead, as Sophie had been knocked off her bike on her way to the gym by a motorist who apparently was not bike-aware. It also requested everyone wear white.

There is unexpected traffic on the way to the service, so when I arrive I am late, but at least it isn't to my own funeral. I don't bother waiting for Clint, who insisted on coming from work to support me, but instead walk straight to the front of the church to a spare seat beside JJ, who glances at me, shifting uncomfortably. In my pink and teal dress I am happy to see I stand out amongst the sea of white and that my choice of seating has ensured the workplace contingency has noted my arrival.

It is a Catholic service, and they have opted for the full mass. A sensible choice, as it makes the whole affair a reasonable length, suited to the sobriety of the occasion. I am not a big fan of the non-secular services which are a bit 'wham, bam, thank you, ma'am' for my liking. I do, however, think the PowerPoint presentation is a little lengthy for someone who, let's face it, had not done very much at all in her short life. The eulogy is suitably moving but sadly lacking in jokes, as is the entire service. I do, however, approve of the way they've indicated the seating arrangements with subtle white ribbons around the entry to the pews, which means everyone, apart from myself, received a clear message as to where to sit.

From my current resting place, I have a particularly good view of the casket and it's obvious no expense has been spared. Unfortunately, no good taste has been spared either. It is a bit too gold-trimmed, bling and gaudy for my liking. I think coffins should be like a practical handbag, big enough to do the job and sensible enough to match their purpose as a container, not a fashion item. Funerals are getting a bit like weddings now and have become too much about keeping up with the dead Joneses.

During the service, most people manage to adhere to the hierarchy of grief and politely wait until the parents, siblings and Sophie's boyfriend finally break down, before allowing themselves to dab at their eyes. However, I did see a few pre-emptive lip wobbles that suggested some people found the inordinate amount of time the relatives managed to keep themselves together to be excessively self-controlled.

As the service concludes I am happy to hear from the very old, and obviously very traditional, priest that everyone is welcome (read *expected*) to attend the burial. I've never liked the new trend of keeping cemetery services for VIPs only. It's too much like a 'get out of grief free' card for hangers-on who have only really turned up for the free feed at the wake.

The family, who are all thin and artistic-looking, opt to have the professionals carry the coffin out, which I personally prefer. There is nothing more nerve-racking than watching a collection of shaking Mr Puniverse male friends and family juggle the box out of the church while praying the corpse doesn't come rolling down the aisle after the Jaffas. The funeral directors are, thank goodness, dressed in black; someone had to be as this is altogether a far too glary service with all the white making it seem very *Brides of Christ*. After the family depart, I'm able to beat JJ out the church door without so much as a backward glance.

If I am going to keep comparing and, let's be honest, I am, the vehicle procession is the best I have ever seen. The funeral directors' precision driving, matched with their ability to get every single car in the funeral cavalcade through the lights before they turn red, makes me scribble down their details onto my short-list of preferred suppliers. It is especially impressive as I was the last car to drive out of the church grounds after I'd searched for Clint, who was still nowhere to be seen. How on earth I haven't found myself separated from the tight-knit grievers anywhere along the way to the graveyard is definitely worthy of a testi-monial on Tripadvisor.

When we arrive at the gravesite, a light sprinkle of rain, just enough to set the mood, falls on the mourners as the coffin is lowered into the ground. *She's been very fortunate with the weather,*

I think to myself. They have sensibly decided to use the local hall located on the same street for the wake, so we are all able to choof off for our cup of tea as soon as we have thrown our obligatory handful of dirt onto the coffin. Like that is going to help the undertakers. I figure, if people are getting paid to do the burial, stay out of the way and let them do their job. Otherwise, if you want to save money, give us all a shovel, let us put in a bit of elbow grease and, with enough mourners, you can get the task done for free then and there.

The wake is very reflective of Sophie. Everyone is polite and professional, and the catering is first-rate. The leaf tea is just the right strength to help you recover from the effort of keeping your lip stiff and the bulk of your grief suppressed for over an hour, without being brewed so much as to bring out an excess of tannin and spoil the whole experience. The sandwiches are an excellent selection of brown and white bread with egg, meat and vegetarian options, and even gluten-free alternatives. There are mini quiches, sausage rolls and party pies as well as two different types of sponge and chocolate cakes to give a decent sugar hit.

Jennifer, as expected, is the first person from work to dare approach me. She and I had been the closest to anything resembling friends during my short time with the insurance company.

'Hey, Viv, nice to see you here. Well, not nice, but you know what I mean,' she says, smiling awkwardly.

'Yes, a bit of a shock for everyone, she was so young,' I reply, wondering why we all seem to need to resort to clichés when we are at funerals. 'But, you know, we've all got to go some time,

I should know,' I joke, deciding to state the obvious to make it easier for Jennifer.

'Yes, it must be a bit difficult for you being here,' she mumbles, then tries to swallow her words.

'You mean given that I'm next?' I laugh. 'It's okay, I picked up a few good pointers, and I'll definitely be using their caterers.'

Jennifer laughs despite herself. Even bad jokes are funny at wakes, as everyone is looking for an excuse for a good belly laugh to let the bottled-up grief and funeral jitters find their way out into the open air. Jennifer is one of those people who throws their arms up in the air when they laugh, but she quickly puts them down again when she and I get a waft of the stress sweat she has built up during the service.

'I always sweat too when I'm stressed,' I sympathise. 'And I don't know why,' I continue without filtering, 'but it has a particular smell about it that you never get at any other time.'

I can tell she would rather I refrain from pointing out the smell now drifting through the room and return to the unspoken rules of funeral etiquette.

'So, anyway, how are things with your family?' I ask, returning to cliché-speak.

Jennifer looks relieved that she can move on to boring me with the latest politics at the P&C, how her kitchen renovation has blown the budget and how difficult it is to find a school in the area that enforces uniforms, so you don't have to argue over clothes every morning. I listen and relax, glad to be immersed in her first-world problems and the day-to-day business of a mum getting on with living a long life.

Glancing at my watch, I realise I've been here for the minimum standard time of an hour and am ready to head off when Clint finally walks through the door, rubbing a tissue aggressively at some grease on the sleeve of his suit. He spots me talking to Jennifer and comes over, flustered.

'Bloody car,' he complains, interrupting Jennifer mid-sentence. 'Of course the head gasket had to choose today of all days to cark it. I even had to borrow the mechanic's car just to get here and then the stupid GPS sent me all over the world.'

He rubs his sleeve even harder to ensure the grease is distributed evenly. This morning I'd helped him find and then iron this outfit, which is his one and only suit for funerals, weddings and job interviews. He bought it for the wedding of an old school friend two months after we met. Due to lack of use, rather than being well cared for, the suit has lasted much longer than his friend's brief dysfunctional marriage.

Being all dressed up has put Clint into free-food mode, so he grabs a plate and starts hoovering up whatever hasn't been devoured by the other ravenous mourners. Jennifer uses Clint's arrival and bad table manners to make her excuses. As she leaves he suddenly realises the hall is emptying of mourners.

'Well, that's just great. Everyone's leaving already,' he whines. 'I've just about missed the whole thing.'

'Don't worry,' I reply sarcastically, 'I'm sure it will come out on Netflix eventually. You can watch it then.'

CHAPTER 18

Not on Clint's list: Fix the car

After yesterday's bloody shemozzle I have decided it's time to find a new grease monkey. I've never been good with cars, and I reckon mechanics can smell it. It's worse, of course, if Viv goes in to get the car fixed because as soon as they see a woman they double the price. They still add about twenty per cent to the bill with me too, though, especially after I open my mouth and they catch on that I can't speak the lingo. When I was younger that was a bit of a problem as even though most women I dated knew nothing about cars they seemed to like blokes who did. That's why I had a hope in hell with Viv – she was one of the few girls I'd met who wasn't impressed by mechanical know-how. Mind you, there was that one time we drove down to her extended family's place for Christmas when I think she would have happily traded me in for a decent used car.

Viv was six months pregnant, and we were sitting in the driveway outside her cousin's house in Sydney, trying to escape Christmas lunch. The car was refusing to start. I had tested the engine; well, I'd turned the key and then shrugged my shoulders because that was the extent of my mechanical abilities. For a little while, we just sat there, looking forward, going nowhere, almost as if we were at a drive-in movie. If we had been, I'd have had little to no chance of getting lucky while we stared at the garage door in front of us.

My dad's pride and joy hadn't even been a beauty back in her day, and by that Christmas she was even more useless and falling apart. I still couldn't part with her though, any more than I could tell Dad to stop giving me tip junk as presents so he could save money on dump fees. The fact the car, which Viv called the 'impotent ride', had got us to her cousin's house only made things worse because instead of being stuck by the side of the road, we were stuck with her huge family with no hope that the motor would spring back to life.

'So much for our bloody ticket out of here,' swiped Viv, giving me the death stare I'd begun to know and expect. 'I mean, what was I thinking? That somehow, magically, your shitbox car would sprout wings and we would fly off singing "Chitty Chitty Bang Bang" over some hellish pastel-coloured sky? I don't suppose you thought to service the damn thing or put oil or water in it before we left?'

I had learnt early on in her pregnancy that when she was in a mood like this it was best to say nothing, so I sat still, barely breathing, wondering how long we would be able to stay put until someone wandered out to find us, or staggered out more likely. With the amount of festive alcohol flowing inside I began to seriously doubt anyone would even notice we were missing. I didn't dare question why we were sitting outside in a clapped-out car instead of inside with everyone else and the Christmas spread, which looked like something out of a *House & Garden* magazine.

When we'd arrived, the dining table had been covered with ham, turkey, pudding, seafood, salads and even more dessert than I could eat. Viv's sister, Catherine, who thankfully had travelled down separately, kicked off the proceedings with her usual plum-in-mouth speech about the true spirit of Christmas. Despite her faked airs and graces, it wasn't long before everyone was skolling their own spirits for Christmas and any attempt at ceremony had been dropped.

When I joined the clan the year before, I hadn't cottoned on to the fact that Viv's entire massive family were actually strapped for cash because their buffet lunch had been so over the top. Viv had explained how all her relos stash what little money they have so during the holy season they can prove how much better they are than the people they grew up with. Viv, being Viv, never played along. That second Christmas, by the time everyone teetered their way to the over-the-top tree, I knew it would be on for young and old.

Catherine was the first to open her present from Viv, which was wrapped in recycled newspaper. She glared disapprovingly. 'I thought we'd agreed that the colours for this year were gold and silver,' she said, tightening her lips.

Her cousin, who was hosting, tried to maintain the Christmas vibe, even though she could barely stand.

'Now, Cathy Bathy,' she slurred, 'just open the present, I'm sure Viv got you something lovely, didn't you, sissy?' she questioned as if she'd never met Viv.

When the discarded wrapping revealed a basket of second-hand beauty products with a ten-dollar price tag from the Vinnies op shop still visible, Catherine froze, too furious to move let alone speak.

Viv's family always put in specific orders for gifts they want from Kmart, with a specified budget of fifty dollars per person; no more, no less. Every year, Viv has broken ranks in one way or another – she never does herself any favours. That Christmas, even though she wasn't playing by the rules, she still managed to get her knickers in a knot about the thank you from Catherine that never came.

'How rude can she get?' she announced half an hour after all the gifts had been exchanged. 'What, just because I don't shop at Kmart, I don't deserve manners?'

Despite Viv's loud indignation, Catherine refused to take the bait and continued to bite her tongue, making it obvious to the whole family who won that particular sibling battle.

'How does she know I didn't spend hours trawling through op shops trying to find her something she'd actually like?' Viv continued, fuming.

Catherine knew as well as I did that gift-giving was Viv's favourite form of payback for any unforgivable act her sibling committed, but I had enough self-preservation instinct left not to answer her question.

'I won't even bother next time,' she continued. 'If they think I'm going to destroy the earth just so they can get another Christmas present to throw away in two months' time, they've got another thing coming.'

Earlier that year, Viv had picked up a copy of *An Inconvenient Truth*, the Al Gore movie about global warming, at the local op shop. Ever since, she'd been back on her activist bandwagon whenever it was convenient. Viv said she was protesting fast fashion so our unborn child would have some sort of future on the planet, but, if you ask me, it was so she could be right and make her whole extended family wrong.

She still hasn't forgiven any of them for failing to step in to help her or Catherine when they were kids. Her family's inability to ever get together without a drink in their hands hasn't exactly helped either. Viv and I were both boozers when we started dating, so when I first met her family at her uncle's third wedding I'd fitted right in, but after we stopped drinking my status went pear-shaped. Apparently our being 'so bloody uptight' stopped everyone else from enjoying themselves. We'd initially gone sober to try to get pregnant and then, when Viv managed to get in the family way, she'd insisted that if she couldn't drink, I couldn't either. And there was no way she was going to change her mind, not after she held an alcohol-free baby shower and realised how uncomfortable the lack of grog made them all feel. I still try to sneak in an occasional beer with the boys when she's not around, but because she has to be all or nothing, she's stuck to being a teetotaller.

That Christmas, after the fifth person tried to sneak booze into my glass, Viv reached her limit.

Outside, I'd tried to start the car again, but it remained stubbornly silent.

'This crappy, useless car,' snapped Viv. 'I know I was born into this stupid family, but does that mean I have to spend every Christmas here? I refuse to get sozzled just so I can spend my day pretending with the rest of them that our family get-togethers are about anything other than trying to outdo each other.'

The sun was getting hotter by the second and I realised my pregnant wife was now well and truly overheated from being trapped in an unmoving vehicle in the middle of summer. A fly flew in Viv's window and buzzed around her head. Things weren't about to get any better.

'I mean, we all know the recipe we got from Aunty Mary isn't the right one,' she ranted as the heat started to boil her over. 'She'll go to her grave with the real damn recipe for her rum balls before she'll ever give it to one of us.'

I nodded, trying to appear conciliatory.

'And don't give me that look, Clint, it's not like you're Mr Neutral here,' she jabbed, wiping away a bead of sweat that had started dripping down her forehead. 'You're the first to whinge every time they buy you a crap present because you're just an in-law. Maybe you should whinge to them for a change and see how far that gets you, instead of sucking up and saying thank you for yet another bottle of grog we have to give away.'

I tried a different nod, hoping this time to look agreeable as opposed to annoying, even though I was still not sure which nod was which. I apparently got it right as she continued her diatribe.

'Or what about that hole in the wall at Uncle Tony's house?'

Her voice was getting louder.

'Is anyone ever going to talk about how that got there or actually, god forbid, fix it? It's probably asbestos, for god's sake, but let's just keep looking at it and letting the kids do drawings on it and pretending it's not there, shall we?'

I half smiled and nodded, unsure if she wanted an answer or not.

'But what I really bloody want to know is why we have to talk for hours about whether we do a Kris Kringle or what colour the Christmas decorations will be, but we never talk about if anyone has bothered to visit Mum lately? We can put up with hours of bitching about how the man next door to my aunty just built his fence over her boundary, but no one will dare say a word about Mum's condition? Or what about talking about why none of us are blue-eyed and fair-skinned, or how, despite all our best efforts, none of us have ever managed to blend in with the neighbours? God forbid we should talk about anything that's actually important.'

She finished at full throttle but then finally must have run out of fuel as her shoulders slumped dramatically.

Every year before setting out for the festering season, Viv and I discuss alternative Christmas options – working at soup kitchens, ignoring that it's Christmas, staying home to celebrate with people we actually like or, my favourite annual suggestion, going to the Arctic Circle to go husky sledding. Every year when we talk about it, she agrees it would be best to avoid her family at all costs, and yet every year she is drawn back to them like a suicidal moth to Christmas lights. Somehow at the eleventh hour, after watching one too many vomitus family Christmas movies, she always hopes for a Christmas miracle and books us on a flight to Sydney, expecting to be welcomed home like some sort of prodigal niece.

That Christmas, while Viv *hadn't* listened to me about not expecting a hero's welcome, she *had* thankfully listened to me about driving down so we could leave when things inevitably went sour. Unfortunately, I didn't listen to her about hiring a car. It's a decision I never heard the end of. Desperate for another choice other than heat stroke or heartache, I tested the engine one last time with no luck. We relented and went back inside just in time to see one of Viv's many drunk relatives trip and push Catherine face first into the Christmas tree. A fitting finish to Christmas up close and too personal.

CHAPTER 19

My list: Clean out my wardrobe

After the funeral, I am reinvigorated and ready to get back on with my list. As a result, my bed is now completely covered in clothes. I have pulled everything out of the wardrobe to sort into piles – still using, have never used, really loved this, why did I ever wear that, what was I thinking and really, these were rags three years ago. I have decided not to leave Clint to pick up after me, despite having spent our whole married life moving his clothes from beside the washing basket to actually in it. While I would be quite happy for him to clean up my mess, when it comes to deciding who gets what even Clint doesn't deserve to ward off the vultures when they fly in after I am dead and burned. Besides, I have always loved a good cull.

Part of me still feels like I should be setting stuff aside for a garage sale as I've never been good at just giving things away, but the wiser side of me knows that's never going to happen.

I did attempt a garage sale five years ago, but after we had boxed everything up, with lots of prodding from me about what we could do with the money once it all sold, I gave in to Clint's and Ethan's unrelenting protests about how precious every bit of junk was to them and called it off. I think part of me was still feeling a bit guilty about my merciless cull of Clint's memorabilia when we first got married.

When we met he had every piece of *Star Wars* merchandise that had ever been made, all still in its original packaging. Apparently, it was going to be worth a fortune one day. I had thrown most of it out a week after we moved in together. He has never really forgiven me and at least every six months for the past ten years has put a piece of news under my nose about the ridiculous prices things he once owned have just sold for. The latest bit of news to come to my attention was about a concept poster for *The Empire Strikes Back* which sold for $26,400. I ruined his investment strategy. But, seriously, who would have thought that and his original 1977 *Star Wars* movie poster would ever be worth anything to anyone other than a nerdy teenage boy? Apparently, all those nerds grew up to have a lot of disposable cash.

In my defence, all twenty of his *Star Wars* posters survived my original purge, but then during the year Ethan was born I had been forced to throw them onto our fire when we ran out of fire starters. Someone had to do something to keep the kid warm and Clint had been away on a boys' weekend. He hadn't noticed they were missing until a year later, so, seriously, how much could he have loved them? But I still feel guilty. So, as my penance to Clint, I will leave Ethan and him with their coveted stash, but my own stuff will be shown no mercy.

I look at the clothes that have covered my body for most of my adult life and pick out the ones I've loved the most to put aside. Then I move on to easier pickings. The rags go straight into garbage bags and will join the other well-meaning but never used rags in our garage. The unworn clothes can be my charitable donation as I'm feeling quite generous now it's all of no use to me. I'm also trying to rack up some heaven brownie points just in case.

I move on to my shoes. I still have the heels I wore to our wedding. I accidentally gave away my meringue dress three years ago when a girlfriend got married. Our friendship and her marriage lasted about the same time, and after six months I never saw her or my dress again. The heels, however, are still packed away in the box where they were lovingly wrapped in tissue paper. They are incredibly high. For someone who has spent most of her life in joggers, I must have really, really been in love with Clint to have chosen those heels for our ceremony.

I remember stumbling through the park for our photos, having to walk like a kid pretending to be a pony, trying to lift my legs high enough to pull the heels out of where they sunk deep into the ground with every new step. Clint had tried hard not to laugh as he helped me make my way to more solid ground, but then he lost it. At first, I didn't want to see the funny side but, in the end, I couldn't help joining him. Back then, with no bladder control issues to worry about, I let go, and we fell about in fits of uncontrollable laughter. I remember his eyes shining and thinking I had done the right thing marrying him. I haven't seen him laugh like that for a long time.

I set aside the wedding heels, along with my daily joggers and slippers, and dump all my other shoes into the donation bag. I try to imagine if there is anyone who would have even the vaguest inclination to want to walk in my shoes. Of course, both Marsha and Sally would be up for the challenge but unfortunately neither of them is average in any way, shape or form, especially not shoe size. Marsha is two sizes larger than me and Sally two sizes smaller, so no shoes for them. Even if I wanted to, I couldn't give my shoes to my B-list friends as they've already given their condolences and think their job is done. They're not about to come back for a soon-to-be dead person's clothes-swap party. My B-listers are the friends I made because of proximity: neighbours, mums from school, gym dropouts, the sort of people I'm happy to have a cuppa with but, really, if there's a new Netflix show I want to watch, I usually give them the flick. Since my diagnosis, TV has moved way up my priority list and I am midway through four different series, which I am determined to watch to the finish, so I really don't have time for endless guilt-fuelled visits.

My sister obviously won't be getting the heels, and while my niece would probably love them for dress-ups, I think I really should leave them to Clint. If I can't leave him with a lifetime of happy memories, I can at least remind him we started off okay. I look at the clothes left in the pile, trying to decide where I would like them to go. My favourite clothes are my pyjamas and dressing-gown so that's what I'll be shuffling off in. I leave out a couple of pairs of jeans, a few t-shirts and sloppy joes I can wear until I get admitted to hospital, and decide charity can have the rest. It feels good knowing I am providing op shop treasures for someone to find amongst Metallica t-shirts, old magazines and polyester dresses. All this effort has tired me out though, so I lay on my bed and, before I know it, I am asleep.

I am dreaming about Ethan and his friend being hit by a car while riding their bikes and am just getting to the good bit where I get to yell at Clint, as obviously this is his fault, when the doorbell rings and wakes me up. I wipe the drool from the side of my mouth and call out, 'Coming,' as I know it will take me a while to get my body moving. I have bed hair, and the house is a wreck. I finally make it over all the obstacles in the hallway and open the door to Clint's mother.

Clint always says he didn't know what hit him when he married me and inherited a whole tribe. Once he'd recovered from the initial shock, he'd imagined this idyllic life hanging out with my sister and the whole extended family and looking after each other's kids, playing happy families. He'd soon learnt that, in my family, we love each other so much it hurts, and anything and everything can be, and often is, misconstrued. In our genetic soup pot, what starts out as warmth often quickly reaches boiling point and blows the lid off the pressure cooker. Clint's family, on the other hand, never even get to simmering. It is all about politeness and keeping a comfortable distance.

Clint is from the other side of the tracks, the expensive side, and I'd always hoped that meant he wouldn't let me fall back down to where I came from. Despite his privileged upbringing he's had enough knocks to need a little rescuing, which I like as it makes me feel superior. His mother, who grew up as a wealthy ex-pat, was determined her son would be sent to the most respected international schools around the globe. That ended when she lost the lion's share of her wealth in a bitter divorce settlement, but she still manages to maintain a smell of money about her. When she holds parties, she always introduces people with a tidbit about them as a conversation starter. She had once heard me talking about a donation I made to a charity I didn't even care about because it was the only way I could get the pestering door-knocker off my doorstep. Since then, she has always introduced me as 'This is Vivian, she likes to help the poor people.' And ever since I have felt obliged to contribute to charity – of course, I make sure there is always something in it for me. I mostly buy Yourtown lottery tickets on the off chance I might win a mansion with a state-of-the-art security system specially designed for keeping backpackers collecting for the needy out of sight and off my doorstep.

'Hello, Isabelle,' I say, self-consciously pulling my skirt down like I am lining up for uniform inspection with the nuns.

'Vivian, my dear, did I wake you? I do hope you hadn't forgotten I was coming?' she says, surveying our utter pigsty over my shoulder.

'Of course not, Isabelle, I was just resting my eyes,' I lie, unable to help myself from talking in a posh voice. 'Do come in.' Mimicking her upper-class demeanour is now an unstoppable habit, but as everyone in her close circle also talks like this she's never noticed my irrepressible derision. 'Please excuse the mess,' I add, leading her inside. 'I am trying to get things organised – I have the charity people coming around to collect some things.'

There are two points in my sentence she should be very pleased about because she loves to be seen as charitable and simply adores organising her own and everyone else's life. Unfortunately, she also has a very astute ear and instead homes in on the word 'trying'.

'That's very admirable of you to keep trying, dear,' she says, brushing crumbs distastefully off a dining chair and sitting down gingerly, as she knows from experience how much my vintage furniture sinks when anyone rests their posterior on its faded upholstery. I smile apologetically. Isabelle has always had a fabulous ability to make me feel less than worthy of being part of the Smithston family, and I am angry at myself because, even though I am dying, I still appear to give a damn. I remind myself that, despite her best attempts to only show her family's good, photogenic side, they are just people. I've yet to meet a family where, when you scratch the surface, the skin doesn't weep. She did, after all, marry Clint's dropkick of a father.

Isabelle has never had a nickname. Everyone is under instructions to always use her full name, which is why Marsha and I delight in referring to her behind her back as Izzy or the Izster.

I make the Izster a cup of tea and sit down opposite. She generally approves of my brew, as unlike most plebeians, I make it in a pot with leaf tea. She picks up the china cup and, as she puts it to her lips, I realise too late that it is chipped. I remember that's the one that my mother put in the dishrack underneath a saucepan during an unexpected attempt at being 'helpful' in one of her rare sane moments, a month after Ethan was born. Izzy has yet to notice my cardinal sin, but it won't be long.

'How is poor Clint doing at the new job?' she asks. Poor Clint has always been poor Clint since he had the misfortune of marrying me. 'He just seems to be working so hard lately, and last time I saw him he looked positively exhausted,' she adds.

Yes, yep, that's me, I'm literally sucking the life out of your son, I think to myself before answering. 'Oh he's doing well, he's quite the superman, your son. He seems to be able to cope with what-ever life throws at him.'

I neglect to add that last night I threw my shoe at him when he changed the TV station in the middle of my favourite show.

'Oh yes,' says the Izster proudly. 'He has the Smithston ability to get on with it, there's no doubt about that, despite his fragile constitution he just pushes through.'

Izzy has always made me want to rise to Clint's defence. She treats him like an invalid child and takes every opportunity to disempower him and chop off his bits. I think she would have preferred him to stay her little boy and be entirely depen-dent on her forever. She is disgusted when I make any sort of demands on him and hates how he has stood up to her ever since I dragged him along to a Tony Robbins conference in a failed attempt to get Clint to up his game for me. I have taken this as fair compensation for the disappointing truth that, in every other way, Tony left him unchanged.

She has now noticed the chip.

'Oh dear,' she says, looking down unimpressed. 'I'm afraid someone hasn't been quite as careful as they should have been with your teacup.'

She assumes it was me who broke it.

'Oh, dear Isabelle, I am dreadfully, dreadfully sorry,' I say, thinking how good I am at my posh voice these days. 'It's just relatives, you know. When they come to visit, they never seem to behave as one would expect them to.'

She gives me her polite smile and a slight eyebrow raise, as if to say, 'Don't think I don't know you are on the attack.'

'Well.' She smiles, baring her teeth politely. 'I am sure your relatives are just trying to do their best. Grief can be very hard on people, and the preparations must be difficult for them. I am sure there is a terribly long list of things that are still far from complete.'

Oh, she is good, I think to myself. *She is good.*

I get up to find her a new teacup, checking over my collection in the cupboard like a forensic scientist before pouring a fresh, extra strong and hopefully bitter tea into it. I must admit I have always been in secret awe of her ability to slap people across the face while serenely smiling and imbibing a beverage. It must feel amazing to wield that much power and never experience the consequences.

I hear the key turn in the front door – Clint is home. He has obviously noticed his mother's car in the driveway as, before he even glances at her, he comes straight up behind me and grabs me in an embrace, kissing my neck. She abhors public shows of affection, so Clint and I are never more enamoured with each other than when his mother comes to visit.

'Hi, baby,' I say, stroking his face and turning to give him a movie star kiss. He loves it when the Izster comes to town.

When I release him, he turns around and says, 'Oh hello, Mother, what a nice surprise.'

'It shouldn't be a surprise, Clint,' she retorts. 'I scheduled this visit over a week ago, but you are correct that it is nice for you to see me. Come over here and let me look at you.'

He stays where he is. 'Mother, can't you see me from there? You really should get back to the optometrist,' he says.

I settle back into my chair, ready for the show. Ignoring Clint's comment, the Izster begins. 'You really shouldn't run yourself so ragged, my darling, and I can see from your pallor that you aren't as buoyant as you make out. Don't you agree, Vivian?' she says, turning to me with no intention of waiting for an answer.

'Okay, Mother, that's enough,' says Clint. 'I'm just fine, the new job is demanding, but I am up for the challenge. And as for my health, I'm perfectly well. I don't suppose you have asked Viv how she's feeling? She is, after all, the one who is dying.'

Izzy sips her tea slowly. She hates that I am dying. It gives me one up on her and nowhere in any of her etiquette manuals does it say anything about being allowed to have a swipe at someone on death's doorstep. Much as I find Clint incredibly attractive when he stands up to his mother like this, I can't help but squirm in my chair.

'Well, Clinton, it is good to hear you *think* you are doing so well. As for Vivian, I was just about to inquire after her when you arrived.' She turns to address me formally. 'So, my dear, how are you going with your list? I know last time I was here you had a lot of things on your plate. Am I to assume you have made any progress with them?'

One would think my mother-in-law is royalty; in fact, she comes from a long line of wealthy toilet paper manufacturers, which I do occasionally like to throw into the conversation. She is happy to discuss the fabulous amounts of money she inherited, which no doubt paid for our spa, but not the shitty relatives who gave it to her. Clinton has always had a love–hate relationship with his mother. He hates that she treats him like a child but is happy to put his hand out when cash is offered, and will occasionally beg and roll over if required. Not that his success rate with begging is particularly high, as Isabelle is of the firm belief everyone should make their own way in the world. It seems, however, that buying a spa for his dying wife may have qualified as an exception.

'No, sadly I don't seem to have made much progress with my list. Unfortunately, help isn't as readily available as one might think.' I am pleased with my ability to put in the word 'one', while also implying that my mother-in-law has been missing in action in the help department.

'Well,' she replies, 'I hope that at least you have been enjoying your spa in your downtime.'

'Oh yes,' I reply, I have been waiting for this. 'Clint worked so hard to give me that wonderful gift on my birthday; he's such a treasure, aren't you, darling?'

I look at him with bedroom eyes and he reaches across and grabs me, rubbing his hands up and down my sides, as close to my breasts as possible. He kisses me again on the neck, and we both relax into watching his mother take extremely focused sips of her tea. Clint understands I now realise his mother paid for the spa, but he also understands I will enjoy it all the more knowing the Izster thinks I am clueless about her being my benefactor.

I shouldn't dislike her, and I certainly don't hate her as she has been nothing but kindly judgemental our whole marriage. While neither of us would ever admit it, Izzy and I have derived considerable pleasure from our ten years of biting repartee and I am the first to admit that without her spartan emergency cashola, my marriage to Clint would have been a financial disaster. By her criteria, she has been patronisingly generous despite having been left struggling, by rich people's standards, after Clint's dad fleeced her for all he could get.

I also owe her a considerable debt for what little sex Clint and I have had over the past eight years. We recognised early on in our marriage, after we both gave up the booze so we could fall pregnant, that when we were sober we were more like friends than lovers. Without her conjugal visits forcing us to act like lust-filled teenagers, our sex life would have ended well before it did. The Izster would, of course, be absolutely horrified to know she's been our own personal aphrodisiac. I am sure her visits would have promptly ceased if it had ever come to her attention.

CHAPTER 20

Ethan's list: Cook us all dinner

Ethan is late home from football practice and races into the house, dropping his jacket, bag and shoes as he goes. 'Nanna Isabelle, are you here, where are you?' he yells, racing from room to room. Ethan's love for his nanna is one of her few redeeming features. She makes him feel like he is the king of the castle and her habit of regularly showering him with money doesn't hinder his affections.

'There you are, my darling boy,' she says, her arms outstretched. He almost knocks her off her chair in his hurry to get to the love and the ensuing cash. Sure enough, she pulls out an envelope.

'A letter came for you in the post,' she says, smiling as she hands him the envelope. He tears it open and pulls out a twenty-dollar note.

'Hey, Mum, Mum, look I got twenty dollars, I can buy that Pokémon game now I've got enough money,' he says.

'What, the one I told you I didn't want you to have?' I tease.

'Yeah that one,' he says, walking backwards and doing a little dance.

'What do you say to Isabelle?' I prompt.

'Oh yeah, thanks, Nanna,' he says, finishing with a dab dance move as if he's an American hip-hopper paying homey props to his elder.

'Now how about you put that away and then come back into the kitchen? We're all getting hungry.'

I turn to Isabelle, hoping she will get the hint that it's almost dinnertime so maybe she should toddle off.

'Ethan has decided he is going to cook dinner tonight,' I say, trying to make it sound as unappetising as possible.

'How delightful, I would love to taste his cooking,' she says, inviting herself to dinner while at the same time managing to look genuinely surprised I have taught my son anything at all.

'You might want to taste it first before you decide if you want to join us,' I warn, hoping to put her off staying. 'Ethan's never cooked baked beans before.'

She settles herself in even further and smiles. 'That will be just fine.'

Dinner actually turns out to be quite delicious as, unbeknownst to me, Clint had taken the initiative of taking Ethan shopping yesterday after school in preparation. So, Ethan's first attempt at cooking involves taking the Aldi lasagne out of the packaging and getting Clint to put it in the preheated oven. When the timer rings, and it is done, his next task is to get his dad to dish it up to prevent any risk of burns or injury. Ethan does, however, help in the plating up of the gastronomic extravaganza by throwing an unwashed grubby handful of mixed lettuce onto each plate and plonking a few cherry tomatoes on top. He also sets the table and decorates it with a centrepiece of leaves, shells, rocks and a feather. I remove the feather despite his protests, telling him I don't think any of us want bird lice as a condiment with our meal.

He has tucked a tea towel into his t-shirt and is pulling out the chairs to welcome us to this fine dining experience.

'Please take a seat, Mrs Nanna,' he says to Isabelle, pulling out the chair for her. She refrains from dusting it off again and sits politely, smiling at her only grandson who can do no wrong.

'Would sir like to sit next to Nanna?' he asks Clint.

'Why thank you, waiter, I have heard excellent things about this restaurant.'

I am waiting for him to pull a chair out for me, but he suddenly gets hungry and climbs up on his chair, sticking his nose down into the lasagne.

'This smells yum, yum, pig's bum,' he says enthusiastically. I make sure I don't catch Isabelle's eye, so she can keep her disapproval to herself, and pull out my chair.

When I sit down there is a sudden tearing sound – the worn upholstery gives way and I find myself sitting with my knees up around my chin and my bottom almost touching the ground. Ethan laughs in hysterics. Clint rushes to help me. I have stopped breathing as the pressure on my tumours has sent a shooting pain through me. He heaves me out of the chair and, as I straighten up, a wave of nausea comes over me. I race to the bathroom to pray to the only god I have ever known. Clint stands in the doorway watching me, not saying anything.

He finally mutters, 'Are you okay?'

I don't reply – *Isn't it bloody obvious?* – but instead say, irritated, 'Yes, yes, I'm fine, go check on Ethan.'

I watch as he leaves with his tail between his legs and then take an extra dose of my nausea and pain meds. I run water over my face and wrists for what feels like hours but is only a few minutes. I start to feel human again. When I return, Ethan is wiping tears away from his eyes.

'I'm sorry, Mama, I didn't mean to laugh. Are you okay?'

'It's all right sweetie, I'm okay now, really I am, and luckily my tummy is much better too, so I hope you made dessert?' I ask, knowing full well the only reason he agreed to cook was so he could put sweets on the menu.

It's good to see he has made slightly more effort with the dessert, probably because there are no health and safety concerns about burns when you're just dishing up ice cream. He has decorated the outside of the bowls with blueberries which have once again been unhygienically boy-handled. Isabelle refrains from any criticism of Ethan's lack of cleanliness, not because I am recovering from my fall but because the one thing we have very much in common is that, most of the time, Ethan is perfect in both our eyes. After dinner, my son blesses us all with a big loud, impolite yawn which gives me the opportunity to say, 'You're tired honey. Go get changed and clean your teeth, it's bedtime.'

Five minutes later, much to the relief of Clint, myself and no doubt Isabelle, Ethan is in his pyjamas, signalling it's time to call it a night. As the Izster beats a hasty retreat, Ethan follows her out to the front porch to see her off and waves goodbye using his twenty-dollar note as a flag. The Beatles were wrong when they said money can't buy you love. When she has driven off, I can't help but let out a sigh of relief, glad to be left alone with my own private dysfunctional family. Clint heads off for a shower to wash that mother right out of his lack of hair, and Ethan comes into our room, ready for his bedtime story. Just as I am about to start reading, he notices the piles of clothes on the floor.

'What are your clothes on the floor for, Mum?'

This from a boy who doesn't know what wardrobes are for and thinks floors are an all-purpose storage unit. I've promised myself to try to be as truthful with Ethan as possible but the problem with that is if I tell him the clothes are being sorted in preparation for my imminent demise he will surely have a melt-down. At this time of night, even telling him I have changed his brand of toothpaste can result in a major fall-out so I deflect the question until I am ready to deal with the big issue.

'That's not a big pile of clothes, haven't you noticed the junk your father's had in front of the French doors for the past year?'

'Yes,' says Ethan, laughing. 'And I even heard Daddy telling Tyson's dad about it and how he never cleans it up no matter how much you nag him.'

'Oh really?' I reply through teeth half smiling, half gritted.

Ethan's favourite hobby is dobbing in his dad. It's a pastime I must confess to encouraging. It's good to have a spy and an ally rolled into one. I know the parenting books all talk about the importance of being on the same page and presenting a united front to your child, who is apparently the enemy, but I've yet to see that play out in real life. In real life, you want your children to love you more than your spouse. You want them to say 'Mum' before they say, 'Dad'. More importantly, you want them to understand that every time they get upset or things go wrong, that it has absolutely nothing to do with your imperfection as a mother and everything to do with your lousy choice in breeding partner. Most of the time Ethan is a willing participant in this game of one-downmanship, but every so often he will take his father's side, especially if I make a broad gender-based criticism, which I guess is fair enough. As a mother to a boy, you have to be very aware that your power lies in your ability to belittle your husband while still building up your son's sense of pride in his masculinity. It's a fine art and one I must admit to having put a huge effort into perfecting.

Ethan snuggles in closer and I stroke his hair and kiss his head.

'You know, darling,' I whisper lovingly, 'your hair is just like your dad's used to be. It's a shame he went bald, but I guess that's what happens when you call someone a nag instead of listening to their advice.'

I raise one eyebrow at Ethan and he laughs.

'Love you Mama.'

'Love you little man.'

CHAPTER 21

Not on my list: Learn how to use a wheelchair

Today I am going for a driving lesson. I've decided I need to learn to use a wheelchair just in case. I failed my motor vehicle driver's test five times before I finally got my licence. I bunny-hopped my way through the first test, went through a stop sign during the second test, rolled down to the bottom of the hill while attempting a hill start on the third test, cried so much I couldn't see in the fourth test and, my pièce de résistance, backed into the instructor's car on the fifth test. I then took a year off and drove illegally in the back streets before I finally sailed through my test with flying colours. I have always been what teachers like to call a kinaesthetic learner, which means you learn by stuffing a thing up enough times that you eventually get it through your thick head. So, I knew wheelchair driving was going to be the same. Still, I haven't learnt anything new for a while, so I am partly excited about it.

When I met my mobility mentor, who kindly offered to teach me how to bend it like Beckham wheelchair-style at my next hospital check-up, I was even more up for the challenge. He is a young, muscly man with unnaturally white teeth. Marsha and I have always joked about growing old together and chasing around young wardsmen in our wheelchairs. Not because we would be vaguely interested in them or any sort of dalliance, but more because we know we could horrify them. We've talked about taking out our teeth and asking them to kiss an old lady who doesn't have long left to live and discussed accidentally leaving the door open while showering to mortify them when they catch sight of our ageing mammary glands. We've even considered faking an affair and letting them walk in on a mocked-up sexual encounter between us.

To kick off today's lesson, I ask my handsome teacher if I can take a photo of the wheelchair to show my husband and sneakily include him in the picture so I can text it to Marsha for gloating rights. While I am doing this, he checks my pedometer. For the past few weeks, I've been counting my steps, but despite my worst efforts my numbers have gone down instead of up. I've realised once I stop walking, I won't leave a trace of me behind. I wonder how many footprints most people make in a lifetime only to have them washed away by the ocean, like a scene out of *From Here to Eternity*. I wonder how many footprints I've left in the sandpit or made when I've walked wet from the bathroom to the bedroom because someone used the last clean towel.

I made a cast of Ethan's feet when he was a baby. His feet were so tiny and delicate, and I'd marvelled at how perfect he was. Death is birth's poor cousin. When a baby is due to be born, you take moulds of your pregnant belly and do soft porn photo shoots standing naked in bushland next to riverbeds. You have baby showers, cut locks of hair, keep first teeth and christening outfits. Everything is precious, and every moment cherished. When you are dying, no one wants your dislodged rotting teeth or samples of your hair as it falls from your head. No one wants to take a photo of you or breathe in your breath or post photos of your withering body on Facebook. Well, almost nobody – I'm sure now I have thought of the idea that Marsha would.

Sitting in the wheelchair feels stranger than I expected and I want to kick and scream and cry. I wish my bestie was here, hooning down the corridor, scattering patients and doing her best to make this lovely young man squirm. He is quite sweet, and part of me wouldn't want her to be mean, but another part comes alive at the thought of it.

A guy in a wheelchair once tried to pick me up at a nightclub. He was funny and good-looking and could do tricks and wheelies and make that wheelchair dance like Lightning McQueen in a Disney on Ice production. I was contemplating how exactly we could have sex and whether or not he was taller than me even though he was sitting down, when he stood up and walked to the bar. It was his friend's wheelchair, and this was his party trick. He did it to try and filter out how caring his pick-ups really were. I had passed the test apparently, so he had gone to buy me a drink at the bar. He returned with a cocktail, a Slow and Comfortable Screw Against the Wall, decorated with an umbrella which had seen better days. I smiled graciously and poured it over his beautifully styled hair. He stuck out his tongue as it ran down his forehead and over his mouth and laughed. His mate, now in the wheelchair, handed him a towel and a clean t-shirt. Payback was par for the course apparently, and I couldn't help but join in with the laughter. I wasn't going to give him the satisfaction of talking to him again, though, so I pulled up a chair next to his friend in the wheelchair.

Five minutes later, I was pouring a drink over his head as well. By the end of the night I'd concluded none of the men at the bar were in any way disabled other than that they were complete dickheads. They had bought the wheelchair at the tip shop and spent most of their spare time learning impressive tricks to try to pick up girls. I now regret not paying attention to their mad skills as my mentor is showing me how to adjust the footrests and explaining how to drive downhill. I wonder if he has ever taken a wheelchair out at night.

'Do you ever take these out for a spin?' I ask.

He laughs. 'No, I'm saving that for my old age.'

He will be one of those men who age well, like James Bond. Very few women, apart from Audrey Hepburn, seem to age well. I don't have to worry about that. People will remember me as forty and bitter instead of eighty-five not out. All those anti-ageing cream ads now make me feel special. Sometimes I do a sing-song dance when those ads come on, 'I'm not getting older . . . I'm not getting older.' There is part of me that also feels like dying has elevated me in the sainthood queue; after all, only the good die young, so I must have done something right.

My mentor wheels me out to reception. Now he has to bill me for the honour of having helped me get one step closer to needing a wheelchair. Nobody likes charging the terminally ill, even people who work in the industry are squeamish about it. They can't even make it easier on themselves by offering after-pay unless it's after-life pay. But now that I have a wheelchair, the cancer freebie racket has been supersized. All I need to do is rock on up in my new wheels and cashiers will take one look at my legs and throw their money into my lap. I pat my newly acquired wheelchair affectionately. When Marsha gets here, we are definitely going out to a bar in this baby.

CHAPTER 22

Clint's list for me: Finish your novel

The group moves across the field as one and then suddenly, I can hardly bloody believe it, Ethan breaks free and is running like the clappers. He's only twenty metres from the tryline. Oh . . . my . . . god! He's not going to score is he?

'Come on, son, keep running,' I mumble under my tightly held breath, not wanting to distract him.

One of the biggest players on the other team has his eyes set on Ethan and is picking up the pace. Ethan, for once, is doing what I'm always telling him to do – focusing straight ahead with his eye on the prize – but that means he is totally unaware of the clear and present danger that's gaining on him from behind.

'Watch the defender on your left, mate,' I yell, jumping to my feet.

He gives a quick glance over his shoulder and for a moment I think he's going to stumble but then he picks up the pace.

'Run, Ethan! Come on, mate, use those legs of yours. Run!' I yell, breaking out in a sweat. It's like the defender is breathing down my own neck.

He's only five metres from the tryline as the player behind him prepares to go in for the tackle.

'For god's sake, run!' I scream from as far forward as I can get without falling onto the field, not caring that my voice has gone up two octaves.

Just as the defender is about to grab him around the ankles, Ethan leaps high into the air, dives over the line and puts the ball down.

I am holding my head in both hands, so it doesn't fall off from the shock.

'You bloody champion, Ethan. That's my boy, that is my boy,' I yell so everyone in the crowd knows exactly who belongs to who.

I punch my hand into the air three times and then turn around to Viv.

'His first try! He got a try, I can't even believe it.'

I look back to the field and see Ethan's little mates all slapping him on the back. He has the biggest smile on his face. Maybe he's not going to be so soft after all.

'Did you see that, love? Did you see that?'

'Yes, yes, I am sitting here watching the same game you are.'

Viv's trying to be sarcastic as she hates every sport except netball because she played it, but I can see she's proud of him too. Ethan looks over at us, and we both give him the big thumbs up and high-five each other. I plonk back down, but I can hardly sit still for the rest of the game.

'His first try, his first bloody try.'

'He hasn't found a cure for cancer, honey, he just put a ball on the grass over a white line,' Viv says, trying to deflate me.

But it doesn't matter what she says or thinks; she can't take the shine off this one. Jason, one of the other dads, comes over and punches me in the arm.

'What a try, hey, Clint? He's got some legs on him.'

'I reckon. I've only ever seen Ethan run that fast when I've asked him to give me a hand with something.' I laugh.

'Well good luck catching him next time you need him then,' he says.

Out of the corner of my eye, I see Viv trying to stand. I turn to help her.

'What do you need, love? I can go get it for you.'

'I'm going to the bathroom, Clint. I don't really think you can do that for me,' she says drolly.

'Okay, sweetie.'

I watch her as she walks off. It's getting harder and harder for her now, but she's still refusing to use the wheelchair. Jason watches her limping away.

'Bloody shame that.'

'Yeah, yeah, it is, but she's still giving me jobs to do, don't worry about that,' I say, trying to lighten the atmosphere.

'Oh, I'm sure she is. My wife will have me digging my own grave and then putting the dirt back on top,' he says.

I wince at the thought but he doesn't notice.

'At least her to-do lists keep her mind off the . . . anyway, I'd rather she spent her time writing her novel.'

'She's a bit of a writer then, is she?'

'Yeah, and a good one too. Even when she writes out chores for me, there's always some clever turn of phrase in there. I've told her she should call her novel *Black* because she's got such a dark sense of humour.'

'Well, you couldn't call it black for any other reason these days, not with all this bloody political correctness around.'

Oh, here we go, time to brace for another racist barrage. I thought talking about books would be safe, but it doesn't matter what I say to Jason; he always finds a way to slip in a random, small-minded comment.

The whistle blows, I am saved by the bell. Ethan runs over to me.

'Dad, Dad, did you see that try, did you see it?'

'You bet I saw it.' I laugh proudly. 'Now I know you can run that fast I sure as hell won't be putting any money down next time you challenge me to a race.'

Ethan's chest swells, and I reckon if he were a peacock, his feathers would blind me with their brilliance. He heads straight to the cooler bag, grabs an orange quarter and devours it. He keeps the skin in his mouth and then smiles a big orange smile at me. He is absolutely stoked.

I turn back to Jason but he's wandered off in search of another beer. Viv is on her way back so I jog to her side to see if she needs help. I feel like a bit of a sportsman myself surrounded by all this youthful testosterone and sporting prowess.

'What did Dickhead have to say?' Viv asks, jerking her head in Jason's direction as Ethan makes his way back onto the field for the second half. 'I don't know how Cecilia bloody stands him,' she snarls. 'She must hate his guts and I can't say I'd blame her.'

'Oh, he's all right,' I say, defending him despite myself. 'I was telling him about your novel.'

'For god's sake, Clint, I've scrawled out a few pages, it's hardly a novel.'

'It's genius, is what it is.'

I can almost recite it by heart. Viv's only written ten pages, but they're amazing. I love the opening line, 'Greed is good at hiding things'. How does anyone come up with lines like that? She gets exasperated when I talk to her about it and tells me anyone could write like that if they bothered to buy themselves a dictionary and a thesaurus, but I know she's wrong. I am useless with words, although Ethan's inherited her talent. I've gotten used to him being better with the books than a footy but after that magnificent try today, things might change if I'm lucky. He's a little bugger though, he doesn't use his smarts to get ahead at school, he just uses them so he can do whatever he wants.

Viv's always made sure he has no qualms about using the power of words to his advantage. Sometimes when he has his little mates over I stand within earshot to listen to him, and he's always got some racket going on. The other day he literally had an idea to sell ice to the Inuit. His play date, who isn't the sharpest tool in the toybox, was talking about global warming and Ethan was convincing him that if they started freezing water and buying eskies, they could send ice to Alaska and clean up when the ice caps melt. Next thing I know they'd snuck into the house and were sneaking ice cubes out to his cubby.

It reminded me of the kind of mischief he used to get up to with his cousins; they were inseparable when they were little. It's a damn shame Viv won't talk to her sister, and it's going to be pretty weird if the next time Ethan and I see them is at the funeral. I don't want that to happen. Catherine looks too much like Viv.

I hear a cheer and look back at the game. Ethan's got the ball again. I jump to my feet.

'Run, Ethan, you little bloody legend, run!'

But he trips and falls, fumbling the ball. A player from the other team snatches it up and heads in the other direction.

'Tackle, tackle. Come on, what are you doing?' I yell, totally frustrated as Ethan's team appears to fall apart at the seams while their opponents pass the ball deftly from one player to the next, heading unstoppably towards the tryline.

'Oh my god, what are you doing? Get him! RUN!'

Viv reaches up and pulls on my arm.

'For god's sake, Clint, sit down, it's only a game. They're kids; it's meant to be fun. This is why I didn't want him playing this stupid game.'

I sit down and look back at the field. That's when Viv and I, at the same time, notice Ethan is still lying, unmoving, where he's fallen.

CHAPTER 23

Not on Ethan's list: Play with his cousins

Ethan is still in hospital. They said not to worry, that it is standard practice to keep kids overnight when they've been knocked unconscious. I still can't believe how yesterday, when Ethan was lying on the ground, Clint had been too busy yelling at other people's children to even notice his son was injured. When I finally got his attention, he had the nerve to tell me I hadn't noticed either. Seriously, that kid's in trouble when I'm gone.

My neck is stiff from sleeping in the chair next to Ethan. Clint has just texted to say he is on his way back with tea and breakfast. I can't eat this hospital food, I swear it's designed to keep the customers here longer. I look over at Ethan. He is just starting to make the screwed-up, gorgeous face he always does before he wakes up. He yawns, rubs his eyes with the back of his hands, stretches his arms and then rolls from one side of the bed to the other before finally opening his eyes. He looks around, startles, then notices me next to him.

'Oh, hello, Mama,' he says, reaching over to me and pulling my arm up to his bed.

'Hello, baby boy,' I say, stroking the hair back from his face. He frowns and pulls his hair over his eyes again.

'I'm hungry,' he complains just as I hear the clatter of the hospital trolley coming along.

'That sounds like breakfast now, but don't worry if you can't eat it, Dad is on his way with cereal from home.'

The orderly bustles into our room and pulls the table on wheels across Ethan's bed, placing a stainless-steel tray on top of it. 'Juice or water?' she asks Ethan.

'Juice! Mum, can I have the juice?'

'Yes, you can have the juice.'

His eyes light up like it is Christmas as he takes each individual lid off the plastic-looking, slightly discoloured food.

'Mum, there's eggs, and there's a little butter packet, and there's toast, and there's tea, hey, Mum they gave me tea, and there's cereal . . . oh, Mum, they gave me Coco Pops, and I'm in the hospital. Does that mean they're healthy? Hey, Mum, if Coco Pops are healthy can I have them every day?'

I smile, take a deep breath and sit back, enjoying watching him destroy his breakfast. I swear he can inhale food. It's making me hungry, despite what the food looks and smells like. Where the hell is Clint? Ethan notices the TV screen at the end of his bed.

'Hey, Mum, can I watch TV?'

Sure, I think, *you're eating shit you may as well watch it too.*

'Okay, honey, just the kids' channel though.'

'I know, Mum, I know.'

He flicks on the TV and it goes straight to the news. I dive across the bed, grab the remote and switch it straight off.

'Mum, you said I could watch it.'

'I know, I know, just give me a minute. Close your eyes, and I'll find your channel.'

I press mute as I turn the TV on and quickly flick past the latest shooting massacre to the cartoon channel where a mouse is trying to blow up a cat. Oh well, at least it's animated violence.

Clint finally arrives with my breakfast and, more importantly, my tea. I start to feel human again. They told us if Ethan's still okay by lunchtime he'll be discharged this afternoon. I wonder how long it will take for the novelty of lying in bed watching television to wear off.

'Ethan, now that Dad's here, I'm going to head home for a bit of a rest. I'll be back later and then fingers crossed we'll all be heading home this afternoon. Did you want me to bring you anything, a book or some games to play?'

'Nah, Mum, I'll just watch telly,' he says, his eyes glued to the screen. I switch off the remote to make sure he has heard the question. 'Oh, Mum,' he whinges.

I turn his face, so he is looking at me, 'Do you want me to bring you anything?' I repeat.

'Huh? I dunno. Nah, I think I'm good.'

'You won't get bored?'

'Maybe . . . are you going to be here?'

I sigh and repeat myself. 'No, I'm going home for a bit. Your father will be here.'

'Oh, well could someone come and play with me? Maybe Jessie . . . Or, Mum, what about Billy and Sarah?'

Clint looks at me. Ethan has asked to see his cousins. My sister and I haven't spoken for almost a month. Ethan and his cousins spent the first seven years of their lives together so, even though I've told him there's some adult stuff going on between me and his aunty, he has still asked after them every few days.

•

When I first found out I might have cancer, Catherine hated me for it, because, as usual, she thought I would get all the attention. I hadn't been particularly worried the day my masseuse told me she'd found concerning lumps on my stomach. I thought she was being a little dramatic, but I'd obediently agreed to get them checked out by my doctor. I organised for Clint to pick me up from the clinic so we could go to Catherine's birthday together. After palpating my stomach, the doctor asked, 'When did you first notice these tumours?' I laughed and said, 'Oh no, that's just post-baby belly fat.' He remained serious and ordered urgent blood work and a biopsy. When Clint pulled up, I was still in shock. He was on the phone to work and wasn't about to start picking up on emotional cues from me for the first time in his life. Ethan was in the car rabbiting on about how it was so unfair he'd gotten in trouble at school for talking because he'd just been trying to help Sophie with her maths question. I wasn't about to say, 'You think that's unfair? Mummy might have cancer,' so I stoically kept the news to myself.

When we arrived, the party was in full swing, with Catherine hyper-vigilant as always, trying to make sure everyone was playing by her long list of unspoken rules. Unfortunately for her, just as she was about to blow out the candles, I stole her thunder by bursting into tears. She tried to press on regardless, opening presents like a child at Christmas and clapping her hands together in delight as she unwrapped each gift in the now silent and uncomfortable atmosphere. When her friends left early to 'leave us to it' she glared at me in disgust.

'Well, that was embarrassing,' she said, closing the door on the last of her friends. 'All right, so what's your latest sob story that absolutely could not wait until after my birthday?'

Still in shock, I picked up my bag, kissed her kids goodbye and walked out the door. Ethan and Clint followed obediently and quickly behind me.

'What's the matter, Viv?' Clint probed worriedly.

'Not now,' I said firmly as Ethan pricked up his ears and put on his seatbelt.

I drove home numb, but not numb enough that I couldn't help but take pleasure in sending Catherine a terse four-word text: Being tested for cancer.

Part of me knew, even as I sent it, that she'd probably think I'd asked to be tested just to spite her and wouldn't reply. She's always had this ability to put up a shield of selfishness when things go wrong. It's been her go-to way of dealing with our traumatic childhood and crazy family, second only to making everything that ever happens, including the sun setting, all my fault.

She eventually called me the next day because she liked to be the one person in our family who, if only in her own mind, could be counted on to do what she thought was the right thing. She justified not getting straight back to me because it had been late, and I would have been putting Ethan to bed, even though she knows I have never been able to go to sleep on an empty stomach or bad news. By the time she called I was slightly calmer and prepared to pretend she was apologising rather than making excuses.

'Don't worry, sis, we all do the wrong thing sometimes. Like last week when Clint broke the vase you got from Nanna and I was too much of a coward to tell you –'

She interrupted me before I could go any further.

'What? But you said you didn't know what had happened to it . . . You lied to me?' she accused, outraged. 'You know how much I loved that vase. I mean, I knew you'd always wanted it for yourself, but I can't believe you'd lie about that. How am I ever supposed to know if you're telling the truth? You probably don't even have cancer,' she yelled, then hung up on me.

Ever since Catherine was a kid, I've always had to be the one to apologise, whether I've been in the wrong or not. It's an older sister thing, I suppose, but now no more. A few days later, when it was confirmed I had cancer and the specialist gave me a three-month prognosis, I knew that even though I looked healthy at first, it wouldn't be long before I would look sick enough to prove my point and make her squirm. Unfortunately, the only way my plan was going to work was if we saw each other, which wasn't about to happen unless I called her. I was in a double bind as Catherine's record at holding firm until I'd give in and pick up the phone was impressive and, so far, unbeatable. Still this time, every time I went to dial her number, I reminded myself I was over playing her game. I figured if we couldn't talk about important things, why bother speaking at all?

Eventually word got out on the grapevine that I was dying. I would have thought things might have softened between us after that, but it only got harder. As the weeks wore on, I could feel her pride taking hold and sense her making a list of all the things I'd ever done in my life to bring the cancer on myself. I shouldn't have been so surprised; when we were kids, every time Mum lost the plot, Catherine blamed me. Every time one of her boyfriends broke up with her it was because I'd said something to them. Every time our kids fought it was because I was raising Ethan the wrong way. We've always both been super sensitive, super prickly and super stubborn but, despite our similarities, Catherine has never been able to accept that I am not the enemy. We both knew we still loved each other, but as the days went by, winning the stand-off became more important and I had no energy left to deal with any more of our screwed-up childhood bubbling its way to the surface.

Even though we weren't talking, we still bought each other's families presents for birthdays, especially the kids. There are so many unspoken rules in our family that I didn't even pretend to understand, such as, it's okay to hate each other but you'd better not miss someone's birthday. That sort of tough ability to enforce dysfunctional love whether it's liked or not runs in our family.

I know Ethan has been missing his cousins as last week he did the unthinkable and agreed to come shopping with me to help me pick out a birthday present for Sarah. He made his way through the department store boy-handling the usual list of things he loves.

'What about Pokémons, Mum? She'd love those?'

'No, Ethan.'

'What about a robot? Hey, Mum, Mum, look at this robot. Wow, this one's cool. Hey, it can walk. And listen to the noise it makes!'

He turned on the sound to the annoyance of the poor, long-suffering woman working in the kids' section. I grabbed the robot and turned it off.

'No, Ethan, we are looking for something for Sarah.'

'What about this, Mum, look at this, wow, this is the coolest magic trick ever.'

'No, Ethan. Uncle David said Sarah wants a hula hoop and fairy wings, I told you that, so that's what we're looking for.'

I don't know how, but apparently I'd forgotten that when shopping *for* children you should never shop *with* children, but I'd been trying to squeeze in as much time with Ethan as I could. In the end, I decided to leave him to it and ducked around to the next aisle in search of pink and sparkly treasures. I quickly located the wings, but when I headed back to where I'd left Ethan, he was no longer there. That kid didn't need magic to disappear. I looked in about three of the toy aisles before a feeling of panic started to creep in. My steps quickened with my heart, but just before full-blown hysteria set in, I saw him heading my way from the confectionary section struggling under the weight of a huge box of chocolates almost as big as he was.

'Here, Mum, she will love these,' he said, proudly dumping them straight into my trolley.

In the end, we compromised on a small chocolate bar to go with the fairy wings. When he asked me if he could go to her party, I'd been forced to lie to him.

'No, honey, it's just for girls this time.'

•

Ethan's eyes are firmly fixed back on the TV screen at the end of his hospital bed, and he's thankfully taken my silence on the topic of his cousins for a 'no'.

I am tired and feeling hungover from my lack of sleep. My nausea is bad this morning, but I know it's not just the tumours. Despite my every effort to let go and move on, my stomach still churns every time I think of Catherine.

CHAPTER 24

My list: Choose songs for my funeral

Ethan came home yesterday and, after a good night's sleep, he seems to have doubled his usual amount of energy. I have sent him out to the cubby with Clint, so I can try and get a bit of downtime, but just then the doorbell rings and, knowing who it will be, I rush to open it.

Marsha is standing on my doorstep struggling under the weight of the parcel she is carrying. It's the first time I have laid eyes on her in over a month. Even though she's been phoning every other day, it hasn't been the same and, despite myself, my eyes well with tears as she greets me.

'Okay everyone, jazz hands at the ready – Aunty Sugar is back!'

She opens her arms and drops her parcel onto the deck. Marsha is the best person in the world to hug. She is full of chocolate, cakes and self-indulgence and feels like a featherdown pillow.

When she lets go, I surreptitiously wipe my eyes with the back of my hands, so my tears don't fall and give her an excuse to follow through on her constant threats to lick them off my face. Thankfully she doesn't notice, as she is looking down at the parcel at her feet, laughing her deep, throaty laugh. I wonder what on earth she has brought with her this time.

'Come on, come on, where's my bloody cup of tea?' she asks, picking up her package and whirling her energy around like a tornado. 'I didn't come here to just stand on your doorstep, you rude cow.'

'Well I don't know if I should be letting people like you into my establishment,' I retort, bustling her through the door and feeling her whirlwind energy blow my imminent death out through the cracks in the walls.

Marsha sits herself down at the dining table just as Clint walks back inside to grab the coffee he left behind. As soon as he sees her, his eyes dart back to the yard, trying to assess if he can escape again before she notices him. He is uncomfortable with boganistas, which only makes her worse. Any remnant of culture she has goes out the window the minute she senses his fear, but that's never stopped her from loving him. Now she launches herself at him. He tries to sidestep her but she pulls his face straight into her chest and winks at me as he tries to find someplace in amongst her cleavage to draw breath. By the time he finally struggles free, I am doubled over with laughter.

'Yes, yes, very funny, Marsha,' he says. 'Please tell me you're not staying long.'

'Oh, you have no idea how long I can stay,' she says running her tongue across the front of her teeth before flicking it in and out like a deranged lizard.

She reaches into the package she's carrying and pulls out two boas wrapping one around my neck and lassoing Clint with the other while dancing around him like he is a pole in a nightclub. He tries to ignore her, but his eyerolls are less convincing than he'd like them to be. She shimmies over to me and grabs two more boas out of her bag, wrapping them around my face so I look like a deranged gumnut baby.

We both look at Clint and chant, 'Stay till you can party no more'.

Just then Ethan, who has obviously heard the commotion, races through the door.

'Aunty Sugar!' he yells.

'Little snotty-nosed brat,' she replies, her eyes lighting up.

He looks straight at her bag on the floor. 'What did you bring me?'

She grips him in a cuddle/headlock combination so he can't get away from her.

'First, you gotta show me the love,' she says, contorting her face and lips as he tries to struggle away from her.

'Come on, give Aunty Sugar a kiss.'

'Oh yuck, disgusting.' He laughs.

'No love, no present,' she says, pouting. He wriggles out of her hold and aims a quick kiss at her which lands on her elbow.

'Okay, that's better than nothing.' She grins, reaching into her bag and pulling out a packet of Pokémon cards and a white paper bag.

'Let your mum know these are one hundred per cent sugar-free, organic, made from fair trade vegetarian reindeer from Uzbekistan, good for you lollies.'

'Can I have one?' he asks me as he pulls out a blue and red additive-, sugar- and nuclear-infused sweet.

'Of course not,' I reply. 'It's not even food, you can use it to throw at your father instead.'

'Cool,' say Ethan and Marsha together.

Marsha and I met at a community choir eleven years ago. I was a soprano, and she was singing bass with the only man in the group. It was besties at first sight. I was in awe of her disrespect and her ability to speak the unspeakable. The choir was new and consisted of an elderly, out-of-tune church singer, a cranky old man, a wannabe opera singer, Marsha, myself, and a particularly depressed choir master. The first rehearsal started with a 'get to know you' exercise. When it got to Marsha she said, 'My name's Marsha and I'm an alcoholic . . . Oh, sorry, wrong group . . .' She chuckled. 'But seriously, I'm an alcoholic.'

I accidentally laughed out loud and that must have encouraged her, because the next thing we knew she was pulling up her top. Instead of flashing her flesh, she revealed a 'Made You Look' t-shirt. Two seconds later there was a blackout and Marsha yelled, 'Quick everyone, hands in the air!' We all obeyed, as that's what you do when Aunty Sugar tells you to do something. 'Many hands make light work,' she chortled and then, as quickly as they had gone out, the lights came back on. We all cracked up laughing.

The choir master tried to restore some order and get us all back to the program for the evening. He looked at Marsha

161

reluctantly, as she still hadn't finished the getting to know you exercise, which also involved describing your musical influences.

'I grew up listening to . . . my mother,' she blurted, revelling in her infantile humour like the primary school kid she was. The choir master tried to move on, but Marsha wasn't about to get off centre stage. 'Oh and . . . my dad.' She cracked up, bent over with the pain of laughing so hard at her own jokes.

I have loved my friend, the class clown, ever since. And she's obviously the best person to help me choose the songs for my funeral. After Ethan takes his stash of lollies and Pokémon cards to his cubby, Clint wastes no time in getting out the door to his shed; leaving Marsha and me to get on with serious sorry business.

Before she will allow me to compile my funeral soundtrack, however, Marsha insists we change into black for what she has dubbed our 'death by karaoke' session. I remind her that I want bright colours at my funeral but it falls on defiant ears.

'No one will listen to that, you watch, they'll all wear black,' she says, heading to the bathroom to change, adding, 'and I certainly will be – because it's positively slimming, darling!'

Not long after we met, Marsha started making me mixtapes. They are now a musical record of our friendship and remind us of exactly what we were doing when and how we both were feeling. They also remind me how old I am, if only because I call them mixtapes. When Marsha turned forty-seven last year, she was lamenting being on the downhill run to fifty, which is why now, I have to confess, part of me is glad this is as wrinkly and aged as I am ever going to get. I've always delighted in reminding Marsha I am seven years younger than she is and plan on rubbing that in even more by choosing a photo for my funeral pamphlet from ten years ago. I used to be proud of how good I looked for my age, but in the last year or so, thanks to my body's early adoption of peri-menopause, my downhill run has picked up considerable speed. At least now I get to stop the clock and, unlike my bestie, will check out looking semi-okay and not too demented. Even though Marsha and I have both joked about life in the retirement home, I'm not sure I would have grown old either gracefully or disgracefully. I would probably have just stayed a grumpy, cantankerous and even more miserable and wrinkly housewife. Clint doesn't realise what a considerate gesture me dying actually is.

Marsha has re-emerged in a slinky sequined black dress with a matching black and silver boa. In protest, I've refused to play dress-ups and stayed in my tracky dacks and pink t-shirt. We settle on the couch with a pot of English Breakfast.

As always, Marsha has thoroughly researched her mixtape. Her suggestions for songs include, 'Another One Bites the Dust', 'Ding Dong the Witch is Dead' (how rude) and 'Death of a Disco Dancer' (obscure but true). Then there are 'Things to Do in Denver When You're Dead' (she wants my ghost to meet her there and go shopping), followed by 'Dead and Bloated' (in honour of my current tumour-filled pregnant belly – something only Marsha could get away with) and finally, 'Like You Better Dead'. I ask if we couldn't have more of an alive than a dead theme as I'm planning to hang around and haunt her. I explain how I'm going to be 'coming through' spelling only the first letter of my name and giving her vague references about our life together via a psychic so she'll never really be sure if it's actually me.

'So how about "Born to Be Alive" for the entry?' I ask. 'Then I'm thinking "Look Alive" for when they have to carry my casket out and "Help I'm Alive" as they draw the final curtain before setting me and my casket on fire.'

The tea Marsha has been drinking spurts out her nose as she snorts with laughter.

'Oh my god,' she shrieks. 'I'd be jumping over old ladies and pushing little kids out of the way to get to you. Then I'd be straddling the coffin and trying to rip it open yelling "It's all right, Viv, I'm coming!" But hang on, shit, they probably nail those suckers shut – so I'd be trying to scratch my way *in* instead of out! But then I'd feel the conveyor belt starting to move towards the barbeque and I'd be thinking, *Fuck, shit*. But there's no way I'd give up. I'd be grabbing everything in my handbag that might help. I'd be using nail files and hairbrushes and anything I could find to try and prise that bastard open.'

I am in tears laughing but manage to gasp out, 'And Clint would just be sitting there looking around saying, "What's happening?" and by the time he'd finally spring into action, we would've both gone up in flames.'

By this time Marsha is shaking uncontrollably, and I am laughing so hard it takes me a minute to realise she's sobbing.

'I don't want you to die,' she chokes out.

She collapses in my arms, and we hug for what seems like a lifetime of friendship and way too many cups of tea. When we slowly let go of each other, we're both drenched in tears. She wipes her snotty nose on her sleeve, and I grab her other sleeve and do the same.

'Bitch,' she says. 'Don't expect me to rescue you now.'

I have been laughing so much I need to rush to the toilet, hanging onto myself like Michael Jackson. These days I give myself a standing ovation followed by an encore when I visit the bathroom. When I think I have finished, I stand up, only to find my pelvic floor is not in agreeance, so I sit down again. It can take me up to four curtain calls before the performance is finally done and, even then, when I pull up my jeans, I can still be caught out by one last flourish, have to sit back down and start all over again.

By the time I'm finished, Marsha has boiled the kettle so a new pot of tea is waiting for me when I return. The cups are warmed, and the pot even has a tea cosy on it. See, that is why we are friends.

CHAPTER 25

Clint's list for me: Play with your son

As much as Marsha drives me completely mental, at least when she's here I get five minutes to myself. So, while they're in the lounge room, I head to our bedroom to see if I can finally do something about that mess Viv made trying to paint our French doors. I wish she wouldn't do things like that. I told her I would paint them. Now I'm going to have to strip them and sand them back before I can do anything, so it's going to take twice as long. And if that's not bad enough, I've still got to deal with all these clothes she ruined, just because she's so bloody impatient.

I've brought a garbage bag with me to sort what will have to be binned. The whole top two layers of the pile beneath the doors are covered in paint so will have to go. Then just below that I discover the photo album.

'Shit, I bloody forgot,' I accidentally say out loud and then look around to make sure Viv hasn't come within earshot. Luckily, she's still too busy with Marsha. I head out quickly to the car, the album under my arm.

'I'm heading out, love,' I call, closing the front door behind me.

I head straight to the photography shop. Our wedding anniversary is coming up soon and Viv always complains that I forget it, so I'm going to get a photo from our wedding blown up and framed as a surprise. I really like the picture I've chosen. My hair looks great in it and Viv is staring at me like she is totally smitten. I wish she still looked at me like that.

I need to find a way to make my hair grow again. When I first started going bald, I tried a few snake oil remedies. I knew how much Viv loved my hair so I thought it would be nice for her if I could at least try to look a bit more like the man she fell for. The prices were out-bloody-rageous, but just six months ago I thought I'd try again and put down $1200 as a deposit for some hair implants. Of course, the shysters went out of business and I did my dough. I should have known when the guy told me to make the payment out to a B. Smith that they were not a legitimate business.

Having exhausted all avenues to try and give Viv back the old me, I figured the next best thing I could do was give her back some happy memories with a big framed photo she can admire every day.

The woman behind the counter is blonde, and if I was into blondes I reckon she'd be a bit of all right, but I've only ever been a brunette man. Besides, most blondes come out of a bottle, and I prefer natural beauty myself. She smiles at me, and I hand over the photo album and open it on the page I've marked.

'It's our wedding anniversary coming up,' I say. 'So, I thought I'd surprise my wife. I wanted to get this one enlarged and put into a nice frame for her.'

'That's so thoughtful of you. How many years have you been married?' she asks.

'Nine years married, ten years together.'

'I can see why you've lasted.' She smiles approvingly. 'If more men did thoughtful things like this for their wives, there would be a lot less divorces.' Then she pauses, frowning down at the photo. 'Is this really you?' she asks, sounding a bit too incredulous for my liking.

'That was when I had a bit more hair.'

'Weren't you good-looking,' she says, smiling again.

I smile back at her, trying to show off my teeth, which after my hair have always been my biggest selling point.

'What size would you like?' she asks.

I ask for the largest size they have, imagining our whole bedroom wall covered with our wedding photo. I reckon Viv would love that.

'The largest we can do here is a fifty by seventy-five,' she explains, 'but we can send it out-of-house and then you can go as big as you like. That can take several weeks, though.'

'I'll just have the fifty by seventy-five,' I reply, not wanting to explain we might not have that long.

While she goes to blow up the photo, I take a look at the frames. There must be about fifty different styles. Bloody hell, can't they make anything simple these days? There are too many choices to make about everything. The size I need narrows it down a bit, as does the colour. Viv loves pink, but I hate it, especially now she's painted the bloody French doors that colour, so I decide to go for plain black or white. There is only one white one and it's marked down because it has a bit of a chip in it, which you wouldn't notice unless it was pointed out so that's it – decision made. I return to the counter and the print is ready. It looks great and I ask if she can put it straight into the frame and gift-wrap it. Apparently they don't usually do wrapping, but she manages to find some brown paper and string. Job done. Viv is going to love it.

When I get home, I hear giggling coming from the lounge room and I quickly hide the present in my bedroom wardrobe. When I come out, I'm happy to see Ethan and Viv playing a game. Viv is blindfolded and has what looks like a donkey's tail in her hand. Marsha, who thank god hasn't noticed me yet, is sitting on the lounge watching. Viv is walking blindly and unsteadily around the room.

'Okay, Mum, you've got this,' encourages Ethan.

'Colder, freezing.' He laughs.

Viv turns around and starts heading towards where I am standing, 'Warmer, warmer still,' says Ethan. 'Getting hot, hotter,' he says, sounding more and more excited as she comes closer and closer to me.

'Boiling, Mum, you're boiling now.' He giggles.

'That's it, Mum,' he says as she reaches towards me.

'Get out of the way, Dad!' he yells. I step to the side just as she lunges forward and tacks the tail onto a poster I hadn't realised was behind me.

Ethan laughs. 'You got his nose, Mum,' he squeals. 'He's got a hairy nose now.' I look behind me and see a picture of me on the wall.

'We're playing pin the hair on the Clinton,' says Marsha. 'They had a special on photo enlargements at the chemist.'

I head out to the shed; it's going to be a long night.

CHAPTER 26

Not on my list: Rewrite our wedding vows

Clint is not exactly a big fan of Aunty Sugar and I suppose it was remiss of me to not include her in our wedding vows – do you take this woman and her best friend to taunt you for as long as you both shall live? My sister, Catherine, would have also liked to have been included from day dot – do you take this woman and her entire family in sickness and mental health? Unfortunately for both of them, I opted for the standard-issue vows.

When Clint proposed, in place of due diligence I'd simply checked my schedule and diary, realised I had nothing on for the rest of my life and booked him in. In my haste to get to the all-you-can-eat buffet, I failed to read the nuptial fine print and from the moment I said I do, I did way more housework than I'd ever done in my life. He, on the other hand, did the same as he'd always done, which was nothing apart from buying takeaway, running out of toilet paper and hiring someone for an end-of-lease bond clean.

But before I said those fateful words, my dearly beloved had needed to prove he was not only capable of passing the best friend test but also the sibling test. In those days Catherine was still single and the longest relationship she could lay claim to had been a four-day passionate internet affair she'd initiated with a man in Sweden. Like every Swedish man ever born, he was super good-looking and didn't want to listen to ABBA music. Unfortunately for him, my sister and I had grown up learning all the steps to 'Mamma Mia' and honed our terrible voices singing 'Dancing Queen'. It was one of our few happy childhood memories and inspired Catherine's biggest romantic goal of finding a karaoke king to play with. When her lover-to-be realised she was incapable of having a conversation that didn't include Benny, Bjorn, Agnetha or Frida, he ended their brief liaison. It wasn't a total waste, however, as now, thanks to Mr Ikea, my little sis knew all there was to know about relationships and could give ignorant advice like no one else.

I decided the kindest way to introduce Clint to Catherine was to go to a show so there was less time for him in the scrutiny chair and less time for me to listen to her unsolicited wisdom. I'd recently started trying to binge on everything I had missed out on as a child, such as fairy floss, showbags and stuffed toys, so the obvious choice for our 'meet the family' date was the circus.

When we arrived at the showground, I realised circuses were not quite the same as they would have been if I had gone to one as a child. Thanks to animal rights activists, there were no more lions and tigers and bears (oh my) for children to torment and the big top looked decidedly small when viewed through adult eyes.

Catherine was not as enthusiastic as I'd initially been so had sandwiched our circus date between business meetings to make sure her assessment of Clint didn't drag out. Despite the breezy day, her sprayed hair hadn't moved, nor had her immaculately made-up face when the dusty crowd eyed her up and down in her high heels and business suit. This was her latest look, having previously gone through a hippy bohemian fad, followed by a 1950s retro housewife look and then a period of pseudo-spiritual white-only styling. Little did I know, her power dressing was not going to be a passing phase. She'd finally found her look. That day Catherine got her first taste of fashion-funded superiority, which wasn't difficult given the tracksuit uniform worn by most of the rest of the crowd. As I lined up amidst the sea of obesity to buy my diabetes on a stick, even I momentarily felt I had my life together.

Clint, god love him, was having a ball. He knew I'd never been to the circus and, as only a man in the early stages of love will do, he dragged me from one wallet-draining stall to the next. Before I knew it, I was struggling under the weight of fairy floss, fairy wings, a giant stuffed panda and helium balloons; and wondering how on earth I was going to nurse it all during the main event. Just then, a dramatic voice boomed, 'Ladies and gentlemen, welcome to the Landling Brothers Circus, please make your way into the big top, where our show is about to begin.' Catherine, who had so far spent the morning complaining about how dusty her patent leather shoes were getting, finally allowed herself to look, just a little, excited.

'Oooh, it's starting! Come on let's go,' she said, grabbing me by the arm and pushing me into the crowd who were now funnelling into the tent.

'It's all right, they won't start until everyone's in there,' I said, trying to stop her pushing me into the old lady in front of me. Clint looked at Catherine and laughed.

'You two are so alike. You both have no time for patience.'

We looked at him and stuck our tongues out simultaneously.

'Jinx,' said Catherine, holding her pinky out to me to pull and make a wish. I obediently obliged, like always.

'If anyone was looking at us now, they'd think we were one big happy family.' Catherine smiled.

'Yep, that's us all right, just ask any welfare worker.' I laughed.

Clint looked at me, clearly puzzled, before leaving me to hold his place while he ducked to the bathroom. Catherine, of course, seized the opportunity to give me her opinion.

'He's way better than Steve,' she said, delivering a fine opening backhand. 'He talks nicely to you, not that you're likely to return the favour,' she continued. 'But he does seem a bit weird . . . I mean who'd want to go out with you? There must be something wrong with him.' She pinched me on the arm the way she used to when she was a kid, trying to look disapproving but knowing I could tell she actually liked him.

'Thanks, sis.' I smiled, rubbing my arm which was still smarting. She was always very good at pinching. Regardless, this was way more approval than I'd ever expected from Catherine, which made me nervous. I think part of me had been hoping for a get-out-of-marriage-free card so I wouldn't have to jump in, hang-ups and all.

Just as we were being shown to our seats, Clint made it into the tent. He'd stopped along the way and bought us all tea and cinnamon donuts. I relaxed back into loving him, but then the clown arrived.

From the minute the red-nosed, big-shoed man drove out in his tiny car and started spraying the audience with water from his bow tie, Clint, and every other under-five-year-old, couldn't contain themselves. The rest of us adults politely smiled at the entertainment, but Clint fell about laughing. Each time the clown fell, tripped or beeped his horn, he doubled over in hysterics, like it was the funniest thing he'd seen in years. And it wasn't just the slapstick that got him, every new terrible joke made him laugh until he was literally wiping tears off his cheeks. I should have known then he was destined for a career in dad jokes. Catherine and I rolled our eyes at him, although we did it more affectionately than either of us would have liked.

The next act was the trapeze. Thankfully they had a safety net as Catherine was close to having a heart attack as it was. She still had a lot of anxiety from when we were kids, and as each performer jumped off the platform to swing gracefully through the air, she gripped my knee tightly. By the time the last leotarded lady gave her final bow and tripped lightly off stage, I could feel bruises starting to form where her fingers had been embedded.

The juggler was next and was the act I could most relate to. I've always had to keep a lot of balls in the air at once, so I was super impressed to see a man could do that too. It probably gave me false hope, and could have even been the final impetus that pushed me over the threshold of my fear into a lifetime of wedded blisters.

I take out my list and make a note to check that the "til death do us part' clause in our wedding contract is still valid.

CHAPTER 27

Ethan's list: Have a sleepover

Ethan's friend has arrived for his sleepover. In theory this was supposed to give Marsha and me time to chat while the boys played; instead, we are watching a kid's concert. Ethan's friend Brodie is one of the cool kids. Not a try-hard cool kid, he's just a hip little dude. He has this adult attitude about him and yet it isn't bratty or rude. Ethan, on the other hand, doesn't even know cool has been invented yet. He is still well and truly floating on the ethereal plane, and yet the two of them have absolute acceptance and love for each other, possibly because they've known each other since they were babies. There is a special bond that seems to form when you have learnt to walk, talk and poo in the potty together, which manages to sidestep judgement.

Clint and I met Brodie's parents, Bria and Ben, in the birthing centre and have stayed connected ever since. We don't see a lot of each other, but they are one of the few families where there isn't a mismatch between any of us. Bria is a full nerd and tea-junkie who secretly loves how I am nowhere near as polite as the rest of the school mums, and Ben and Clint can talk about nothing interesting for hours. If our kids had met each other for the first time now, they're so different they might not even want to be acquaintances, let alone friends, but here they are side by side, ready to audition for Only Your Parents Think You've Got Talent.

Brodie is first to take to the stage. He is doing a pretty impressive, if worrying, impersonation of Donald Trump.

'We're going to build a wall and make America great again,' he says, sounding scarily like el Presidente.

We laugh out loud and applaud, which is all the encouragement Ethan needs to jump up beside him and start doing a less professional impersonation of Donald Duck. Realising his quacking is being trumped by Brodie's strutting, he throws in some flossing and a dab to try and compete for our attention. They are giggling their little heads off. For at least the first five minutes, Marsha and I are laughing too, but half an hour later we have no fake laughter left in us. They are ramping it up just when they should be calming down, so it's time to call it quits if we are to have a hope in hell of getting them to sleep anytime this century.

'Okay, that's enough now, time for a bath you two,' I say.

Marsha leans into me and whispers, 'And . . . cue whingeing.'

True to form, the boys start their protests.

'But, Mum, I'm not even dirty, I've hardly been outside today,' says Ethan, hooking his feet up under the couch to hide the obvious dirt.

'Yeah, yeah, we've just been inside playing Pokémon,' says Brodie, joining in the game of 'let's see if we can wear her down tonight like we usually do so we get our own way'.

I am well aware of this game and also well aware the ninja shower-avoiders are banking on me being easy prey because Marsha is here, which makes me less inclined to argue. Knowing how Brodie's mum would feel about the ferals going to bed in their filth, I yell for reinforcement.

'Clint . . . Clint, what are you doing? Can you come here and help?'

The boys run, hoping to get to him before I do.

'Dad, Dad, we don't need a bath, we've only been inside,' yells Ethan before Clint has time to reach me.

Ethan knows he only has a narrow window of opportunity to secure a bath-time exemption pass from Clint, who will do whatever it takes to escape child-nagging duty.

'Show me your feet,' he says to the boys, who quickly try to rub the dirt from their paws onto the backs of their tracksuit pants. 'They're pretty dirty,' he says.

I am momentarily impressed until I hear, 'But I tell you what, why don't you just grab a washer and if you clean your feet and show me you've done a good job, you can skip tonight, and your mum can put the bath on for you in the morning.'

I am furious. Marsha starts to rise to my defence, but I know it's too late. Once one parent is down, it's all over.

'When I am dead can you come over once a month and use the pressure cleaner on my son?' I ask Marsha, exasperated.

'Will do.' She gets out a pen and paper. 'Right, let me start a list. Number one, pressure clean child, tick. Number two?' She looks at me for instructions then answers her own question, 'Sterilise husband to ensure no more children get dirty. There, all taken care of,' she says solemnly, making a sign of the cross. 'May God on high now grant unto you eternal rest.'

Something smashes in the bathroom.

'Not in this house,' I groan, getting up to put the kettle on. Time to ignore the fact I am a mother before I go completely insane.

'Anyway, we've talked about me to death. How about we change topic and you can finally tell me what's been happening at your madhouse?'

'Oh, same as usual. The neighbours still look over their fence at everything I do, so I'm keeping myself busy trying to come up with new things for them to gawk at.'

'Any success?'

'I accidentally set fire to the washing the other day when I was bringing it in while having a fag.' She smirks at me.

I laugh. 'Impressive.'

'Yeah, but luckily it wasn't any of my clothes, just a couple of shirts of the old man's, so that earnt me bonus points.'

'I'm sure he appreciated it. How are things with Phil anyway?'

'Oh, he's still there,' she sighs. 'I'm not sure if he's alive or not, though. If he is, I think he's been super-glued to the couch. The only time he doesn't look like a corpse is when his phone dings and he automatically salivates. When I left to go away, he was there, and when I came home, he was there. I think I am going to use him as a hat rack,' she says slumping down in her chair.

'What does Phil think about that?'

'Wouldn't have a clue, we haven't spoken since he told me he wasn't talking to me, and that was months ago.'

Phil and Marsha met each other twelve years ago on a comedy cruise and found each other hilarious. Unfortunately, their biting wit consumed their relationship until all that was left were teeth marks. They are two lovely people destroying themselves, and I wish there was something I could do. But I'm not exactly in a position to pass on wise relationship advice, so I pour her a cup of tea.

'He hasn't said anything since then? You're joking,' I say.

'I wish, but you know what he's like. He's so bloody stubborn, and he'll do anything to prove a point. I think I'll just move out and wait to see if he notices.'

'Where would you go?' I ask.

'Well, I thought I'd wait until you're dead and then move in on your husband and into your bedroom.'

'Sure.' I chuckle at the thought. 'But when you do, can you at least take on Ethan's bath duty?'

'Too easy. I'll wash down Clint too if you like?' She pulls out her list. 'Number three, use the Gerni on Clint.'

CHAPTER 28

My list: Amend my will

It is four o'clock in the morning, and my brain has decided now is the perfect time to review my whole life. Every single person who has ever pissed me off is now flashing before my eyes, and I am rehearsing what I should have said to them, imagining tossing back my hair, telling them how these days my life is so much better than theirs. I am, of course, carefully leaving out the part about being on death's door. After about ten minutes of ranting to myself, I'm starting to get a headache. A better use of my insomnia would be to use my early morning to tick something off my list. I really need to amend my will, so, with a choice of fighting my ex-nemeses in my head or digging through paperwork, I get up and take the less disturbing option.

All of my paperwork is 'neatly' filed in the lounge room in five overflowing boxes comprised of actual paperwork, mail that is yet to be opened, receipts I forgot to submit for my tax return, junk mail and recycling that never made it out the door. Finding my will should be easy. Two hours later, I look up and out the window to see the mist still clinging to the valley, hanging onto the last of the darkness for dear life. All I have managed to do before sunrise is distribute my neglected paperwork into vaguely sorted piles all over the floor, and start reading an old journal.

It's the journal I began writing at my first Tony Robbins seminar. Like every other desperately unhappy woman in the room, I fell instantly in love. Tony, unfortunately, was never available when I was, so the poor man had to settle for who he could get in the meantime. The seminar had sparked the beginning of my obsession with lists, only instead of long, tedious notes of daily chores, I called what I wrote in my journal back then 'goals', which made them sound far more impressive. My ambitions at that point weren't anywhere near as lofty as they are today. Instead of wanting a clean recycling bin or to be so organised that I never ran out of toilet paper, I focused on petty things like saving the planet for my son, leading the charge to revolutionise childcare, and emanating love wherever I went.

The Viv I used to be would have easily and effortlessly written her will in no time flat, leaving everything to the first good-looking, hard luck story she came across. It's easy to give everything away when you only own enough hand-me-down clothing to fit in your car boot. Now I have to think about who I want to leave all my debts too. There's my horrendous credit card bill. I'd like to gift that to Marsha, not because she deserves to pay lots of interest, but because she'd be mighty impressed at how much I've managed to rack up on hormonally driven shopping sprees. It will make her feel better about her own feeble attempts to purchase beyond her means. She'll also get a big kick out of chopping up my plastic fantastic and not returning calls, so a sheriff has to turn up on her doorstep. Despite having heard all my evidence to the contrary, she still thinks sheriffs look like they do in the movies.

The mortgage, boringly and unsurprisingly, I will leave for Clint. The house has gone down in value since we bought it, which reflects how badly we've taken care of it, so it is only fair he should be heir apparent, as he worked just as hard at neglecting the property as I did. As the mortgage goes hand in hand with the house, I am a bit worried that without me keeping an eye on things, Clint may end up losing our Australian nightmare and end up homeless. While Ethan does love camping, I can't help but be sensible and want to protect my son from spending the rest of his life in sleeping bags, star-gazing next to urine-scented alcoholics. I make a note to tell my solicitor to make Isabelle the executor. The Izster will no doubt embrace taking charge of all the financial responsibilities and, much as I hate to admit it, in this case mother-in-law knows best. Clint and I have spoken about it and should he die of a broken heart shortly after me, I also have no other option but to leave my most precious possession, my son, in the hands of Clint's mother. Sadly, she is the most stable, not only financially, but mentally as well. Of course, Ethan's teeth will fall out of his head from eating lollies day and night, but at least she will be able to afford the dental bill. Her house is lovely and, unlike anyone else I can think of, her friends are all sane, fine, upstanding, charitably judgemental citizens. While I could personally think of nothing worse than living in a world of politeness, it is still the best option for Ethan should he ever be left orphaned by his two less than deserving birth parents.

As for my to-do list, Sally has had her eye on that ever since we met. It's a shame to leave it to her really, as she will have everything ticked off in no time flat, with no regret, no guilt and no nagging. A wave of sadness hits me as I consider leaving my women's work behind. My never-ending chores have been a constant and while the thought of having no leftover Life Admin should be a relief, I can't bring myself to abandon my legacy. I will have to think of something else to leave to Sally as I know in my heart of hearts my list needs to go to Marsha, whose high-level procrastination skills will ensure I am kept alive and unfinished for all eternity.

CHAPTER 29

Not on my list: Beg in public

After my early morning attempt at will writing, I put my list aside and finally manage to go back to sleep before being woken by Clint trying to get Ethan out the door quietly. When he gently slams the door behind himself, I somehow manage to doze off before being rudely awakened by Aunty Sugar shaking my toe.

'Come on, girlfriend, up and at 'em, have I got a scheme for you,' she says, dancing around like a maniac.

If she was Clint I would punch her right now, but she's Marsha, so despite only having one eye open and feeling like I have been hit by a truck, I indulge her.

'Oh god, here we go, at least get me a cup of tea first.'

'Already on it,' she says, pointing at a steaming mug of tea on my bedside table. She grabs a pillow so I can sit up in bed and waits impatiently for me to take my first sip. She knows me well enough for that at least.

'Three little words,' she says animatedly. 'Go . . . Fund . . . Me.'

'How about Go Fuck You instead,' I respond wearily, knowing that once she's got an idea in her head she's unstoppable.

'No, really,' she says without missing a beat. 'All those cancer fakers do it to rake in the cash, why don't you?'

'For a start, I don't want to share pictures of me looking crappy and depressed as all hell.'

'Of course not, we'll do glamour photography.' She winks. 'You only have to look sick if you're faking it. That's objection number one sorted . . . Next?'

'I hate Facebook, I haven't been on it for ages and I'm not about to message anybody. Remember what happened last time you made me get online?'

'Oh yeah, Tinder . . .' she says, looking vaguely guilty. 'Good to see you've moved on though, and you're not still keeping score! But, listen, you're going to love this.' She sits down on the bed.

'God help me,' I moan.

'No, god help *Clint*.'

Now she has my attention. 'What have you got in mind?'

'Not just in mind, I've already organised a special surprise for you both.' She pauses, loving building the suspense. 'It's a sponsored chest wax where everyone has to pay money to watch Clint get a bald body to match his head.'

'Oooh . . . You are evil, I love it.' I laugh. 'But there's no way in hell he'll agree to it.'

'Oh, you underestimate me, my dear friend, it will be – wait for it – a surprise waxing marathon party at his work.'

'Are you kidding me?'

'No, I've been organising the whole thing and two days ago I finally got his boss to agree to it.'

'Get out of town.' I slap her.

'Nup. I won't even get out of your bedroom.'

'I've noticed. So when are you thinking we do your crazy scheme number five hundred and forty-two?'

'How about now?'

'What the hell?'

'Yeah, you don't think I'd just wake you up for nothing, do you?' She's already pulling the quilt and sheet straight off my bed. 'Come on, you've got half an hour before you miss the show, and, trust me, this is a show you don't want to miss.'

She's right, of course, I would never want to miss anything Aunty Sugar has organised. Life with Marsha is never boring. No wonder I chose someone more predictable to marry, I needed some Yin to balance out her supersized Yang. I shower, dress and follow her obediently to the car.

Clint is going to kill me.

•

When we arrive at the motel where Clint has recently started working, the receptionist greets me with a conspiratorial smile.

'We've booked the conference room and it's all ready to go,' she says, handing us the keys.

The conference room is located on the top floor of the building and when we go inside, there is a massage table set up in one corner with a microphone, a large whiteboard and a projector screen. The screen is hooked up to a laptop showing the

GoFundMe donations so far, and I am surprised at how generous Clint's new workmates have been. The largest pledge is for five hundred dollars and there are multiple donations of one and two hundred dollars. It's amazing how much people will pay to witness public humiliation and physical torture.

The whiteboard appears to be for betting how long Clint will last, and people have put their names next to various time periods. I put my name next to the smallest possible time, thirty seconds after the first strip is ripped off, but am surprised to see that most of his colleagues are betting on him to last a lot longer. He obviously has a different personality at work than he does at home. A woman called Mariah has put him down for an hour. I hate to burst her bubble, but he's never lasted an hour with anything physical, especially when there's pain involved.

The door opens, and a crowd of people rush in, jostling for front row seats. Clint is with them but is obviously clueless as he's totally surprised when he notices me and Aunty Sugar. He looks at me questioningly and I just shrug my shoulders, trying my best to look like I am as clueless as he is. His new boss, Peter, an old friend of Clint's, loves public speaking, so he grabs the microphone and, after closing the door behind the last staff member, stands in front of it to ensure there is no escape exit.

'Well, Clint, I know what a hard time you and Viv have been having,' he says, nodding towards me.

People shuffle their feet and look down. I think they'd forgotten this was a cancer fundraiser. They're really only here for the bloodletting.

'So, when I told everyone here what was going on, they were all keen to do whatever they could to help.'

Like hell, I think, *none of them volunteered for the torture table.*

'I know what a good sport you are, and you've always said you'd do anything for Viv, so now's your chance to prove it.'

Clint is starting to look nervous.

'We've got some really generous pledges up here on the board as you can see,' he says, pointing to the screen. 'Now all you've got to do to encourage more donations, and turn these promises into cold hard cash, is to man up and jump on that table.'

'Am I getting a massage?' asks Clint, confused.

'Not quite. Let me introduce you to Eloise.'

From out of the crowd steps a woman in a white coat. She looks around at the crowd and then holds up a waxing strip theatrically, walking around the room for everyone to see it.

'Are we ready people?' she yells.

Clint's workmates cheer and their eyes light up.

'That's right, Clint, you've been "volunteered" to wax your chest for your wife,' she says, continuing to gee up the audience.

Clint turns pale.

'Now, now, I'm sure your wife's done enough waxing of herself for you in her time, am I right?' She turns to me. For once I am lost for words, but Aunty Sugar steps in and yells, 'Hell, yeah!' Clint looks at her with murderous intent.

'All right then, let's get started.'

Clint looks around the room. There is no way out, so he gingerly removes his tie and shirt and climbs onto the table. The beautician puts on the warm wax and he relaxes, thinking it isn't so bad after all. She gently rubs the strip of fabric on top of it and, just as he closes his eyes – probably wondering what women are always complaining about – she rips it off, removing a lifetime of chest hair from above his nipple. The crowd cheers, drowning out Clint's screaming and Marsha's hysterical laughter. I can't help but join her, although when Clint glances at me, looking betrayed, I have to admit I feel guilty. I point to Aunty Sugar and mouth, 'She did it.' He isn't convinced but doesn't have time to hold the grudge before the next strip is ripped off a second later.

Halfway into the job, the crowd's cheers start to wane and even the men who started out with the most bravado begin to wince. The audience is losing their enthusiasm and the beautician appears to be losing her stride. Clint sees her waver and, for a moment seems to think she will give up halfway, but then watches in horror as she regains her strength and continues to tear strips off him.

Fifteen minutes later, just as I am getting ready to call Amnesty International and even Clint's bloodthirsty workmates are starting to feel sorry for him, Aunty Sugar decides to liven up the party and steps up to the pulpit.

'Phwuh, phwuh, is this on?' she says blowing into the microphone. She smiles at me and I give her a tentative thumbs up.

Here we go, I think to myself.

'Most of you don't know me from a bar of soap, but I'm Marsha, Viv's best friend, so don't go hustling in on my territory,' she says, laughing and heading straight for me, mic in hand while she pulls me into a cramped hug.

'As you all now know, Viv has gone and got herself the big C, so I want to be the first to congratulate her and say . . . Well done, Viv!' She puts her hand up to mine, which I obediently high-five. 'She's never been first at anything in her life so she thought she'd give dying a go.'

While she's on a roll I try to wriggle out of her hug, but she tightens her arms around me, like when she's drunk and telling me how much she loves me.

'You have to admit, she's done a bloody good job of it. I mean, look at her.' She holds me out at arm's length to make her point. 'Her tumours are so ripped they look like a sixpack, and I know thin is in, but she's wasting away to nothing.'

I hear an uncharacteristic falter in her voice and see her surreptitiously swat at an unwanted tear like it's an annoying fly.

'Anyway, we are here today to join this man and this woman,' she says, putting on a fake compere's voice to regain her stride. 'Oh, hang on, wrong gig.' She laughs at her own joke. 'Correction, we are here today because Viv, like me, has never had two cents to rub together.' Her voice cracks again but she doesn't miss a beat. 'And I think that also deserves a bit of recognition.'

She lets go of me and starts clapping, overcoming her emotion the way she always does, by going well and truly over the top.

'Come on, folks, show some enthusiasm,' she implores, upping the volume and walking around invading people's space. She stops at one particularly unenthusiastic woman and claps her hands together for her. After that everyone else quickly joins in to avoid their own public humiliation.

I quickly retreat to a seat, but my eyes remain fixed on my sad clown friend.

'See, Viv, I told you you'd get the clap one day, you just had to get cancer first,' she says as another un-swatted tear rolls down her cheek, streaking her make-up.

'If this is making you all feel uncomfortable, don't worry, you'll feel much better when you hand over your guilt money,' she continues, still managing to pretend she's headlining Vegas even though I've never seen her so heartbroken.

'Now, just to be clear, this money is not going anywhere sensible like doctors' bills because, one, how boring is that? And two, she's dying, so what's the point?'

She falters again, and I stand up, ready to walk over to her, but she gives me her death stare, so I sit back down.

'I reckon Viv should be able to spend your hardly earnt cash on whatever puts a smile on her dying dial, and I will personally supervise to make sure she only spends it on something that is going to be fun, fun, fun! So, step right up, folks, and hand over your cash for Viv to waste before she wastes away.' She is really starting to sound like a carnie now. 'And if you don't hand over any money, well, you'll have me to answer to.' She punches her fist into her hand and then shakes it like she's really hurt herself.

Job done, Marsha finally exits stage left and I comfort her the only way she's ever let me, by giving it back as much as she dishes it out.

'Are you done, you great big leg of ham?' I taunt. 'You really only organised this GoFundMe so you could put on a performance and amuse yourself at my expense, didn't you?'

'Why change the habit of a lifetime?' she chortles.

Just then, Clint, who has all but been forgotten, gives a loud groan. He is starting to look like an exhausted, plucked chicken. The beautician has worked up a sweat and appears to be running out of steam but luckily, after forty-five minutes, her job here is almost done. While Clint is still embarrassingly breathing the way our Lamaze course taught us, I am impressed he has managed to hang in there. Two minutes later, when the final strip rips out the last of his masculinity, I feel an unexpected wave of pride that my not exactly brave husband has lasted so long.

He sits up shakily, putting his shirt back on, and there is visible relief in the room that the torture is finally over. One by one, his workmates come up to him, patting him on the back and saying, 'Well done, mate,' and 'Looks like I've done my dough.' The praise starts to ease Clint's pain, even while little droplets of blood begin showing through his white shirt. By the time the last person has paid their respects and Peter has given him an extra strong tea with two heaped spoons of sugar, Clint is looking more his normal pallor. When he looks up at the screen and realises we have raised over ten thousand dollars he looks even better again. The smile returns to his face as he joins in the jokes which have already started to circulate.

I make my way apologetically towards him. 'I swear I knew nothing about it until I got dragged here this morning,' I say, once again trying to dob in my bestie.

'Oh really?' he replies, thinking for once he has the upper hand. 'And I'm supposed to believe that, when you've only been saying I should wax my chest ever since we met?'

'Can I help it if Marsha listens to everything I say and takes it all literally?' I reply.

'So, seeing I got waxed, do I get to spend this money on whatever I like?' he asks cockily.

'Yeah, nup, I don't think so.' I shut him down before he gets carried away.

'You've put up with being waxed once, I've been doing it ever since puberty. One time on the beautician's table isn't exactly going to get you nominated for sainthood you know.' My guilt is wearing off and my years of putting up with his whingeing are kicking back in. 'Anyway, I'm the one with cancer,' I finish, reminding him who still holds the ace card.

Clint looks defeated. He knows when it comes to arguments these days, he will always be defeated by 'I'm dying, you're not – I win'.

CHAPTER 30

Not on Clint's list:
Stand up to his dad

Ever since bloody Aunty Sugar launched her stupid fundraising campaign the other day, every man and his dog has come out of the woodwork. Viv and technology are not exactly friends so I'm the one who's stuck fielding all the dumb messages from everyone. Number one on the list of people I'd rather not have to deal with is my dad. He's been blissfully missing in action for the past six months, but as soon as moronic Marsha posted those damn photos of me with a hairless chest he crawled out from under his rock.

Before he left Mum for younger pastures, Dad was a crap drummer who earnt a crap living. He's never had money and has always been a gold digger, which is probably why he turned up unannounced when he saw the donations hit the ten K mark online. Thankfully, he so far hasn't found out about the extra two K we made in cash on the day.

When I was a kid Dad always used to walk into my room without knocking, especially when I had girls over. Entering unannounced is a bad habit he's never managed to overcome, so when he lets himself into our lounge room to find me rubbing cream into my very sore, plucked chest, I am startled, but not surprised.

'Bloody hell, mate, that looks even redder than it looked online,' he yells.

Dad only has one volume and that's loud.

'I'm right here, Dad, you don't have to yell,' I reply futilely.

'We ought to put you on stage with us as our support act,' he announces to the huge audience that doesn't exist. 'You can be the understudy for the bearded lady.' He laughs loudly at his own joke.

'Okay, Dad, what do you want?' I ask, refusing to even pretend to be amused.

'Well, not your miserable company that's for sure.' He pouts.

'No kidding,' I mumble under my breath.

When Dad met Mum, she, like every other woman, fell for his good looks, charming stage persona and status as the drummer in the coolest up-and-coming band of the era. Mum was rebelling against her strict upbringing and assumed Dad was too, as he dressed well and talked the talk, although he did seem a little rough around the edges. Still, he'd convinced her, by splashing money around like water, that he was an ex-pat investor who played music for fun and had been brought up studying at an international school in Hong Kong. The money, of course, wasn't his, nor were the brand name clothes he'd strutted around in. He'd 'borrowed' them from his flatmate who was away on holidays.

By the time his housemate returned, Dad had already quick-stepped Mum down the aisle after a whirlwind romance. He managed to keep up the pretence for a year, saying his funds were tied up in a lucrative investment that, like him, hadn't yet matured. But when Mum's long-lost cousin from Hong Kong came to visit, Dad's pack of cards had come tumbling down.

Despite his lies, Mum had tried to make the most of it. After all, he wasn't a violent drunk like my grandfather had been, so she'd hung in there trying to convince herself and the rest of her family she'd made the right decision. After all, when you are a Smithston, marriages are forever. Mum certainly wasn't going to be the first to ruin the family's unbroken reputation for enduring horrendous marriages no matter what. In the meantime, Dad persuaded Mum he had untapped management potential, so she gave him a job as a powerless executive at our family's toilet paper company. The only real potential he ever had was spotting untapped wallets.

Despite all his faults, Mum still sticks up for the man who swept her off her feet before dumping her in the dustbin. She still has the personalised toilet paper roll he bought her for their first 'paper' anniversary, which reads 'I know I give you the shits, but thanks for marrying me anyway', and the chopping board with her name spelt wrong that he gave her for their fifth 'wood' anniversary.

The door finally closed on their one-sided marriage a week after their tin-th anniversary, when Mum found him drunk in the arms of a woman fifteen years his junior, after having spent the earlier part of his anniversary drinking tinnies with his ageing, welfare-recipient band members. As karma would have it, Dad packed his bag and moved into his mistress's home, only to find out she was a con woman and owned less than he'd started out with. He tried to get Mum to take him back but by then she'd suffered the public humiliation of their break-up, so, despite still loving him, she refused. In retaliation he tried to take Mum for all he could get, but luckily Mum's friends from boarding school days made sure she kept her home and the family business. He still got plenty of payola though and didn't seem to care that he'd left her with a huge dent in her bank account.

After Dad left I think Mum was hoping I would become heir to the family business. I did work for her for a bit, but after a year of listening to the staff complain about how bad Dad had been to work for, I left. Viv had given me the heads-up about a holiday relief position behind the bar in a local hotel and even though it was only for a couple of months, it was the excuse I needed to finally give Mum two weeks' notice. I don't think my mother ever forgave Viv for that, but I was glad to be out of the family business, even though I could never quite get away from the old man.

Dad sits himself down on the lounge and grabs the remote, switching the television on. Our relationship has always had a soundtrack of the races, football or cricket, regardless of whose house he's in. Viv figured out early on that he couldn't function without background noise, so she used to hide the telly in the cupboard when she knew he was coming. That kept him away for a while, but whenever he hit desperate times he would work around his addiction to sports and his hatred of silence and turn up anyway, creating his own backing track by drumming on the table and belting out old songs from the 1970s. This time he's caught us off guard, so is feeling right at home in front of the unconfiscated TV set.

'I never took Viv to be the kind to put her hand out,' he yells to the neighbourhood, getting up and helping himself to leftovers from the fridge.

I clench my teeth and wait for it.

'Mind you, she did all right out of stripping you bare.' He chuckles. 'Ten grand, phew,' he says, looking astonished and shaking his head. 'That's more than I've ever bloody made in a year.'

I hold my tongue.

'I reckon I ought to do something like that, because you know times are a bit tough right now,' he carries on, like it isn't bloody obvious to me where this whole conversation is going.

'No one wants to hear decent music anymore, only that hip-hop rap crap. Anyway, you know me, I'm not one to whinge, even though your mother left me high and dry.' He empties our fridge of eggs, milk, orange juice and the last of the veggies.

I want to tell him to get the hell out of my house, but I just stand there and watch him, the way I've done ever since I was a kid.

'I can always rely on you to help me out,' he says, patting me on the back and winking as he heads to the door.

Five minutes after he leaves, I notice the envelope I'd left on the coffee table has gone and with it the two thousand dollars of cash donations from the fundraiser.

'Fuck.'

Viv and Marsha are going to kill me.

CHAPTER 31

Add to my list: Make sure Ethan doesn't take after his grandfather

After an unexpectedly long appointment at the hospital, the patient transport officer helps me inside. I am desperate for food and a lie-down. Clint is looking guilty and when I open the fridge, there is nothing there. I know immediately his father has been to visit. As much as I dislike the Izster, she is like Mother Teresa compared to Mr Psycho Pop.

'What did he take?' I ask.

Clint responds by opening and shutting his mouth like a goldfish, before finally managing to speak.

'The envelope with the cash from the GoFundMe. I accidentally left it on the coffee table.'

'Bloody arsehole,' I fume.

'I'm so sorry, love,' he mumbles.

'No, not you, you idiot. Your waste of space father.'

He looks at me, confused I'm not attacking him, but he can't help it if his mother bred with a scheming bastard. Besides, ever since I was an accomplice to his wax torture, I've been way too guilt-ridden to be hard on him. I didn't actually think he'd go through with the waxing, especially not after that first strip came off. He's braver than I thought. His dad, on the other hand, is horrendous. He thinks he's a FILF (a male version of a MILF) but he's just a creepy old cretin. The worst thing about him, which proves karma is a crock, is how he's managed to maintain his good looks like he's in Hollywood. I've been waiting for him to start looking as ugly on the outside as he is on the inside, but age shall not weary him like we, who he rips off, are wearied.

The front door opens, and I brace myself for his father's encore performance, but instead it's Ethan, home from school and looking shattered. He heads straight for the fridge and a no-food meltdown. To avoid catastrophe, I implement my standard emergency intervention, digging my phone out of my handbag.

'Who's for pizza?' I ask. 'Put in your orders.'

Clint's face lights up almost as much as Ethan's.

'The usual thanks, Mum,' Ethan says, giving me a big hug. I like how I can buy his love so easily.

I call our local pizza joint, hoping for a speedy delivery. Unfortunately, the boss is away and has hired what sounds like a five-year-old to take the orders.

'No, no, that's not what I ordered, I wanted two supremes and a vegetarian on a gluten-free base . . . No, I don't want extra ham on the vegetarian. The vegetarian has no meat on it,' I say through gritted teeth as I feel myself getting hangry.

Ethan sits down at the table and starts drumming with his fingers. He does that when he's happy. It makes him look exactly like his thieving granddad.

'For god's sake, Ethan, do you have to do that?' I bark, ravenous and triggered by the family resemblance.

'No, I wasn't talking to you,' I turn back to the phone frustrated, 'no . . . no, don't put me on hold . . .' I realise it's too late and I'm already speaking to piped music.

Ethan is losing himself in a drum solo, looking way too much like his grandfather when he's drunk for my liking. His drumming reaches a crescendo and the vibration shakes a glass off the table, sending it shattering on the floor.

The dial tone hums in my ear. They've hung up on me. It is all too much.

'Bloody hell,' I mutter through clenched teeth. 'I spend my whole life trying to organise everything for everyone else.' I'm attempting to maintain composure and keep my voice at a reasonable level. 'Ordering pizza, shopping, cleaning, cooking, booking holidays and play dates and what does anyone do for me?' I rant, my volume involuntarily rising.

Clint looks up and spills the coffee he's just made for himself on the floor. I feel myself losing it from low blood sugar and exhaustion.

'Not much, not much is the answer!' I scream as I grab a cloth from the sink and throw it in Clint's face.

That's all the energy I have. I start sobbing.

Clint quickly wipes up the coffee before pulling me to his chest. He is wearing the blood-stained shirt he wore after he was waxed, which instantly makes it obvious my argument is a moot point.

'Come on, love, it's all right. Let's get you into bed for a good lie-down and we'll sort out the food and bring you in some pizza when it gets here, won't we, mate?' he says to Ethan.

Ethan nods. 'Yeah, Mum, don't worry, it's okay,' he says, joining us in the hug and giving me his cheeky grin. 'I promise I won't eat *all* the pizza when it gets here.'

I laugh and squeeze my gorgeous son tighter into our group hug, before holding him out at arm's length and looking him seriously in the eyes.

'You just make sure Daddy doesn't eat all my dessert,' I say before walking obediently through the bedroom door Clint is now holding open for me.

As Ethan gets ready to put on his pyjamas that night, he pulls his t-shirt up over his head revealing his little bare chest. For the first time ever, I see how much he's starting to take after Clint.

CHAPTER 32

Clint's list for me: Take a hot bath

Viv hasn't been in the spa since her birthday. It's too much effort for her to climb the stairs to it now, even though she'd love to get back in the water. Catherine told me enjoying long soaks in the bath is a girl thing.

If Viv knew Catherine and I had been communicating, she would kill me, and she would dismember me if she knew the spa was Catherine's idea. Her sister said it was the perfect gift because Viv's always loved the water and it would help take the pressure off her body. Catherine's a physio, so I guess she'd know. She started emailing me when Viv first got sick. I've never gone behind Viv's back before and communicating with her sister feels a bit like cheating. Not that I've ever been unfaithful, although I have done the occasional window shopping – but what looks good at the stores is often cheap rubbish when you get it home. I'm yet to meet any woman who has a tenth of the fire Viv has, apart from maybe Catherine. Now, with the two of them not speaking, I'm caught between a rock and a hard woman, but I will be the one left to deal with Catherine when Viv is gone, so I'm trying to cover both bases. The truth is they've both got too much bloody pride.

Recently Catherine has stepped it up a notch. She's always been one to push the barrow out just that bit further, probably so you do your back in and have to see her for treatment. She told me I need to go over to hers but she won't tell me why. I've had to take an extra-long lunch break and instruct the motel receptionist to tell Viv I'm in a meeting if she calls. I told her I was organising a surprise. I'm weaving a tangled web of bullshit that I hope doesn't trip me up.

When I get to Catherine's house, I'm surprised but happy to see the kids are home. I haven't seen them in over two months, and they've grown like they've been planted in fertiliser.

'Uncle Clinton,' they call out, their little faces lighting up when they see me. I've always been their favourite uncle and they must have missed me, poor kids.

'Where's Ethan, Uncle Clint?'

'Oh, sorry, kids, he's at school today. What are you two doing home anyway?'

'Mum said we could have the day off because you might be coming over. Can Ethan come for a sleepover tonight?' asks Sarah.

Billy shushes her but looks at me hopefully.

'Not tonight, darling, but don't worry, you'll see him soon, I promise.' It's a promise I know I'll be able to keep, but not the way they are hoping.

'Oh, okay,' they say, looking crestfallen. 'Will we see Aunty Viv soon too?'

Luckily Catherine swans down the stairs before I have to answer them. She's always reminded me of a cross between Viv and my mother. She's got Viv's ability to tell it like it is, but she manages to look like butter wouldn't melt anywhere near her at the same time.

'Hello, Catherine,' I say as she reaches out to me with an air kiss.

'Clint,' she coos. 'It's been too long.'

As I kiss the vacant air near her cheek, I am already starting to feel like it was a bit of a dog act to come here without talking to Viv first. Catherine leads me out to the back deck, so we can watch as the kids jump into the pool.

'How's my sister?' she asks.

'Same as usual,' I can't help but answer truthfully. 'Tough on the outside, but it's starting to wear her down.' The kids do a bomb right next to us, and the water splashes Catherine's hair.

'Oi, what have I told you two?' she yells, her refined façade falling away, as it often does.

Unlike my mum, everyone who knows Catherine is aware she can go from first class to cattle class in a single sentence.

'So, what's up?' I ask, aware my lunch break can only last so long. Plus I want to get out of here as soon as possible.

'It's Mum. She's back in the clinic again.'

Oh terrific, just what we need.

'She's asking for Viv.'

'Oh, shit, Catherine, you know Viv's on the downhill run, don't you? She's not exactly up to a visit to the funny farm.'

'She never was, but it might be nice if she just said goodbye to her.'

'Goodbye to her?' I put my head in my hands and take a deep breath. 'Bloody hell, Catherine . . . Please tell me your mother doesn't know. I thought the family agreed not to tell her.'

'Some of the family agreed,' she replies, her lips tightening. 'But Viv, whether she likes it or not, is her daughter, and I believe Mum should know.'

Viv has often said that, despite being the youngest child, Catherine has always acted like she's the oldest. She is well known for making executive decisions that go against the whole family – the trouble is no one apart from Viv has ever questioned her right to do so.

'When did you tell her?' I ask.

'I told her yesterday after I got your latest email. I thought it would be best if Viv saw her while she could still walk in there on her own two feet.'

'Great, that's just great. Viv doesn't even know we're in contact,' I say, exasperated, 'so I don't know how I'm supposed to broach the subject.'

'Oh, Clint, don't tell me you've been emailing me behind Viv's back?' She looks smug. 'I wondered why you'd been using your work email address . . . Why don't you just tell her you got an out of the blue email from me today at work letting you know?'

I run my fingers through where my hair used to be. 'Yeah, right, good idea.'

I wonder if I can get the IT people at work to delete all traces of our previous communications. I am now picturing Viv as a

Russian spy who, even after I get the techies to wipe my cache or whatever, manages to track down evidence of my ultimate betrayal. I feel sick. I know she recently went through my personal inbox . . . *Why does she have to try to bloody control everything all the time?*

I must look terrible because Catherine suddenly reaches out her hand and touches mine.

'It's okay, I won't tell her,' she says. 'She's my sister, and she's dying and, much as I want to hate her for being so stubborn and not admitting she is wrong, I still love her. I'm not trying to make things harder; it's just that Mum has a right to know.'

I head back to work, driving slowly as a throbbing headache starts to pound behind my eyes.

CHAPTER 33

My list: Give my husband a list

I am making a comprehensive list of everything I do on a daily basis. It's comprised of both pre- and post-diagnosis activities to ensure there are no loopholes. The list includes washing up, dusting, vacuuming, mopping, nagging Ethan to get dressed, picking up after Ethan, picking up after Clint, cleaning the toilet, writing grocery lists, restocking the loo with toilet paper, packing school lunches, getting Ethan ready for school, taking out the rubbish, doing the laundry and hanging it resentfully on the line, folding and putting away the clothes, ironing albeit on special occasions only, cooking, doing the banking, paying bills, collecting the mail, filing, buying birthday presents, sending cards, liking Facebook posts from people in the family I don't like, cleaning the windows so I can see what the neighbours are doing, watering the plants, pulling out the dead plants I forgot to water, nagging Clint to mow the lawn, booking hairdresser appointments, buying clothes, throwing out odd socks, taking Ethan to after-school activities and then forgetting to pick him up, organising social events on the weekend, booking annual holidays, booking the car in for servicing, changing the bedsheets and towels, buying Christmas presents to put away for the end of the year, replacing broken crockery, turning the compost, cleaning the oven, cleaning out the fridge, cleaning the microwave, cleaning the bathroom, returning phone messages unless they are from Catherine or Isabelle, booking doctors' appointments, booking dentist appointments, organising every one of Ethan's birthday parties, reminding Clint about my birthday, our anniversary, his son's and his mother's birthdays, changing light globes, shopping online, shopping in general, rescheduling gym and yoga appointments I never get to, writing down and then crossing out what day I am going to take up meditation, calling friends, procrastinating by drinking endless cups of tea and, of course, the two most time-consuming things of all, writing lists for myself that I never get through and nagging my husband to do all the things on his list.

Just as I hear Clint's car pull into the driveway, I finish and put down my pen. I give the list a quick check over. There is absolutely no way he is even going to attempt to do a tenth of these jobs when I am gone. He comes in, gives me a peck on the cheek and looks over my shoulder at what I am writing.

'Another list?' he asks.

'Not just any list. This is the master list.'

'God help me,' he says, looking sheepish.

'Okay, what gives?' I can read him like a book.

He takes a big breath in and then lets it out with a massive sigh. 'I got an email from Catherine at work today.'

'Oh great, what does she want? I assume she wants something?'

'She told your mum about the cancer.'

I can't even breathe, let alone utter a reply. I am burning hot and can feel flames of fury bursting out of every orifice in my body.

'She thought your mum should know,' Clint says spinelessly.

'Of course she thought Mum should know. She always thinks she bloody knows best. Great, this is just great.'

I can't sit down and can't stand still. I pace around like a madwoman, like my mother.

'It gets worse,' he mumbles under his breath, scared shitless. 'Your mum wants to see you.'

I sit down and hold my head in my hands. I breathe in and out for a full five minutes, trying to calm myself down. Finally, I can speak.

'And let me guess, she's back in the clinic?'

'Yes.'

'And I wonder what shock might have put her back in there?' I get up and start pacing again. 'The stupid freaking cow! All right, as usual, I will go and clean up the bloody mess.' I grab my handbag and the car keys.

'Wait, Viv, you know you're not up to driving,' he says, running after me with the spare keys, but carefully keeping a safe distance.

He overtakes, giving me a wide berth, and reaches the car before me, claiming the driver's seat and opening the passenger door for me from inside. I sulkily get in. I hate not being able to speed off and leave him in my dust.

He is about to start the car.

'Have you forgotten your son?' I ask sarcastically. I look at his face and realise he has. 'He's inside playing on the computer.'

'Oh, I thought he must have been at a play date,' he mumbles, trying to act like he hasn't forgotten he is a father.

'No, he's not.' I sigh. 'But you might want to organise one as he can't exactly come with us to the clinic, can he?'

Two minutes later, Ethan, who apparently had his headphones on the whole time and was oblivious to the fact that his father and mother were about to drive off without him, hops into the back seat. Immune to adult dramas, he is super excited to hear his dad has organised to take him to Brodie's. We listen to a Paddington Bear audiobook all the way to Bria and Ben's house and then change to ABC news after we drop him off. I like listening to the news now. For years I avoided it, as it was all too depressing, but now I love listening to stories about people who are having a more shit time of it than me.

When we pull up to the clinic, I get the familiar feeling of dread I have come to associate with my mother's illness. There is no real way of separating my mother from her disease, the two have always been one. As a kid, I never knew the difference between her unpredictable personality and her mental illness. I thought her diagnosis was an excuse for bad behaviour; and as an adult, I'm not too sure I feel any differently. I trained myself early on to brace for the unexpected. Some days I would greet her with my armour locked tightly around my heart; at those times, she would be soft and gentle and the kindest mother a girl could wish for. On other days, when I went to her like an innocent child longing for connection, I could almost guarantee she would be at her worst: distant, unfeeling and hostile.

Today, predictably, I don't know what to expect, but delusion lives eternal. So somewhere, very deep down in my heart, I am hoping to see her soft underbelly exposed by her immense grief over the imminent loss of the daughter she has never been capable of loving. I am setting myself up for a fall, I know it, but I can't help but hope my final goodbye will be like it always is in the movies.

Clint settles himself down in the waiting room with a sports magazine and a coffee, and I follow the signs to Ward B, looking for Room 5, trying to ignore the erratic beating of my heart. When I walk into her room, she is lying in bed looking at a picture on her bedside table. Catherine planted it there for sure. It's a photo of Catherine and me laughing and hugging in the pool together when we were kids. She was five, and I was seven. My sister looked so cute back then.

I remember that day. It was my birthday. I had been given more presents than usual so, by the time I was on to the fourth and final present, Catherine was beside herself with fury that none of the presents were for her. While I was ripping open my last gift, she picked up the Enid Blyton book I'd just unwrapped and tore out page after page in a fit of jealousy. When I jumped up to grab the book out of her hand, Mum noticed us and came flying in our direction. I grabbed Catherine by the hand, yanked her away from Mum and started running. Even as I dragged her to safety, Catherine went into default survival mode, yelling over her shoulder, 'It wasn't me, Mummy! Vivian did it.' Our neighbour, Mrs Martine, who had heard Mum yelling and spotted us coming her way, quickly opened the gate for us. I didn't know it at the time, but the minute she saw us heading her way, her family would go into formation and react like a well-oiled military machine. She would bring out the cake and cookies while her husband called triple zero. It wasn't until a few years later that I fully understood I could make Mum go away just by visiting the neighbours. Up until then, I had only known two options: run and hide, or try not to cry during the beatings. Occasionally we were accidentally saved if the phone rang or her favourite ad came on television, or some other random occurrence distracted her and snapped her back to some semblance of rationality.

Mrs Martine had spare clothes, cossies and pyjamas for us at her house. Every year she took us shopping to buy new spares of anything we had outgrown to keep at her house. The first thing she would always do was to feed us, and then, when she knew the coast was clear, she would hand us both our cossies and fluffy towels to take out to their pool. That day, after she had rubbed sunscreen gently onto my face and under my eyes, she pulled a hat down onto my head and said, 'Let's make this the happiest birthday ever.' Catherine and I swam and played for hours. At the end of the day Mrs Martine took a photo of us with our arms around each other giggling.

My mother is running her fingers around the edges of the picture frame.

'You look like such nice children in this photo and now look what's happening to you,' she says. Tears start to well up in her eyes, and for a moment, our eyes meet, and I remember times in the bath when she would wash my hair and gently sing to me. I remember how on my first day at school she packed a special meal in the new lunch box she'd bought me. She made a mayonnaise and egg sandwich cut into quarters instead of halves, with the crusts cut off because she knew I liked it that way. There was an apple with the peel still wrapped around it which I could pull off in a long, unbroken spirally swirl and she decorated the whole thing with nasturtiums from the garden. I remember a day when we planted a flower together to mark a burial site after my first fish died. I was so distraught. I'd loved Bubbles so much. When my mother came into the room and saw the tears streaming down my face and the fish floating belly-up, she cupped my face in her hands and said, 'I'm so sorry, baby.' She was the proverbial mother with the curl in the middle of her forehead; when she was good, she was loving and very very good, but when she was bad . . .

I look at her in bed in the clinic where it seems to me she has lived half her life. She looks frail and helpless in her nightie, and the nightwear's girlish floral pattern makes her seem all the more fragile. Her hair is greyer than the last time I saw her and I notice her start to clench and unclench her fists. Her mouth twists into an angry, ugly ball of hatred and I instinctively brace. Her eyes bulge out of her head, and she jerks herself up to sitting.

What little muscle tone she has left on her body ripples with fury. 'SLUUUUT!' she screams out. 'Who let you in, who let this bitch into my room? I'm going to kill you, you little slut.'

I startle and step backwards away from the bed.

'The devil's in you. I can see him hiding in there trying to pretend he has the face of an angel, but I can see right through you. You're not going to get to me, you spawn of Satan, with your perky breasts hanging out of your dress, don't think you're fooling me.'

She is screaming the ward down and edging her way down the bed towards me. Her face becomes familiarly unrecognisable as she starts to foam at the mouth. By the time a team of nurses has rushed into the room to sedate her, I find myself cowering in the corner. They give her an injection, and a few minutes later, she is lying back on her pillow. The nurses return to business as usual, except for one who notices me on his way out. He gently crouches down and stretches his hand out to me. A groan escapes from somewhere deep inside of me, and he discreetly withdraws his hand but continues to talk to me in a soothing tone. I can barely hear what he is saying through the fog.

Hours – or is it only minutes? – later, loud voices outside are followed by the comforting rattle of the tea trolley heading towards the room and breaking through the numb silence in my head. I hear the nurse say, 'They're bringing afternoon tea, would you like some?' I am able to nod, and he beckons to the tea lady who hands him two cups of tea in plain white cups with saucers. He sits down on the floor, a generous distance away from me.

'It's my tea break, mind if I join you? It can get a bit hectic out there,' he says, jerking his head towards the rest of the world.

He doesn't wait for a response, and I can't give one, so he sits there like an old friend and quietly drinks his tea.

The warm steam rises from my cup, and I watch it swirl in front of my eyes and soften my view. In the background, I can hear the nurse as he starts to talk about the weather and what his children do after school and how well his garden is growing. Clint, who must have witnessed the whole affair from the hall, is now standing at the door looking helpless, trying to decide whether to come in or not. It annoys me, and as the tea warms my blood that had run cold, my irritation at Clint walking through our life as a bystander crawls under my skin, prickling me, until I feel myself coming back into my body. The nurse is looking at me.

'Feeling better?' he asks, hand outstretched to take my empty cup.

'Thank you,' I manage to say. The nurse beckons to Clint to take the cups and then reaches out a hand to help me back onto my feet.

'Take your time,' he says.

I am unsteady and so willingly accept his assistance as he walks me out of the ward. The doors open automatically to the outside, and I feel the fresh air against my face and take my first breath in what feels like forever. He opens the car door for me and helps me into my seat, buckling me up and then gently touching me on the top of the shoulder. He talks to Clint for a few moments then squeezes his arm before waving goodbye and heading back inside. Clint sits down in the driver's seat, holds my hand, turns on the car, then withdraws his hand to take the steering wheel, and we head back home.

CHAPTER 34

Not on my list: Reach spiritual enlightenment

Today is the day I reach spiritual enlightenment. I've had to squeeze it in between amending my will and writing a letter to my son as I don't have much time left. The chances of me achieving this on my own are zero to none, so I've enlisted the aid of Sally. If anyone can do this, she can – she's sweet and kind, and kind and sweet, and sweet and kind. She doesn't need more adjectives than these two. There's no point in getting clever about it and pulling out the thesaurus to check if there are more intellectual, witty words to describe her, as that's always been my downfall – trying to be too smart. At least that's what all my teachers said, 'Don't be smart, Miss Walker,' but I'd ignored them and gone to uni for a whole two weeks anyway. That was plenty long enough for me to realise that only crazy people study psychology and to drop back out as quickly as I'd enrolled. Sally has always kept it simple. She's the only person I know who I can confidently say is going to heaven, thanks to climbing her way up the enlightenment ladder one pyramid scheme at a time. Unlike her peers, she has managed her ascent by helping everyone, including her competitors, to navigate their way to the top. Sal's not motivated by greed, but need, and honestly believes the whole world desperately needs whatever she is selling. If there's a product out there that fills a need, Sal will have it, so I'm hoping somewhere in her bag of tricks she stocks something called Reach Nirvana in a Day. If she does, then she's just the gal to help me multitask today and pick out a casket while paying off my karmic debt at the same time.

As always, Sal's six minutes early and bubbling over. She's driving a sparkling clean car that looks like it's just been detailed. Her chariot doesn't disappoint on performance either and is the smoothest ride I've ever had, which, given my current pain levels, is much appreciated. We arrive at the funeral parlour with one minute and thirty seconds to spare. The funeral director comes out oozing warmth, compassion and love. I don't know what it is with this profession, but something about putting make-up on dead people seems to bring out the best in humanity.

After my research at my workmate's funeral, I originally decided to not be too showy when it comes to caskets but when I walk into the showroom that idea goes flying out the window. Especially after I learn you can have absolutely anything you want printed on your coffin. There's one casket covered in racing memorabilia, one adorned with VB beer cans (for those who drank themselves to death) and a particularly eye-catching coffin featuring a picture of someone trying to scratch their way out of it. When I point out my preferred escape vehicle to Sally and see the look of horror on her face, I recognise my error in not bringing Marsha along. Sally not only doesn't have a black funny bone anywhere in her body, but she is also, quite sensibly, concerned about my spiritual future. By now, the funeral director can tell I am definitely interested in the printed casket option.

'Are you being cremated or buried?' she asks, as kindly as anyone can ask that question, but still managing to sound like a guard in Monty Python's *Life of Brian* asking, 'Crucifixion or freedom?', as if I get to choose between the two. I want to answer 'Freedom' and then say, 'Just joking, crucifixion,' but before I can reply, Sally jumps in with 'Cremation'.

Spoilsport, I think until I realise she has just been my muse. Five minutes later, I am signing the paperwork on my cremation-themed casket, with flames down the side like a hotted-up panel van. I have also chosen a few choice quotes for mourners to read as they gently place their hands on my coffin and bow their heads, including, 'Burn, baby, burn', 'Light me up' and 'Who brought the marshmallows?'

Despite her many reservations, Sally, who spent years as a wedding planner, is delighted to learn my choice is not actually totally random but will fit in perfectly with my funeral theme, colours and music, especially with my funeral waltz, 'Help I'm Alive'.

Now my casket is chosen, it's time to get on with the less interesting job of evolving as a soul. Sally has a full day's schedule planned out for that dubious task, but my energy is already starting to fade, along with my enthusiasm for being even vaguely well behaved. Still, it is on my list, so I have to at least pretend to participate.

•

The first stop on our tour is the church I was baptised in, where I also spent many a night making out in the confessional with my first boyfriend, who went on to be a priest. I'd helped him find God (he was in the church – surprise!). Every night for the whole two weeks we dated, Jayden and I would wait until everyone was asleep and then climb out our respective windows and run down the road to St Matthews, which was conveniently located between our two houses. Twenty-odd years ago, church doors were left open for people in need of 24/7 spiritual refuge, or in our case refuge from under-protective parents. Holding hands, kissing and touching each other's naughty bits made us both worry we would go to hell, but it was just innocent first love, trying to find somewhere safer than home to push the boundaries.

When I follow Sally reluctantly into the church, the smell of incense and candles taps into something so deep and intangible, I almost fall to my knees. I came here for years. It was one of the few places, apart from my nanna and poppa's, where I'd felt some sense of belonging. Everyone was welcome and our priest had been a rare gem who was not only a man of the cloth but also a man of the heart. He seemed to genuinely notice who needed what and always did what he could to make a difference. Somehow, he sidestepped all the corruption and abuse breeding in the church at the time and managed to maintain a sense of what was right and good in the world. When he passed away, I left the church. My belief in all things bright and beautiful died with him and I quickly regressed to Monty Python's 'All Things Dull and Ugly' instead, bypassing religion in favour of mix-and-match spirituality. Now here I am, decades later, with no one to confess to except Sally.

First on her list is forgive the past. Let's start with something easy, shall we? When I assigned Sally this task, I'd hoped she'd do something like get me to chant 'I am enlightened' and 'dib, dib, dib, dob, dob, dob' three times over, make me some herbal tea and then pass on the secret to eternal life via a forty-minute podcast and be done with it. As usual, she is always more thorough than really necessary.

'Okay, Viv, let's start with lighting a candle,' she says, smiling gently and sounding so soothing she manages to root my feet to the ground so I can't bolt out the door like a startled horse.

I step up to the votive holder and grudgingly pay the inflated price of one dollar for a tiny white paraben candle, trying not to swear out loud as each hundred-year-old match refuses to light.

'Very good,' she says after my fifth attempt finally manages to ignite a wick that looks like it has been there since the Reformation.

'Now just sit down in front of the candle. I want you to imagine the flame is the light you have brought to the world by being here,' she continues, channelling one of those fake TV hypnotists people find themselves obeying no matter what.

'I know, Viv, that you don't think you have brought any light to the world, but you just being you has been perfect and enough.'

She's delusional but I do love her. Sal also apparently reads minds, so pushes the point.

'You have made us all laugh, you have given birth to Ethan, you have told brave, hard truths to everyone you know and that, Viv, is what helps people to grow: the truth.'

In my mind, I hear my parish priest, 'I am the way, the truth and the life.' I guess that makes me about one-third as good as Jesus – impressive.

'So, with all that in mind, do you know who you are here to forgive?' Sally asks.

'Not Catherine, no way,' I reply petulantly. 'You know it's her turn to say sorry first this time.'

'No, not Catherine,' Sally replies. 'You're here to forgive yourself.'

'Oh, well, that's easy, I haven't done anything wrong, just ask me,' I joke.

'Joking isn't going to help you reach enlightenment,' she instructs as sternly as someone like Sally can manage.

'But you said making people laugh was part of how I bring light to the world,' I argue, defaulting to a backchatting high school student.

Unlike Clint, Sally, my enlightened friend, does not bite or buy into my distraction techniques, instead she kisses me on top of my head and coos, 'I am just going to leave you here for a few minutes while your candle burns down and then I will be back.' She heads down the aisle and out the door.

I stare at the door she's closed behind her until my neck gets stiff from twisting in the pew, then unenthusiastically turn my attention back to the candle. Thanks to cheap, imported holy merchandise, it seems to be burning a lot quicker than I remembered, thank the Lord.

All right, I think to myself, *you asked for this, so stop being a sooky la la and play along.* I start to mumble, 'I am enlightened, I am enlightened, I am enlightened,' then, before I know it, like a monkey in a science lab, I am praying.

'Hail Mary full of grace, the Lord is with thee, but not with me, because apparently I'm not good enough for him to hang out with. Holy Mary, mother of Ethan, blessed is the fruit that he eats but it would be more blessed if he would put the bloody skin in the compost the first time I tell him to rather than the last.'

When it comes to prayer and any form of meditation, my attention is somewhat deficient, which is something I don't appear to have grown out of. Before I know it, I am going through a long list of all the reasons I am not enlightened and never will be. Attempting to refocus, I turn my attention back to the candle; it is almost burnt down. My light is almost gone. I will not feel sorry for myself, not in here, but a single tear ignores my determination and rolls merrily down my cheek just as Sally returns.

'Okay, I'm enlightened now, can we go home, please?' I ask, standing up. Sally reaches up to my face and wipes the tear from my cheek.

'Yes, we can go home.'

CHAPTER 35

Clint's list for me: Recuperate

Viv is still trying to get through her bloody list when what she should be doing is preserving her energy and trying to rest. It's like she doesn't even want to admit she's got cancer. She's always been like this. I swear she runs on Eveready batteries. I've been waiting for her charge to run out since the day I met her, but it's only since she became sick that there's been any hint she's running out of energy.

Last night we got to bed later than usual so she'd promised to spend today recuperating, but now she's just remembered it's Ethan's prize day at school. She's asked me to come because it will be the last one we can go to together, so I've had to call Peter to see if I can start work a bit later today. I still haven't forgiven him for hosting the waxing incident, but he's been really good about everything with Viv, so I'm trying not to push the friendship as I know I'll need more time off further down the track. I personally don't see what the big deal is about a school assembly, but Viv seems to think it matters, and she's determined to exhaust herself, so at least if I go along, I can drag her away early.

Ethan's school isn't the one I would have chosen for him. There's not much of a sports program, and it's a bit too airy-fairy for me when it comes to the basics of reading, writing and arithmetic. I caution myself to be prepared for a prize day where all the kids get a prize and no one's baby gets their feelings hurt or, god forbid, a reality check.

When we get to the school hall, I'm knocked over to find that not only are they giving out firsts, seconds and thirds, but Ethan is up for a guernsey.

As always, we are late. Viv notices a couple of seats right up the front are still vacant. This is her specialty. She doesn't care who notices her, and she's certainly never given a damn about anyone else's opinion. I'd prefer to sneak in up the back, even if I have to stand, but instead I find myself walking straight up the middle of the aisle close on Viv's heels as everyone stares at us disapprovingly. I know she needs to sit down, but I'd rather have sent her up there on her own. Ethan is on stage with the other kids up for awards. He looks away, trying to pretend he doesn't recognise his own, embarrassing parents. Viv waves at him and he can't help but wave back despite his better judgement and the elbow in the ribs from Miss Goody-two-shoes next to him. I settle in for the duration. I know how long these things can drag on for.

After the first half-hour, you can already see everyone shifting in the school's standard-issue, highly uncomfortable seats. By the time we reach the forty-five-minute mark, everyone, including myself, is getting out their phones to book appointments with their chiropractors. Viv and I have no choice but to wait until the end as Ethan is the last cab off the rank. His award is for Most Improved Student. Maybe he's getting it for PE because of that awesome try he scored before he got concussion. He looks nervous when they call him up to the podium, and even more scared when he finally gets there and can't see over the top of it. The poor little bugger then has to wait until someone brings him a booster step. When he is finally good to go, he looks at his mum, who gives him the thumbs up and then he clears his throat, ready to start his talk. We've already had to sit through god knows how many stilted, long-winded acceptance speeches from a whole bunch of other kids as, apparently, talking in public is part of their education. Call me a dope, but in my experience getting them to take a breath so adults can get a word in edge-ways is the harder thing to teach them. I vote we go back to kids being seen and not heard. Let's hope Ethan has learnt from the vacant stares on the adults' faces during the speeches so far not to drag it out too much.

'Mr Pepper said I should thank everyone who helped me get this award,' he starts, his voice sounding shaky. 'So, I want to thank Sir and my other teachers, but I couldn't have improved without my mum.'

Viv looks up at him in surprise and smiles. I am surprised too. His mum? How in the bloody hell has she helped him with footy?

'My mum is super smart with words, and that's why I've improved so much with my English.'

Oh, it's an English award, well that makes more sense.

'My mum is awesome, and she is fully sick as a mum, but she's also sick with a disease . . . that's why I've been trying so hard to be good,' he says, stumbling over his words and staring at the piece of paper he is gripping on to.

'Oh shit,' I say accidentally out loud.

'The doctors have said she is going to die, but I don't believe them because Mum is too young. She's always told me that people only die if they are old or drink or smoke too much. Mum doesn't do either of those things. The only thing she does too much of is writing long lists of jobs for my dad and me to do.'

The audience chuckles and Viv squeezes my hand.

'She's not that old either for a mum. Tyson's mum is way older, you can tell by the clothes she wears.'

Viv laughs and looks horrified at the same time.

'But the other reason I know the doctors are wrong,' he continues, 'is because Mum loves me too much and has always said there's no way she'd leave Dad on his own to look after me because he's bloody useless . . . So anyway, I just wanted to write this speech to tell everyone Mum's okay and to tell the doctors they should stop lying about people.'

There is stunned silence, and then Viv starts to clap. I join in, but the rest of the parents just sit there. Viv shakily rises to her feet and continues clapping until, one by one, the rest of the audience uncomfortably joins in. Viv remains upright, and I think about getting up to stand next to her, but she sits before I find my feet.

While the principal is ushering Ethan off the stage and finally wrapping up the assembly, Viv tells me it's my job to set him straight about the cancer. She wants me to pull him aside later for a quiet talk, but for once I put my foot down and tell her it's better to do it now, like a band-aid and rip it straight off. She's too tired to argue.

So when Ethan comes running down the stage stairs and goes straight to his mum for a hug, Viv gives him a cuddle and then heads to the morning tea at the back of the hall to grab us both a cuppa. I decide to get straight to the point. After all, it's her mollycoddling him that's led to this confusion.

'Hey, mate, good speech about Mum, she does look way younger than Tyson's mum that's for sure,' I say, choosing on second thoughts to start with an ice-breaker.

Ethan is distracted. His little mates have just run past, hassling him to join them for some handball outside.

'Ethan, listen, I just wanted to check in with you about what your mum has told you the doctors have been saying,' I say, trying to be sensitive despite being irritated by the fact Ethan is looking straight past me to the windows leading to the playground.

I push on regardless, as I reckon Ethan always listens best when he looks like he is ignoring you.

'You know that the doctors have said your mum has cancer,' I continue. I find myself talking to the back of his head as he walks towards the windows.

'And we probably need to have a bit of a chat, buddy, as things aren't looking that –'

'Later, Dad. I'm king in handball, I have to defend my place.'

Knowing what I am about to say, Ethan opens the window and jumps out and down to his friends.

Viv walks back over with two cups of tea in hand. She hands me my cuppa and says, 'That looks like it went as well as could be expected for a man who has refused to read every parenting book I have ever left on the bedside table.'

I take a sip of my tea and stare at a particularly interesting looking poster on the auditorium wall that had previously escaped my attention.

CHAPTER 36

Not on my list: Become completely dependent on Clint

This morning when I woke, there was no Clint leaning over to whisper good morning and no noise from Ethan racing around the house running late for the bus. Clint is supposed to be helping me monitor my meds because I've been put on all new dosages, which is making me so foggy I can't remember what I have and haven't taken. Today, however, he has let me sleep in, and seems to have managed to get Ethan out the door to school without my all-important nagging.

For the first few moments after opening my eyes I blissfully enjoy the peace of my empty house, but then pain comes washing over me. I look around in desperation for my meds, but they are not beside the bed and nowhere in eyeshot. Clint must have left them in the bathroom. Trust him to leave without making sure I've taken them. I go to sit up, but a searing pain shoots through me, pinning me down. I suck in air like I am in labour, hoping

I can roll to the side of the bed, but even breathing proves too much. I'm too scared to try to move again. Instead I watch the seconds then minutes tick by on the clock. I feel more alone than I've ever felt in my life. I am steadily soaking my pillow with silent tears but when I try to move to somewhere dry, grief, self-pity and pain stockpile. When I can no longer contain the agony, excruciating sobs escape me. I am screaming uncontrollably, no longer able to see, think or hear, so it takes a moment before I realise a nurse is standing by my bed.

'It's okay, darling, it's okay, I'm here, sweetie,' she soothes as she urgently but gently pushes a needle into my arm full of the miracle morphine.

'Hang in there, darling, it will be better in just a minute,' she says, stroking my head with deep concern on her face.

My palliative care nurse has been coming more regularly lately and yesterday she brought up more home care. I told her it was all good and 'Clint's got this' as I'd been hoping he might come good, despite our whole married life being evidence to the contrary. It was never on my list to become completely dependent on Clint because, obviously, I can't depend on him. In his defence, he has picked up his game recently and is at least trying, even if he's not getting it anywhere near the ballpark. His epitaph will say he meant well. He wants to do the right thing, but being obsessed with *Star Wars* for most of his life has scrambled his brain, so he now hears every instruction I give him in Yoda speak – little wonder he gets everything back to front.

When the emergency meds hit my veins, they bring instant relief, and I love my nurse so much in this moment, I could kiss her.

'What happened, darling?' she asks as she watches the colour come slowly back into my face.

I show great restraint by refraining from telling her I missed my meds because my husband is from a far-off distant galaxy and remind myself it was his idea to make sure the nurse had a house key in case of an emergency. After helping me sit up, she gives me the best cup of tea I have ever tasted.

Even though the pain meds have kicked in and I am now once again perfectly capable of dressing myself, she still helps me put on my shoes and brushes my hair like Mrs Brady used to do to Cindy. I resist a sudden urge to ask her to put my hair in bunches and curl it into ringlets. She brings me over a mirror and, despite my harrowing morning, I am surprised to see I appear vaguely respectable. She helps me out to the dining table, bringing with her yet another perfectly brewed tea in my favourite cup. She has also brought home-baked cookies, and I hope some adoption papers. She sits me down, and I know we are about to have 'that talk'.

'So, Viv, you were pretty uncomfortable when I got here, and I can see you aren't necessarily getting the care you need for your situation,' she says empathetically.

She turns her attention to my surroundings. We are sitting at a table covered in unwashed dishes from last night's dinner and she is trying carefully to keep her feet away from a pair of Ethan's dirty undies that have been left lying under her seat.

'Now, we could get some more home care in to try and help you keep on top of things,' she continues in what is obviously nurse speak for 'How in hell's name do you live in this pigsty?' I hope she's not smart enough to figure out the state of our house has nothing to do with my cancer and everything to do with how we have always lived our lives.

'But while that will help a bit, I really think you might want to consider whether or not you need a bit more assistance.'

I shrug my shoulders, so she changes tack and begins to wash up.

'I know everyone tries to put off going to the hospital these days, but there is something to be said for being in professional hands with people who know what they are doing and what to expect,' she continues, trying to beat the world speed record for doing dishes. 'It might also be helpful for your family to have fewer demands placed on them and to be able to speak to social workers and nurses about their concerns.'

If I'm honest, I hadn't at any point considered making it easier on Clint. Somewhere in the back of my mind, and even at the front of it, I'd considered this as payback for all his years of shirking responsibility and running away to his job. In his mind, he only ever had one thing on his list: to be a provider. I finally have the perfect excuse for why he should up his game, and now this lovely, well-meaning woman is trying to get me to give it up.

'It's also obviously vitally important we keep your pain under control,' she says firmly hanging up the tea towel before sitting back down to face me. 'Now I'm a great believer, as you know, that at this stage of life any drug is a good drug, but they are no good to you, my dear, if someone isn't making sure you take them.'

She has a point, and I certainly don't want a repeat of this morning.

'In hospital, when the time comes, we can also look at putting you on a syringe driver. It will administer your meds subcutaneously, so you won't even have to think about them, which will keep you on a nice even keel instead of your pain going up and down.'

Now she has my attention. I like to think I have pretty good pain tolerance, but when those meds wore off this morning, I thanked the lord for western medicine. The thought of avoiding an encore performance is all I need to agree and sign on the dotted line.

'I think I'm ready now. If hospital will help me get off this pain rollercoaster, let's do it.'

'Okay. Are you sure you're happy with that decision? Because I don't want you to feel pressured and you can always change your mind.'

'Once I make a decision it's made,' I say, surprised this statement actually feels like it's true.

'That's a good way to be. Well, now you know your next step, hopefully it'll be a relief for you. There's no rush though. How about I organise to come back in a couple of days so you can take your time getting ready? I can also organise for a social worker to come and talk to your family about your decision.'

'Do you have any anti-social workers, as I think they might be more fun?' I ask, not at all politely.

She laughs. 'No, we don't, but perhaps that's something we could look into.' She's as professional as always, but for the first time allows me to see a hint of the party girl hiding beneath the uniform of every nurse I have ever known.

Seeing the crack in her façade, I decide to ask a question.

'You know the system, so you know the real deal. Be honest, what would you do, if you were dying? Would you want to stay home, or would you go to hospital?'

She doesn't hesitate. 'I've thought about that a lot, and I'd go to hospital. I'm a nurse, so I like things to be efficient. Some people come into hospital then they go back home then they come back again, and that's okay because that's their choice. But I think of it more as going on a trip, and I've never liked stopovers, so I'd just go to hospital, check in at reception, and then sit back and watch the inflight movies. Plus, it would be nice to be waited on hand and foot for a change.'

'Sold,' I say. 'Book me my ticket.'

CHAPTER 37

Add to my list: Get Clint professional help

Since making my decision to go to hospital, I have realised Clint is going to need professional help if Ethan is to survive without me. I have texted the Izster, who is relishing the idea of replacing me with hired help and has happily agreed to pay for someone to come once a week. I am, however, going to maintain as much control as possible, starting with personally interviewing my replacement. I want to make sure they are not only up for the job but are also as unattractive as possible. This is all part of my plan to influence Clint's life as much as I can, now and when I reach the other side.

I have started a post-expiration-date list, which includes not only jobs from the master list but also a carefully edited set of rules around grieving. Number one states: Clint must wait at least one year before handing over anything other than domestic duties to another woman. This first rule came from overhearing

Izzy say that, in polite circles, women should allow at least one year before dating after a bereavement, whereas for men it was only six months. In protest, I have opted for equality between the genders and ignored her recommendation that no one expects widowed men to last the distance. I intend to let my friends know the timeframe during which I expect them to disapprove of Clint getting down and dirty with someone else, unless of course, it is with Marsha, as she would hose him down afterwards.

To help me pick the right replacement, I have enlisted the help of my cousin Jane, whose nickname is Janal. Janal has always run a perfect house where there is a place for everything and everyone is put in their place. When I told her proudly about my master list, she laughed out loud and said that while she was glad to see I had made a start, my version would only be a foreword to the magnum opus she has written on the subject. She told me the key to hiring the right person so you could delegate, delegate, delegate, is knowing the right questions to ask, so this morning, as promised, at precisely 8.29, an email arrives. After reading her extensive list of exactly how a household should be run, I am armed with enough knowledge to be able to thoroughly screen my would-be-me candidates. I print out the interview questions and am ready to meet genetically modified and improved versions of myself.

At nine o'clock, the first interviewee arrives precisely on time. Sue is suitably overweight, unattractive and, at fifty-six, much older than me. While I approve of her physicality, I am concerned her inability to walk to the kitchen without puffing like she has run a marathon may mean her employment, like her, could be short-lived. She sits down at the dining table, and I begin with the most important of life questions.

'So, Sue, when you stack the dishwasher, can you please describe to me how you arrange the cutlery?' It's news to me, but according to Janal, there is actually a correct answer to this, which is with the forks and spoons standing upwards. Being unaware of the science around this important issue, I had always previously put them downwards, but apparently this is the reason they have never yet come out as sparkling clean as those of all my domestically superior friends.

My possible replacement looks at me, apparently a little confused as to why I am asking her to state the obvious but then quick as a whip answers, 'Well I would, of course, rinse them first, then wipe them with a cloth and put the forks and spoons facing up but the knives down. I always sort the cutlery into separate compartments so when it comes time to empty the dishwasher there is no need for unnecessary and time-wasting sorting.'

I mark down an A-plus for Sue, for not only pre-washing the cutlery before putting it into the dishwasher but for also taking the importance of knife safety into account. I am now beginning to understand why whenever I unstacked Janal's dishwasher, she needed to explain that the sparkling dishes I was removing were actually dirty. I feel Sue looking over my shoulder at the, I now accept, horrendously stacked dishwasher behind me. Apart from the food-coated cutlery, the open drawer reveals my complete ignorance of the necessity of rinsing dishes before haphazardly stacking everything on top of everything else. She stares in horror at the broken glasses lying cracked under saucepans I shoved in there during my last-minute attempt to clean the kitchen before she arrived.

I follow her gaze and lie, 'Yes, I know . . . that is why I am interviewing for *new* help.'

She looks at me suspiciously and I am very impressed she is such a good judge of my bad character.

I've never been a good liar, so I admit, 'Well, okay, the old help was me, but I am dying so I thought it would be nice for my family if they could finally get someone who knows what they're doing to run the house.'

The 'I'm dying' line works a treat, as always, and she immediately softens.

'Don't worry, dear, I'll get this all sorted. You obviously need a hand, and I am sure there are more important things for you to be doing right now than keeping your house tidy.'

Her last line wins me over. So, before asking her any more of Janal's essential questions about clothesline peg choices, the best cleaner for grout or how to ensure colour-coded cleaning cloth protocol is adhered to by visitors, I have hired her. I am delighted to know I'll be leaving Clint in her highly capable and unattractive hands.

CHAPTER 38

My list: Write a letter to my son

The nurse is coming to take me to palliative care this afternoon. There is one last thing I have promised myself I will do before I leave the house where Ethan was accidentally born.

Eight years ago, after watching some scarily graphic home birth videos, I'd decided to ignore the theory that giving birth is in any way natural and had planned for a hospital birth with all the possible medical intervention on offer. On my shopping list was gas, an epidural, morphine, a general anaesthetic (not negotiable) and a caesar. Instead, the little bugger came early and, after the fastest labour on record, was born at home without me even managing to lay my hands on a Panadol. Clint had been out when I felt the first contraction. I'd looked around the house for the invisible assailant that had kicked me in the stomach before I quickly realised what was happening, but it was too late. I couldn't get to the car and I only just managed to stagger to the phone to ring an ambulance.

The ambos arrived an hour later after having been held up in traffic behind a horrendous crash. By the time they got to me, I had given birth in a frenzy, like a cross between a wild animal and a feral hippy, and was holding my baby in my arms, sobbing, breastfeeding and covered in bodily fluids I never knew I had. For eight years I had not been able to look at our spare room, where Ethan was born, without feeling traumatised. So, in theory, this should have made it much easier for me to leave my house for the last time.

It's been weird packing for the hospital. It's not like packing for birth. That bag had been packed weeks in advance and included all sorts of things I'd purchased for the new chapter in my life. Instead, I now find myself packing the morning I am leaving and looking at all the things that won't be following me on this next adventure. If I were a pharaoh I'd be packing my entire tea collection; instead, I decide to take just one cup and saucer, so I have something civilised to drink out of. It's an easy decision to make. I carefully wrap the chipped cup I used as a little girl when I visited Nanna. It is an espresso cup and so small it can hardly hold a decent cup of tea, but it's the one I want beside me. I pack four pairs of pyjamas and all my underwear. I pack lavender oil and camomile tea but leave my tarot cards and any inkling I'd had to kill my husband behind. I no longer need my future.

I wish I had written the letter to Ethan earlier. It feels much harder now I am leaving home. This is where our memories were born, and his first breath taken. My heart tightens, and the tears fall as I start to write the hardest letter I've ever written.

Dear Ethan,

From the day you were born, you brought me joy, so I am so sorry I will now be bringing you sorrow. Everyone will try to give you advice about how to cope when you feel really, really sad. Ignore them. This is your journey, and I want you to know that, if it's at all possible, I will be with you. I've never lied to you about anything important so I won't now – I don't know if there is a way for me to reach you from where I am going, but if there is I will fight my way back to you no matter what it takes.

If I can't make it, I want you to know that you already have me inside you. For a start, you have my hilarious sense of humour, and you and I both know you get that from me as your dad's jokes are, well, they're dad jokes. You have a fighting spirit like no one I've ever met, and I know you will use that to your advantage. Don't ever be scared to disagree with anyone and everyone, no matter who they are. The more people who disagree with you, the more on track you probably will be. Most people will want you to be like them as it makes them more comfortable, but be like you. Make people uncomfortable and do it regularly. I know me giving you advice is probably a bit ridiculous as, let's face it, I haven't been the most successful person on the planet, but I want you to know, just because you might not achieve anything big, doesn't mean you aren't worth anything. If you never write a great book, if you never climb a tall mountain, if you never buy a castle to live in, you will always be the most important person in the world because you are my son.

I am so, so sorry, I am leaving you. That is my biggest regret about going. You deserve to have had a mother for a lot, lot longer and you definitely deserve to have had a far more perfect mother than me. You have my eyes, and you have my heart beating in your chest. You are the most divine creature on earth, and how I had the privilege of being your mum, I will never know. The fact you exist gives me hope that there may just be a god; otherwise, how did you ever come to be? If there is a god, I will be crash-tackling him until he puts us both back together. Try your best to put up with your dad, he will be a mess and will probably be totally useless, so just call Aunty Sugar whenever you need to. Play lots of Pokémon and make those robots the best in the world.

Love you, my darling,

Mum

CHAPTER 39

Ethan's new list for himself: Eat blended food through a straw

Even though I have only been in the hospital for less than four hours, Ethan has already made friends with most of the nurses. His favourite one is Larissa, who we dub Lovely Larissa because she is all smiles and took Ethan under her wing the minute he arrived at the hospital.

When I was admitted today I was pretty happy to find that, despite being put in a twin room, I had the place to myself. Ethan had straight away checked out every gadget he could find. He climbed onto my bed and grabbed the patient help buzzer, pushing it before I could stop him. I expected it to take at least three or four buzzes before receiving any sort of response from ward nurses, but Larissa had come rushing straight into my room. When she saw who had called her, instead of reprimanding him, she made a game of it.

'You must be the new patient,' she said. 'Oh . . . but you do look a bit off colour. It's a good thing you called me.' She took his temperature and put her stethoscope on his chest. 'Hmmm, yes, oh I think I can see the problem,' she said thoughtfully. She turned to me, 'You must be the patient's mother, has he been eating a lot of ice cream lately?'

'Yes,' I said, looking at her as if surprised that she knew all about his diet. 'He did eat a lot of ice cream last night.'

'I suspected as much.' She turned back to Ethan. 'I think you might have frozen part of your belly.'

For a minute, he looked worried, and then she winked at him, and he laughed. 'I'm not the patient, you silly,' he said. 'My mum's the patient.'

'Really?' said Larissa. 'Oh dear, well in that case you're right, I must be a bit silly, mustn't I? Okay then, if Mum's the patient you'd better get off her bed and let her get tucked in. But I tell you what, if you need to press any buttons in future why don't you try using these ones instead?'

She handed him the TV remote at which point I rolled my eyes. 'Oh, he'll press those buttons, don't you worry,' I said. 'And he'll press my buttons and probably yours too eventually.' She laughed and left us to get settled in.

My spare pyjamas, undies and toiletries are unpacked in the side table and my dressing-gown is hung up in the locker. Even though I'd dreaded the day I would have to leave home, part of me relaxed as soon as I arrived at the hospital, and everyone rallied around to look after me. I have clean white sheets on the bed, there are no piles of washing waiting to be put away, there's a telephone and a buzzer beside me if I need help and they have drugs on tap, so I don't have to worry about running out of my pain meds. The nurses mark off the chart at the end of my bed every time they give me medication, so I don't even have to worry what pills I have or haven't taken. The bed is comfortable and can be adjusted with the push of a button, and as I lie propped up against the pillows, I find myself breathing a sigh of relief that I am finally in the hands of professionals who know how to get me to my end destination as comfortably as possible.

The fluorescent lights are a bit bright and glary, so Ethan turns them off for me and we rely on the natural light coming in through the window. The walls are bare and unattractive, and I make a mental note to ask Clint or Marsha to bring in some of Ethan's drawings and some pictures from home. Lying in bed with my feet up, I wonder if this is the first time I've done this since becoming a mum. Even when we've gone on holidays, I've still always had jobs to do, like tidying up our motel room before the cleaner comes so they won't see how we actually live at home, or organising the next leg of our journey. I should have booked myself into hospital years ago.

A woman arrives with a trolley with my lunch on it. The food is pre-blended, and although I have always complained about hospital food, I am happy to have something someone else has made that's easy for me to eat. Ethan, of course, is super excited about the delivery service and immediately starts trying to decipher what all the blended colours are made of.

'The orange is either pumpkin or it's carrot,' he says. 'And the green's definitely peas, or it could be beans, but I think it might be broccoli, yuck.' He sticks his nose over my tray. 'Oh, Mum, Mum, what's this yellow stuff here? It smells sweet, yum, I reckon that's custard and apple, can I have that, can I, can I?'

They've neglected to leave cutlery on the tray, but Ethan has the perfect solution.

'No, Mum, you're not meant to use cutlery, look there's a straw, this is how you do it.' He tries to suck the blended food up into his mouth. His eyes look like they are going to pop out of his head as he uses every inch of the power in his little chipmunk cheeks to suck the food up through the narrow confines of the straw.

Just as he is mid-suck, the tea lady arrives. I am delighted to see a large steel teapot, like the ones the CWA ladies used to use after church when I was a kid, sitting in pride of place on top of her trolley. The older woman, who is a volunteer, notices what Ethan is doing and smiles at me.

'I assume you don't want to eat your lunch that way?' She smiles. 'So sorry they forgot to leave you your cutlery, dear, but here's a spare teaspoon, will that work for you?'

'Yes, thank you very much,' I reply gratefully. 'But I think my son's enjoying using the straw, which is a good thing – if he had cutlery I don't think there'd be any lunch left for me. Apparently the Vegemite sandwiches I packed are far less appealing than sucking hospital food up through a straw.'

She gives a chesty, smoker's laugh and then pours me my tea. It is good strong black tea with regular cow's milk. There is no offer of herbal tea or soy or almond or oat milk here, and I relax even further, happy to have all my decisions made for me. As I look down at the standard-issue white cup and saucer, I remember I brought my special teacup, so I pull out Nanna's porcelain and put it on my bedside table for next time. For now, though, I am happy with tea, being waited on and the silence that only comes when your child is completely focused on impersonating a vacuum cleaner.

CHAPTER 40

Things Clint forgot to put on his list: Write Viv's eulogy

I'm not a writer, and I've never been a public speaker, so I don't know why in hell's name Viv thinks I should be the one in charge of her eulogy. Even though it's driven me completely up the wall, I've always done most of the things on her bloody lists, but this is too much. I'd normally put off things in my too-hard basket but today Viv's gone into palliative care, so I'm trying to make a start.

I just don't know what to say about her, at least not in public. I love her body, but I can't exactly talk about what bits I love and why. I can't talk about how we've always loved bitching about everyone in the family and how that's one of our favourite pastimes. I can't talk about Ethan, because, well, I won't be able to get any words out. And I can't exactly talk about her achievements because, let's face it, she hasn't had any. She dropped out of uni and started heaps of courses she never finished. She half-finished some Bunnings workshops, but I banned her from those as they taught her just enough to make her dangerous. We've never made any money and she hasn't been a good housekeeper. I know I drive her up the wall because she tells me as much every day. We've never been poster parents for a happy family, although we have managed to stick together. When I think of Viv, it doesn't feel right to try and sing her praises the traditional way, so I'm not really sure what to do.

I know her friends don't like me that much because they only ever see me the way Viv wants them to see me: totally bloody useless. I swear she likes it that way so she can be doubly sure I'll never cheat like that dickhead Steve. Maybe this is my chance to let them know, despite her prickles, she actually loves me. I know her in a way none of them ever will. She's always controlled what-ever she can, even if that's only me, because life rubbed her raw. It's not like she even hides it well. Sometimes, I swear, she'll have tears in her eyes or rolling down her cheeks, and she'll still be trying to get me to finish something on one of her bloody lists.

Maybe that's what I'll talk about, her super-power ability to project this image of herself as someone who can cope with whatever life throws at her. It's like her personality is a shield of steel. I remember one day early on when we were standing in a queue at the bank because we'd fallen behind in our rates to the point where the sheriff had turned up on our doorstep. I'd left her at the teller to duck out to change Ethan's nappy because Viv knew more about our money than I did, and by the time I got back she was arguing with the bank manager and her eyes were brimming with tears. He was talking in customer-service speak, and barely even noticed her crying. I guess I can't blame him, when she's in survival mode sometimes all you can register is her sarcasm. I only remember one or two times when she actually really let her guard down with me and I bloody loved it. All the walls between us came down and I got to be Superman to the tough, troublesome woman I love.

God, this is hard. I still haven't put pen to paper. Okay, let's just keep this short and sweet.

Viv. What can I say about Viv? I loved her, and for some reason, she loved me back. She adored our son and loved him more than me, or even herself, as she was convinced that's how mothers should be. If she loved you, she was never going to let you get away from her. If you hurt her, she'd act like she'd never forgive you, but if you believed that, then you didn't know her, and there is no way you could have loved her as much as I did. She could be bossy, we all know that, but she had to put up with all of you lot and me as a husband, so who could blame her? She really wanted to be a good woman, a good friend, a good wife and a good mum. I think she always felt she fell short of perfect, but she was still more than enough for me. She was great at writing out instructions, even though she knew there was no way I would ever get around to finishing anywhere near enough things on those damn lists of hers. I let her down a lot, but, despite that, she never left me until now. She was funny, complicated and so, so smart. She could be as soft as she was hard, and I bloody loved her.

CHAPTER 41

Not on my list: Talk like Chewbacca

I can no longer talk. The doctors haven't told me why, and I can't ask them. It's most likely because the tumours have spread to the part of my brain that controls my ability to tell Clint what to do. I can still think whatever the hell I like though and, in my head, I am as articulate, witty and intelligent as ever. I can tell by the looks on my visitors' faces, however, that I now sound like Chewbacca. Clint, being a *Star Wars* freak, should be finding me very attractive right now.

My mouth is so dry. I've been trying to get the staff to bring me some water for about half an hour, but they keep bringing me food. I resort to miming, and someone finally gets the message. I thought this would be the easy bit. The bit where I can no longer do anything for myself and everyone is feeding me, bathing me and showering me. I don't even have to get up to go to the toilet anymore and my three favourite drugs of choice – morphine, Maxolon and Midazolam – are now on tap, via my syringe driver.

I hoped this loss of capacity would mean I wouldn't need to try anymore and that, maybe, Clint and I would finally start to understand each other. I envisaged him turning into a cross between Florence Nightingale and the Dalai Lama. Instead, he is more like a movie extra who spends most of his day sitting around eating and waiting to be told when to walk on and off set. Thank god Marsha is on her way. She will make me laugh at myself and find my current Marcel Marceau predicament hilarious. She will also have the sense to bring me a pen and some paper.

When I'm not sleeping, I've been watching a lot of television, in particular renovation shows. I have always loved the idea that someone could walk into my house and, in a week, bang out all the home improvements on my list. Despite my current predicament, I'm surprised to find I am still as passionate about house makeovers as ever.

A lot of people have regrets when they're dying. I am no exception. My regrets are having put up with a rotting vanity and manky toilet for way too long, never having been 'on trend' with my kitchen and having had a garden that resembles a cross between a tip and a compost heap. I also regret never having slightly lifted, let alone flipped, a property and I am particularly bitter that TV tradies never even considered turning up on my doorstep.

The housing market is one of the few things Clint and I share a passion for, and he's left a copy of the real estate section of the paper on my bedside table. I start to flip through and see he has circled a couple of his favourites. They are, of course, nowhere near our price range, totally in the wrong suburbs for capital growth and definitely no renovator's dream. It is unfortunately not a conversation worth having when it takes all my effort to sound like Chewbacca, but I still decide to cross off Clint's choices and replace them with a few of my own. That way, when he heads off to do our regular, pretend-as-if-a-bank-would-actually-lend-us-money Saturday morning property inspections, he will at least be looking at Viv-approved listings.

On one of my last days when I was still mobile, Clint was at work and I was in dire need of distraction, so instead of giving in to thoughts of hiring a hit man, I booked myself in for some real estate therapy. Unlike our previous investment expeditions, this time I had very specific buying criteria. When you're told you have cancer, you can no longer opt for a long settlement and any renovations need to be quick and superficial. The first property I went to that day was set in the middle of the bush, with a winding track leading to the front door. It looked great in the photos but when I got there it was the sort of place Clint had always dreamt about but I'd always hated. The agent was waiting on the doorstep.

'Vivian? I'm James, nice to meet you,' he said, extending his hand. I reached out to shake it and he twisted it sideways to make sure his hand was on top. Even though I was a woman he wanted to show he was the alpha male. He actually just showed he was a dickhead.

He opened the front door and waved me inside with a thousand dollars of dental work.

I made myself at home while he pointed out the workman-
ship in the raked ceiling. The walls were lined with dark timber
and the place was decorated with the type of heavy furniture
you'd expect to find in Miss Havisham's house, but without the
olde-worlde charm. There was really nothing about the house I
could even pretend to like but Clint, coming from money, would
have loved this solid, boringly well built home.

I followed the agent through the house, pointing out every
fault I could find in the posh voice I usually reserved for Isabelle.
Thanks to hours of online study in real estate jargon, I excel at
that game. Clint and I both have numerous PhDs from Google
University, which we've used at every opportunity to prove we
are experts in areas we have no actual clue about. We initially
enrolled when we were first dating so we could sound smarter
when ordering wine in restaurants. When we gave up the grog,
we visited more and more open homes and decided we liked real
estate better. It was impressive just how quickly we managed to
build our imaginary property portfolio.

'Let me show you the den,' said the agent.

'A den? Do people still have those?' I blurted incredulously,
forgetting to use my posh voice.

Luckily the agent didn't notice the slip in my accent – he
was too busy pointing out featureless features as he led the way
downstairs into the dimly lit man cave. It was the ugliest place I'd
ever seen and looked like it was straight out of a 1970s hunting
magazine. There was a chunky hardwood desk with antlers
on the wall above it, four rifles in a locked antique cabinet and
a Chesterfield lounge sitting on a deerskin rug. It was getting

difficult to even begin to feign interest, and I was starting to want a distraction from my day's distraction when he pointed out the feature wall. There, in pride of place, showcased behind thick picture glass, was every *Star Wars* poster ever released. They were in pristine condition and in the centre was an original poster from 1977.

'The vendor has indicated they are willing to sell the property as is with all the furnishings, including the *Star Wars* memorabilia,' pitched the agent, realising I was finally showing some interest. 'Did you notice the poster has been autographed by the whole cast, including Carrie Fisher?' He smirked.

'Who is Carrie Fisher?' I asked innocently, despite being no stranger to the woman Clint had been in love with ever since she first stepped onto the screen as Princess Leia. I was glad Clint wasn't with me as he would have been drooling and elbowing me in the ribs. Ignoring my comment, the agent raised one eyebrow and gestured to the back door.

'After you,' he said, leading me outside. The treed backyard was huge and housed a massive trampoline, pool, sandpit, climbing wall and double-storey cubby. If Ethan was here he would already be on the trampoline, yelling, 'Mum, Mum, can we move here, puh-lease, it's so much better than our house. Wow, really rich people must live here. Can we buy it, can we? I can put in some money, I've got five dollars.'

'Okay, let me be honest,' I said, lying through my teeth as the agent led me back inside. 'The yard needs a lot more landscaping than I'd be prepared to do and the house isn't really on trend enough for me, but I do have some interest in the *Star Wars* memorabilia.'

The agent paused, feeling a sale slipping through his fingers, but smoothly changed tack, determined to at least make something for getting out of bed on a Saturday morning.

'The memorabilia? Well, the vendors *were* hoping to leverage the unique emotional value of those items to secure top dollar for their property, but what price did you have in mind?' he asked with a smile that made sure he continued to get value for money out of his dental work.

'Ten thousand for the lot,' I replied with my budget-priced smile.

The GoFundMe money had been burning a hole in my pocket and it would feel good to spend it by unburdening myself of at least one thing I'd always felt guilty about before going to my deathbed.

'That's my first and final offer,' I said firmly. 'Oh, and another thing, I need a quick sale as I have cancer,' I added, warding off the possibility of any further negotiation.

The C-word did the trick and he shook my hand uncomfortably, no longer able to flash his smile or look me in the eye, mumbling, 'I'll be in touch.'

I handed him my contact details on a free Vistaprint card I'd done up five years ago to show agents how serious Clint and I were about our time-wasting strategy.

Now, with no time left to waste, I make a mental note to follow up with the agent and circle a few more properties. They are being sold by distressed vendors and I am now officially a distressed purchaser, so that makes us a good match. A nurse comes in to check my vitals and syringe driver. I'm glad to have had a break from visitors this afternoon because if I'm ever going to expand my burgeoning portfolio I'll need to be in an uninterrupted morphine stupor with no distractions. Having narrowed down the listings for my tycoon legacy, I am now exhausted. I rest my head to the side and close my eyes on my great Australian dream.

CHAPTER 42

Not on my list: Reunite with my estranged sister

What seems like only five minutes later, the door swings open, but it's not the Marsha I was hoping for; instead it's my sister and a priest. Catherine has trumped me. We haven't spoken for all this time, and she's left it this long to make sure she gets the last word in when I literally have no right of reply. My sister sits next to my bed and picks up my hand, looking at the priest. She starts talking, but her eyes remain fixed on the man in black. I am furious. How can I give her a Paddington Bear hard stare if she won't even look at me?

'She tried to be a good sister, Father,' she says to him. 'I guess it wasn't her fault she was always doing the wrong thing by everyone.' She is stroking the hand my brain no longer knows how to move.

'She won't admit it, but it's just so sad that at the time when she most needed her loved ones around her, she insisted on isolating herself.'

I have made the bird with my other hand but am too weak to lift it off the bed high enough to get her to notice.

'I wanted you to come here to help her forgive herself before she dies,' she croons to him, her eyes welling with tears.

Me, forgive myself? I yell inside my head, desperate to be heard. All they hear is Chewbacca. The priest nods, as if my groans are confirmation the baby of the family should be believed, yet again, despite having lied her whole life. Catherine picks up the picture of Ethan sitting next to my bed and stares at it sadly.

'Poor Ethan, he's going to miss his mum,' she says, carefully placing the picture back on the bedside table. 'She tried so hard to be a caring mum, it must have been hard for her to see me being such a good parent to my children while she struggled so much with her hormones. It must have been stressful to have to blame her lack of control on post-natal depression.'

I am willing my blood pressure to go through the roof and set off alarms to send the nurses running in.

Outside a kookaburra starts laughing, then is joined by two of his friends, so my sister has to up the volume to be heard above them. Even though I really want to stay angry, I start to laugh as she yells over them.

My mirth sounds like choking these days. It's the first time my sister has heard me make this sound, which my regular visitors have become accustomed to. Catherine looks at me with genuine terror.

'Get the nurse, do something!' she shouts at the priest.

The priest rushes out the door, and I laugh even harder.

'Please don't die, Viv, please don't die. I'm sorry I haven't spoken to you, but you were so wrong, and I don't know why, but you just wouldn't admit I was right. You normally call and when you didn't I just didn't know what to do. You're my big sister, and . . .' She starts to sob. 'You upset me so much . . . I just kept waiting for your call. I know you couldn't possibly understand this, I really do, but . . . but . . . even though I really hate you for not calling, I still love you. You're my sister . . . Please don't die.'

Before I know it, my little sister is lying on my chest racked with grief.

'Please don't die.'

The bird in my hand unclenches and I find myself patting her on her back, the way I used to when she was a little girl. I remember the first time she cried when Mum left me looking after her when I was only six years old. She had started with a whimper and then howled and howled. I tried everything I could to comfort her – patting her, making her laugh, hugging her, getting angry at her and yelling at her to please stop, but the howls kept coming from somewhere so deep inside her little body no one could reach it. Despite myself, the tears start to fall.

She sits up and looks deep into my eyes, recovers herself and says, 'It's okay, I forgive you,' and then rushes out the door into the arms of the waiting priest before I have time to reshape the bird in my hand.

To add injury to insult, Catherine tag-teams the Izster on her way out.

After spray-and-wiping the chair beside me, Isabelle gingerly sits down. No one has told her cancer isn't catching. She has her infamous Tardis handbag with her and it doesn't disappoint. Apart from cleaning products, it contains a complete professional make-up kit and a supersized hair dryer, a full packed lunch, a Wedgwood crystal glass and an extra-large photo album which she plonks unceremoniously on my bed. She doesn't bother to make eye contact, so I assume she is here to give a lecture.

She opens the album to the first page, which is of Clint, naturally. Staring at the photo of the tiny, hairless baby, she breathes in shakily before letting out a heavy, tired sigh.

'I've been working on this because I wanted to show you that your life has not been "without purpose",' she says, regrouping so as to sound as emotionless as one does when describing how to correctly fold a fitted sheet.

I have seen these snapshots on numerous occasions, so am not sure I can muster up what little energy I have to look at one more 'absolutely adorable photo' of little Clinty. She props the book up like a kindergarten teacher about to read a story.

'Here's your darling Ethan, at only one hour old, when I first met him,' she says, softening into Nanna Isabelle.

'And here's Clint when I first held him in my arms.'

I realise she has rearranged her collection to contain side-by-side images of her son and mine. There's my favourite photo of Ethan at two years of age sitting in a muddy puddle with a look of pure, unadulterated joy, and next to it is two-year-old Clint, with the same expression, sitting in his first toy car. Then there's a photo of Clint (or is it Ethan?) weeing onto a bush and giving the dirtiest look to whoever is behind the camera, as if to say, 'Is there no privacy?' Oh and I love this one, Ethan on his first day at school, with his new backpack and lunch in hand, too dignified to smile on such a momentous occasion. Isabelle is quick to point out the accompanying photo of Clint, with an even more serious face and his hair slicked and parted on the side so he looks like a little Adolf. What some mothers do to their children! Still, I can't help but join the Izster in her proud mama smile.

She turns page after page, and my eyes start to mist over as my kind, unreliable, sweet, exasperating, loyal, lazy, vulnerable, irritating, selfish, bundle of joy son and husband blur into one.

'One day someone will marry Ethan, and I want you to know, I will be as hard on his wife as I have been on you, because that's what you do when you love someone,' she says, closing her photo album before lifting the heavy weight off me.

She reaches into her bag and pulls out the Wedgwood crystal glass, placing it on my bedside table and filling it with the water from my hospital-issue plastic cup.

'No one in the Smithston family, by marriage or otherwise, should ever have to drink out of plastic.'

She squeezes my hand then packs up her bag and any notion I ever had that we were different.

CHAPTER 43

Not on Clint's list: Learn how to nitpick

These days life is a bit of a blur – between work, hospital visits and getting Ethan off to school on time, I don't seem to be getting any time to just chill out and take a load off. At least I'm sleeping well, partly because I'm tired and partly because Viv's not stealing all the blankets half the night then kicking them off for the other half. She's never had any temperature control so while I miss giving her a cuddle I don't miss her lack of thermostat. Tonight, Mum's got Ethan, Marsha's visiting the hospital and I got out of work early, so I can be home in time for my hot date with the footy final.

When I turn the corner into our street I see Sally's car parked out the front. What the hell? I turn the key in the door, but it is quiet inside. Thinking she must have parked here and got a lift to the hospital with Marsha, I head to the kitchen to look through delivery menus for my man's night in. Just as I reach for the drawer where Viv keeps the menus, Sally and Ethan, who have obviously been hiding behind the island bench, jump out and nearly give me a heart attack.

'Surprise!' they yell in unison before cracking up laughing.

'I heard from your mum you were going to be home alone tonight so we thought we would keep you company, didn't we, Ethan?' chirps Sally.

'Yeah, Dad, and after dinner you and me can still get to watch the footy together,' enthuses Ethan.

'I thought you were meant to be at Nanna's tonight?'

'Yeah, but I got nits again,' he says happily, scratching his head.

'Hang on, didn't I spend a whole five minutes combing those out this morning?' I ask crankily.

'Five minutes? I don't think that's quite enough,' Sally blurts out before back-pedalling, 'I mean, I'm sure you gave it your best shot. Anyway, your mum rang me because she saw him scratching. She was in a bit of a panic, poor love, she seems to have a real thing about creepy-crawlies.'

No kidding. I've inhaled more pesticide in my life than a farmer and a crop duster put together.

'But every cloud has a silver lining,' continues Sally brightly. 'This will be the perfect opportunity to try out my latest product. Ta-da,' she says, pulling a large bottle and a nit comb out of her handbag. 'And we can kill two birds with one stone by teaching you how to do it, too. That way, you'll be able to treat Ethan properly in the future.'

Unlike Viv, Sally's criticisms are only ever accidental and not designed to barb, so I can't help but smile at her enthusiasm, even though I can see my quiet night in front of the box disappearing before my eyes.

'Now, I'm sure you've come home starving so – oh I've always wanted to say this,' she pauses, giggling, 'here's something I prepared earlier!' She gestures towards a big metal container on the kitchen counter and takes off the lid with the flourish of a game show host. 'And thanks to the Thermoserver, it's still piping hot, so please . . . enjoy.'

I've got to say, Sally is a great cook, even if every meal she prepares is an advertisement and a subtle attempt at guilt, because Viv never did get around to buying a Thermomix.

I look at my watch. It's forty minutes until the match. I reckon I still have enough time to eat, get rid of Sally and settle into my recliner before it starts. I begin to help her set the table. She looks at me, surprised, but then delightedly abandons me to finish the whole thing while she sits Ethan on a stool and organises a bowl of water and a bottle of conditioner.

'Ethan and I have already eaten,' she explains, 'so we can get started on the nits while you eat dinner, and then you can have a try.'

My mother would be horrified that nits are being exterminated in the kitchen, but with the clock ticking down until kick-off, I am grateful for Sally's time management skills. I pull up a chair and quickly dig into the curry she's prepared.

'Now the trick,' explains Sally, 'is to absolutely drown his head in conditioner first.' She pours what looks like half a bottle of goop on Ethan's head. 'But not just any conditioner,' she continues with a sales spiel at the ready. 'Take Up Nitting is a brand-new product that I'm very proud to be selling, because it not only gets rid of the little blighters in one treatment, but it's also made of pure essential oils from the purest place on earth, the Himalayas.' She waves the bottle under my nose, which confuses my tastebuds so much that when I put my next spoonful of curry in my mouth, it tastes like peppermint. My digestive system is now totally weirded out, but I keep throwing the food down my throat as fast as I can.

'Now, and I know you put in your best effort this morning,' she says kindly, 'another trick is to attack the hair in sections.'

Fifteen minutes later she is still talking and combing out nits and I have finished my meal and am very aware the minutes are counting down until the opening whistle. I push out my chair and am on my way into the lounge room when she intercepts my exit, saying, 'Okay, now it's your turn,' and hands me the comb.

'After each time you comb, remember to rinse the Take Up Nitting comb thoroughly in the bowl of water as we don't want a re-infestation.'

I look down and notice what looks like a hundred head lice floating in the bowl beside Ethan.

'Bloody hell,' I say, then get on with one of the biggest joys of parenting. Thank god he has short hair and we didn't have a girl. After much supervision and correcting of my technique, Sally approves my nitpicking and Ethan runs off to rinse his hair under the shower.

'If that doesn't make me miss Viv I don't know what will,' I joke, standing up and straightening my back, which is now aching like mad. Unfortunately, Sally thinks that's an invitation to start an important conversation about how I am going to cope once Viv's gone. I could do without a bloody counselling session from one of Viv's friends right now, especially when I'm trying my best to just get on with things and not think about any of it. I nod and give one-syllable answers to her questions, as I figure if we get this little chat over and done with quickly, she might notice it's dark outside and take her little ray of sunshine home with her. But I should know by now that Sally won't be dissuaded when she is on a mission to 'help' someone.

'I mean, you are going to have to think about these things, Clint,' she says gently. 'Ethan is going to need you for a lot more than you might realise. And have you thought about yourself, how lonely it might be?'

Her words hit me. *Oh god, I'm going to be single again. Bloody hell, I'm not up for that.* Viv's not even dead yet so there's no way I want to even start to contemplate what I'm eating for afters. That is, if anyone would have me. I mean, I don't have hair anymore and I've got a kid now. Is having a kid a good thing? Maybe, if he doesn't have nits. I wonder if being a widower is an asset or a liability? *Bloody hell, thanks a lot, Sally. Time for you to go and the match to start.* I decide to politely remind her I have other plans for the evening.

'So, I guess you're not interested in watching the football final with me?' I ask, picking up the remote.

'Oh, my goodness, I am so sorry.' To her credit, Sally has always been good at taking a hint. 'I forgot about the game. Let me just say goodbye to Ethan and then I'll be out of your hair . . . like the nits.' She laughs, embarrassed at her own bad joke.

Just then Ethan bounces out, smelling clean and fresh in the new pyjamas Viv bought him before she went to hospital. Sally kisses him goodbye in the kitchen, then Ethan insists we follow her to the front door to wave goodbye, where she gives him a big hug. Not content, he now has to walk her out to the car for the final outside farewell which involves a kiss, a hug and a high five.

After the long goodbye, we make it back inside and I switch on the telly just in time to hear the commentator yelling, 'Well that has got to be the play of the century, folks, and you can say you saw it here, live and in real time.' I hold my breath, waiting for a replay, but they have obviously just finished the last of them and, as the broadcast goes to an ad break, I hang my head.

CHAPTER 44

Not on my list: Go back to sharing a room

My sister and I used to share a bedroom when we were little. I swore I would never do it again, but now they have wheeled another woman into my room. I should have paid for private health insurance. My new roomie does, however, come with the bonus of at least fifteen gorgeous and very expensive floral arrangements. She must have had shares in Interflora as surely no one has that many friends. I look over at my bunch of wilting flowers wrapped in tinfoil and shoved in a jam jar. Ethan hasn't visited me since he brought them in last week, hand-picked from our garden. I didn't have the heart to tell him they were weeds. He's finding it hard, he's just a kid, but he's not the only one whose visits are getting fewer and farther between. I'm at the stage of dying where people don't want to watch the decay.

The woman next door to me groans; she is in a bad way. Says me. I wonder if I look that bad? She hasn't opened her eyes since they brought her in here and I wonder if she can even smell the flowers around her. Her breathing is laboured, she probably won't be my roommate for long. I'm not really up for watching someone else die. That's a little too weird, even for me.

The door opens again and an obviously exhausted but very good-looking man, who has aged as well as George Clooney, tiptoes in so as not to wake the soon-to-be dead. I try to lift my hand to tidy my hair, as if that will make me the catch of the day. My roommate makes a horrendous guttural sound. I don't think I have very stiff competition, but as he makes his way over to her, it is obvious she has been the love of his life. He sits by her bed and kisses her hand like she's Scarlett in *Gone with the Wind*. She makes no response, and he settles into a chair for the long haul. He hasn't noticed me or my newly coiffed hair.

Just then, Marsha blusters in. He looks up at her. She is wearing a loud scarf and kaleidoscope jacket with so many sequins that Mr Clooney unconsciously pulls his sunglasses down from the top of his head.

She gives him the once-over and says, 'Welcome to the house of fun.'

He smiles politely and looks away.

She comes to my bedside, glancing back over her shoulder. 'Love your new decoration.' She winks at me.

I smile as she brings the air back into the room.

'So,' she says, reaching into the many pockets of her jacket, 'I've got you more paper and pens. There's stripy paper, pink paper, plain paper, dotty paper . . . there's purple pens, green pens, orange pens.'

She loads up my bed like she's doing a stocktake at Officeworks. She knows how much I love stationery. Then, with a flourish, she pulls from her bag a crazy-looking coat with even more clashing colours than the one she is currently modelling.

'Straight from the op shop to you,' she says. 'Thought you could use a bit of brightening up.' The coat is torn and smells of mothballs. She drapes it over the crisp white hospital sheets and then ties her scarf around my head.

'There, much better,' she says, snapping a quick shot. 'I'll pop that straight onto Facebook, and you watch how many more likes you get than your vegan friends showing their gluten-free breakfasts.'

I laugh and start choking. The man looks across at me, worried.

'You know how to get attention.' Marsha winks. 'Come on, sit up,' she says, pulling me up with ease with one hand while holding a straw to my mouth with the other.

I look at her gratefully. I wish *she* was my roommate. She's here every day. If they would let her stay at night, she would, as she knows I find nights the hardest.

I pick up a pen and one of the pads of sticky notes and write, 'Ready to let me finish wiping the floor with you?'

She sticks the note to my forehead.

'Unlikely,' she says, but pulls out our unfinished game of Monopoly and plonks it in amongst the stationery.

I own Mayfair and Park Lane, and Marsha pretty well owns the rest of the board, so it's just going to be a matter of luck. If she lands on me, she's cactus, but in the meantime, she's slowly sending me broke. She's never been one for showing mercy, no matter what's going on. I roll the dice and try to make my move, but I am tired. I lean my head back against the pillow. She gently strokes my forehead.

When I open my eyes, the Monopoly and stationery have been put away, and Marsha is snoring in the visitor's chair. I turn on the television with the remote. I've never watched so much TV in my life. There is a choice between two depressing reality TV shows, a police show and two hospital shows. I decide I like the idea of lying in bed watching someone else lying in bed watching television, so I opt for an oldie but a goodie and tune in to *General Hospital*. Sonny and Carly have just remarried, which I am sure is what was happening when I last watched the show five years ago. Before I know it, I am asleep again.

My favourite soap is long over when I next wake to see Clint has replaced Marsha snoring in the chair beside me. My mouth is so dry. Clint looks exhausted. I wonder how long he has been sitting there. I try to reach for the water on my bedside table. The latest drugs have stopped my one good hand from shaking, but it still doesn't seem to want to obey me. I feel like I am lying under a layer of heavy, wet blankets. I manage to lift the dead weight of my hand to the side table, but just as I'm about to grab the water, my hand gives an involuntary jerk, and the Wedgwood crystal glass falls, shattering on the hard hospital floor.

Clint wakes up with a start and Irene, the crankiest nurse in the ward, sticks her head in to see what's happened.

'You'd better clean that up,' she barks at Clint before leaving again.

I don't know what she's being paid for, but apparently it doesn't include cleaning up after patient accidents. I am also unsure why she became a nurse as she doesn't appear to like sick people, their relatives, doctors, other nurses or even sanitising her hands when she comes into the room. She does, however, like criticising every-thing and everyone, and giving people drugs, ideally via the most painful injections possible.

I need to use the bedpan, and if I were on my own I would try to wait until Lovely Larissa walked by, but luckily Clint is here and well and truly awake. Over the last few days, I have given in to using a pan instead of attempting to walk to the toilet as I no longer have the strength to make the epic journey from my bed to the bathroom. I try to get Clint's attention, but he is down on the floor, picking up pieces of glass with his hands. Irene storms past throwing a broom and dustpan at him, almost hitting him on the head. I want to yell at the stupid cow but am too busy concentrating on trying to stop myself from having an accident. Just then, I see Larissa walking past the room. I struggle out a strangled call, and Clint looks up at me. His face seems to have aged and is lined with worry. Larissa hears me and turns on her heels towards us. I relax, but when I do, I wet myself.

They have upped the morphine, but it still doesn't help when they need to remake the bed. Rolling me onto my side is the worst part. Larissa, thank god, is the gentlest of them all.

'It might be time to catheterise you soon, darling,' she says, stroking my head. 'You just let me know when you are ready.' I nod.

I prepare myself to let go of control of yet another part of my body that is no longer obeying me. When it is all done, I lie back exhausted. I am not sure how I look, but Clint looks like he should crawl up into bed beside me. I would actually like that. I know I'm on drugs, but I'm not delusional yet, so I haven't completely forgotten he would drive me up the wall within two minutes; still, the thought of being held in his arms again feels like going home. I do, however, understand that the idea of lying next to someone who regularly wets the bed may not be as appealing to Clint, so I opt for holding his hand instead. After two minutes I pull my hand out of his as he has been distractedly stroking it while staring out the window and it's giving me the shits. He can't even pay proper attention to me when I'm dying.

With his hand released, Clint decides it is time to do some stretching. He stands up and reaches his hands above his head, giving a loud groan. Then he puts one foot up on the bed and leans over it, squashing his paunch against his leg. The pressure is too much apparently, and he lets out a loud blast of wind just as the George Clooney lookalike enters the room to sit beside his beloved. I try to roll my eyes to show I am in no way condoning this impromptu Richard Simmons aerobics class, but Clint stretches over in front of me, grabbing the headboard of my bed to stretch out his pecs, and blocks me from making eye contact. My desire to have him crawl up in bed beside me is now well and truly shelved.

After using me and my bed as a Danoz Direct gym, he then proceeds to make his way down to the floor where he does a few yoga moves followed by two push-ups and a couple of sit-ups. He sits down on the bed next to me, gives me a self-satisfied smile, then realises there is still a mouthful of tea left in my special cup and drinks the last of it.

I've never been a big eater, but now I can hardly eat any of the food that's brought to me. As his way of helping, Clint is doing what he's always done, and is eating my leftovers. I wouldn't mind this so much, except for the relish with which he does it. Because it's free food that's not meant for him, he acts like he's living on the wild side. However, let there be absolutely no question in anyone's mind that he has never, ever had permission to drink my tea. There is no precedence for this. Prior to my hospital stay, every mouthful of tea has always been sacredly swallowed by me. But now he has got it into his head that because he can eat the slops of leftover hospital food, he also has full permission to drink my tea. And to drink it out of my special cup. Seriously? Where does this husband of mine get off? Not off my bed apparently. I try to give him a shove as he sits there, drinking my tea, but my hand once again fails to obey. I close my eyes in despair. He sees my eyes shut for two seconds, assumes I am asleep, grabs the remote and changes the channel to sport, before finally getting off my bed and plonking himself in the chair for the duration.

My fellow inmate is still asleep – lucky her. Mr Clooney, however, has not been so lucky and is trying to escape his current reality by flicking through what are probably happier memories on his phone. I am hoping Clint's antics will give him the incentive to ask for a room change so I can be returned to solitary confinement to suffer the indignities of my body and family in private.

CHAPTER 45

Ethan's new list for himself: Play one-sided Pokémon

Clint has brought Ethan in to visit. I can tell it's a shock for him when he sees me. I've gone downhill quicker than they expected and while seeing him is like oxygen for me, I wish Clint had made him stay away. I don't want my son's last memory of me to be like this.

Luckily my roommate has been taken away. I'm assuming to the morgue, but no one has told me. It would have been too much for the little man to see two near-dead bodies at once. He has bought his Pokémons in with him and is telling me all about a new card he has, and trying to show it to me without actually looking at me. I can't lift my head enough to see him properly, so I press the button to make the bedhead rise. He is focusing on spreading the Pokémon cards out all over my bed.

The ward is quiet, so I buzz for Larissa as she always seems to know what I need instinctively. As soon as she sees Ethan, she is onto it. She knows how much he loves technology, and she was here the other day when Marsha finished pre-programming my laptop with photos we took of me pulling funny faces when I looked well. Larissa gets it out of my drawer and puts it onto the portable table beside my bed. She wheels it over to me, places my hand on the keyboard and adjusts my pillows to make sure I am comfortable.

I slowly type in a message to Ethan and then Larissa turns the screen around to face him.

'Hello, gorgeous boy, are you ready to battle?' He reads out loud, before spying the photo of me looking much healthier but with my tongue hanging out to one side. He laughs, and I can feel the relief in the room. He is on to this game.

'Prepare to meet your doom,' he types back, partly because he has forgotten he can talk, but mostly to seize the opportunity to get his hands on a device.

I notice he is still not looking at me but I'm happy he is at least talking to the photos of me as they come up on the screen. Seeing him in here breaks my heart into a million pieces, and I just want to transport him outside into the fresh air, to a park where children are laughing and being lifted into the air by their mums. Instead, I make my move with a Pikachu card and cause him twenty damage.

After months of listening to Ethan talk in a language I didn't understand, I had finally given in to his obsession. I was totally crap at my first few Pokémon card games, but by the time I played five times, I surprised myself, and him, by not only enjoying it but also by whooping his arse. He knows to expect no mercy because, while the card I am playing is an evolved version of Pikachu, I am in no way an evolved version of his mother.

'Ha, ha,' he says whipping out a new card I didn't know he had in his deck. 'So, I am going to swap this one to my bench and now I am going to do 120 damage to you.'

That puts me out of action, and for a moment, I am irked that my son is trying to destroy his dying mother. I have taught him too well not to take any prisoners. There is no one else needing Larissa in the ward at the moment, and she knows my stamina will last for less than ten minutes, so she stays with us until she starts to see me fading.

'Ethan,' she says to him, as per our plan. 'Your mum has some pocket money she thought you might like to spend on ordering some more Pokémons, and there's also a little bit of extra money she gave me so you can get chocolate from the vending machine. Did you want me to show you where it is?'

'Yes, please,' he says, beaming. 'Thanks so much, Mama,' he says to the photo of me on the computer screen, then he spontaneously grabs my hand and kisses it before skipping off down the hallway.

I fall back on the bed, exhausted. When I next wake, I buzz for Larissa, and she tells me she packed up Ethan's Pokémons, so he didn't have to come back in and disturb me. I am grateful as I know coming back in and seeing me again would worry him. She tells me Marsha has taken him home so I type a message asking her to let the family know that, unless he begs to come in, I think it's best that today is his last visit. She squeezes my hand and leaves the room. I know in my heart he won't want to see me like this again, so I say out loud in the tortured voice of Chewbacca, 'Goodbye, my most gorgeous little man.'

CHAPTER 46

Clint's new list: Claim the waiting room for himself

Since Viv moved into the hospital, I've claimed the waiting room on the palliative care floor as my man shed. It's the only place I can get a bit of headspace. It's tucked away from the rest of the hospital, and for the first week we were here, no one else seemed to know it existed. When Marsha swaps shifts with me it gives me somewhere to retreat to. There's a telly and a hot chocolate machine so I've been taking the opportunity to overdose on the sweet stuff.

When I get there today, Marsha is still with Viv and the nurses are doing something with her catheter, so I escape to my cave. But when I get close to the waiting room, I can hear noise coming out of it, drowning out the sound of the building going up next door. I've been enjoying drinking a hot choccy while watching the tradies work as it makes me feel like there's still a normal world out there, but when I open the door today, the outside has come in. The room must only be three by three, but somehow a whole extended family has moved in. There's a mum breastfeeding, a couple of kids sitting on the floor playing a board game, two moody teenagers by the window, a pissed-off dad and an old, old lady who has taken over my hot chocolate machine. What the hell are they doing in here? There isn't even a spare chair for me to sit on, let alone any air left to breathe. Great. What am I supposed to do now to get some time out? If Viv were here she'd say something smart and sarcastic and make them all feel uncomfortable so they'd find an excuse to get up and leave; instead I apologise for interrupting and head back out into the ward.

I start walking up and down the hallways, but can't help but look in every time I see a door open. It's a reflex action, like when you visit someone whose TV is on and you end up ignoring them and tuning in to the cartoons. I head towards the lift. There is no one inside, so I press the button to go right to the top of the building. When I arrive, no one gets in, so I press the button for the ground floor. It is giving me time and space and I have it all to myself. Unfortunately, when I get to the ground floor, people are waiting, so I step out. While I try to decide what to do next, the other lift comes down, and no one else gets in, so I hop in, pressing the button at random for the fifteenth floor. I manage to get three more rides up and down to myself. I look at my watch. Marsha usually stays for at least two hours so I can't go back in there yet if I want any peace. In the palliative care ward everyone apart from Marsha and Ethan talk in quiet, solemn voices. The only noise you hear is when the food trolley comes around.

285

Viv isn't eating anything now, but the food still gets delivered every day, so I am eating it for her. The first couple of days I felt a bit uncomfortable about it and was waiting to be bawled out by someone, but then yesterday the tea lady noticed, and the meals started arriving unblended.

I'm starting to feel hungry now. Until today, I've avoided wasting time and cash at the hospital cafeteria as it's always packed and so noisy you can hardly hear yourself think. Today's crowd is made up mainly of hospital staff along with some blow-ins from surrounding offices. People are laughing and chatting, and after I get used to the bright lights and clamour, I realise I've missed being in the land of the living. I order my meal, and when it arrives I wonder why I haven't come here more often. At first, after a week of only eating blended hospital food, when a non-pre-digested meal arrived it tasted like it came from the best restaurant in the world. But now, scoffing a burger, chips and milkshake, I know why everyone complains about hospital food. I sit back with a full belly and lick the burger juice off my fingers, feeling normal for the first time since this whole crazy thing started. One of the nurses from our ward walks towards my table with a tray and stops beside me.

'Beautiful day,' she says, nodding towards the sun streaming in the window.

'Yep, she's a beauty,' I reply with a huge, satiated smile and then back-pedal. 'I mean, apart from Viv and all that, obviously.'

She looks at me. 'It's okay for you to have some happy moments in amongst all this.'

I shrug my shoulders.

'You feeling good doesn't make you a bad person, you know,' she continues, pouring two sachets of sugar into her coffee. 'And it doesn't mean you don't care.'

I feel a lump coming up into my throat and scrunch the wrapper from my burger into a tight ball. I must have eaten too quickly as my stomach is cramping. I push the chair out from the table, scraping it on the floor. One of the other diners gives me a dirty look that is just like the looks Viv gives me.

I choke out, 'Enjoy your lunch,' and head towards the elevators. There is no one waiting. I hit the button repeatedly until the lift arrives and then ride back up to Viv's floor. When the lift door opens, the family who were in my man cave are standing there waiting. I look down, trying to hide my reddening eyes. I head into the waiting room, relieved I can disappear and make myself my usual hot chocolate, this time with extra sugar. It is back to normal in here. The tradies are packing up for the day. Just as I am about to settle in, I get a text from Marsha to say she is leaving now and that Viv is asleep. I take my hot choccy back to Viv's room, which now feels like home.

It's three days until our wedding anniversary and I'm planning to hang up the framed picture I bought for Viv the night before, so she gets a surprise when she wakes up and sees it opposite her bed. Once she's asleep these days nothing wakes her. It's not like when Ethan was little, and you couldn't even move a muscle without waking him up. Viv sleeps like babies never do. I grab my blanket and pillow and plonk down in the bedside chair, which, thank god, is a recliner, and switch on the telly. Luckily, there's sport on – it always makes the time pass quicker. I swear I hardly sleep a wink here. There's always someone buzzing or doctors talking, or the noise of machines or fluorescent lights flickering on in someone else's room. I try not to watch Viv sleep as she looks so fragile that, when I do, I can't take my eyes off her, just in case, so it's best to pretend she's not here. On the screen, my team, who haven't won a bloody match all season, are about to put down a try and level the score.

'You bloody beauty,' I say a bit too loudly, and Viv pulls a face. I mutter it again under my breath when they kick the conversion. 'You bloody beauty.'

CHAPTER 47

Not on my list: Get permission from Sally to say goodbye

When I first got my diagnosis, I had a moment of spiritual inspiration and went out and bought all my dearests and nearests a copy of *The Tibetan Book of Living and Dying*. Of course, I only expected Sally to take her spiritual task seriously and do the 'I now give you permission to die' malarkey.

I have lost track of time, so I don't know if it's morning or afternoon when Sally breezes into the hospital room like she is stepping into a sitcom. I half expect there to be a bell above the door that jingles happily as she enters.

'Well, here I am, sorry it's a bit late in the day,' she says, trying to hide her shock when she sees how fast I have gone downhill.

'I've come straight from the Sales and the Soul conference I told you about,' she says, managing to remain sunny while squeezing the life out of the Tibetan book she is gripping tightly under her arm.

'Viv, I can't tell you how much you would have loved it,' she says, like she has forgotten who she is talking to. 'It was all about how our souls are designed to evolve every time we make a sale as long as we maintain a true focus on serving and loving our customers.'

I smile at my naive and positive friend, knowing she was surely the only person at the conference thinking of her customers as anything other than wallets on legs. But before she can regale me with her latest insights, the senior doctor and his entourage sweep into the room.

He is an old-school doctor, which means he only ever refers to me as 'the patient' and doesn't bother to talk quietly or tactfully about anything. He picks up my chart, gives it a quick once-over, then holds court for the pimply, pre-pubescent medical students who used me two days ago as a practice pincushion when my canula needed replacing.

'As you can see, the patient is in the very late stages of a highly aggressive malignant melanoma that has metastasised throughout the lymph system, organs et cetera, et cetera. The patient, a female, is also currently nil by mouth due to the progressive failure of the gastrointestinal tract, one of many indications the bodily functions are breaking down. Of course, she is catheterised to make it easier on the nursing staff. We have increased both the Midazolam and morphine dosages to ensure any anxiety about pending mortality does not become a problem from a staffing perspective.'

Finished with the specifics of my case, he completes his oration at double-speed, with an obviously well-practised indemnity chaser.

'It is imperative any concerns from family and care-givers are recorded for administration purposes, to ensure we maintain the hospital's superb reputation. We, of course, remain committed to medical error reduction in our statistics, especially in the lead-up to our annual funding round. Any questions?'

The students look at the ground, well aware of the vitriol dished out yesterday to an inquiring mind who dared to make their superior late for his weekly game of golf.

The doctor gives me an obligatory pat on the head and, in doing so, notices Sally exists. He nods in her direction to show, despite everything he has just said in front of her, he is aware she is human. Job done he marches his troops out the door.

Sal, who looks even more frazzled and uncomfortable than when she first saw me, tries to change the mood by getting straight back to business.

'Now, Viv, I've read this book by the Tibetans,' she says, patting the hardcover, 'and it's very good as I am sure you know, so I am here to do my job and help you on your way.' Sal sounds like she is sending me off on a day's shopping.

As always, her timing is perfect, as everyone is starting to get bored with waiting for me to die. But instead of continuing, she walks quietly to the window, runs her hand along the curtains, adjusts a pot plant on the windowsill and inspects a painting on the wall before returning to sit down beside me.

'You, my very dear friend,' she whispers with an aching amount of effort, 'have lived a wondrous life. I don't know anyone else so funny who is such a dedicated mum and friend and I . . .' She pauses, regrouping. 'I definitely don't know anyone who has cared about me so much, or managed –' she chokes then clears her throat, 'to see through to everything . . . underneath.'

Her joyous eyes well with tears and my heart implodes.

'I know you,' she says, putting her hand on mine. 'And you probably think you have wasted your time and haven't done enough, but, Viv,' she says, her eyes intensifying, 'I need you to hear me now: that is not true. I love you, and Clint and Ethan love you, so, so much . . . and that's enough.'

I can't blink away the tears, so Sal wipes them for me.

'You have been more than a friend to me . . . you have been the only family I ever had,' she continues, drawing on the strength I love her for. 'So, if you need permission to let go and leave for somewhere way better than here, then you have it.'

She holds my gaze with so much love that, even if I could look away or be sarcastic or make a joke, for the first time in my life, I don't want to. She squeezes my hand then rests her head on my chest, and I know she is silently weeping.

After a few minutes she pulls herself together, sits back up with her Sally smile in place, gets to her feet and kisses me on the forehead. Without so much as a glance backwards, my gracious friend walks courageously out the door.

CHAPTER 48

Last drinks, last rites, last list

They have called last drinks. Every time I try to swallow now I choke, so my fine teacup has been replaced with a sponge for me to suck on. It reminds me of playing lick, sip, suck at tequila parties during my two-week-long university days. Back then, we were too smart for our own good, so it made sense to kill off as many brain cells as possible. I wonder how many brain cells Ethan will kill off once he is legally allowed to do so. I wonder if he will die of a diabetic sugar overdose once he is free to spend his entire week's earnings on whatever lollies he chooses. I wonder if when he gets married, he will really be in love. I wonder if he will remember to wear condoms. Shit, shit. I haven't made Ethan a list for when he grows up. I can't rely on the list-making abilities of some future generation Z girlfriend who may be asleep on the job.

I am suddenly wide awake. Marsha is on chair-sitting duty and instantly senses the change in my laidback approach to dying. She puts her hand up to me, and I start to squeeze it, and play charades. She has always been way more on my wavelength than Clint, so our games are a lot easier to play. Yesterday when Clint was on duty, I was still drinking from a cup and was desperately thirsty. I squeezed his hand, and the guessing game began.

'Toilet, you need to go to the toilet?' was his first guess.

No, Clint, I yelled in my head, *I am catheterised.*

'Do you want the nurse, are you in pain?'

For god's sake, Clint, I have a constant morphine fix, or haven't you been paying any attention at all to what's involved here?

'Ethan, do you want Ethan?'

I shook my head and gave him the look of death; he at least still understood that. He then proceeded to bring me the television remote, a magazine, my teacup and an extra blanket, then he moved the bed up and down, randomly got out my dressing-gown and slippers as if I were suddenly about to rise up like Jesus and walk, turned the lights on and then off, opened and closed the blinds, before finally getting me some water. If it had been up to him, I would have died of thirst.

Thankfully it only takes one squeeze of my hand and a stare in the right direction for Marsha to grab me a pen and paper. I have to write this list. I start attempting to scrawl out an R-rated list of advice for my future teenage son. Unfortunately, my hand is not doing anything it is meant to do. After about what feels like ten minutes, all I have managed to scribble out is something resembling the word sex. Marsha reads the word then looks up at me.

'Sex?' she asks. I blink my eyes for yes. 'After all this time.' She laughs. 'I thought you would never ask.'

I smile and look towards the photo she has put up of Ethan.

She nods at me and says, 'It's okay. Aunty Sugar is in charge of sex, drugs and rock and roll, and I'll make sure he gets at least as much of that as you and I combined.'

I roll my eyes, then she looks me square in the face and says, 'I've got this. I'll keep him safe and bring him home to you in one piece, Girl Guide's honour.'

I let go of the pen, and it rolls off the bed onto the floor. She folds my new list and shows me she is putting it straight into her wallet. I am already tired.

When I wake up, it is night-time again and the chair is empty. Clint must be walking the aisles. I think I am asleep now more than I am awake, but with the morphine, I am finding it harder and harder to tell the difference between the two. I have always wondered if my dreams are the reality and this crazy life with all its nonsensical cruelty and random acts of cleanliness is the dream. My hospital dreams aren't of flying, being a superstar or even deep philosophical insights. Instead, they are simple, wonderful visions where I am whole, still capable of drinking, chewing, swallowing and running to the toilet to empty my fully functioning bladder.

In my dreams, the hospital room is larger and there are enough chairs for everyone to sit on; no one is relegated to standing on sore, tired legs. There are two extra beds, one on either side of me, so when I wake in the middle of the night, I can reach out to touch Clint and Ethan and make sure they are still breathing.

I look out the window; the moon is full. My inner Chewbacca urges me to climb outside and run through the streets howling. I attempt to lift my head off the pillow, but it is full of cement, and my mouth is full of chalk. I try to reach out to buzz the night nurse to wet a sponge on my lips, but the morphine haze drifts back over me and the weight of my body pins my hand to my side and reality once again melts away.

CHAPTER 49

The end

It is five in the morning when I next wake. Clint is asleep in the chair beside me. He is holding the remote in his hand but has forgotten to turn the TV off. It is playing re-runs of cartoons I watched when I was a kid. I look out past the TV to a gap in the curtains where I can see a glimpse of a magnolia tree.

I can't remember the last time I took a breath. I feel my lungs struggle and rattle as I pull in what little fresh air there is in the room. I look down at Clint's hand, holding mine like it has done for the last ten years. He has always been there, holding my hand regardless of how much I have yelled at him or how annoying I have told him he is. My lungs rattle again, and I struggle to focus my eyes. I look up at the picture Catherine put up against my wishes when she came to visit, of us as kids playing in the pool. Next to it is a picture of Clint and me on our wedding day. A ray of the sun's first light squeezes through the blinds and shines on the photo of me holding Ethan on his first birthday. It is done. Clint wakes up, and his eyes are drawn straight to the TV screen just as the circle around Porky Pig starts to shrink. 'Th- th- th- that's all, folks.'

A note from the author

Over the past decade I have lost, on average, at least one close friend or family member every year. Not because I am careless, but because they have died. As a result, I have achieved quite the career boost, switching from wedding singer to funeral singer and, most recently, writing this novel.

Luckily, most of my dead friends left me with a sizeable inheritance via the gift of their fabulous senses of humour. Most notable among them was my dear friend Rebecka, who gave me the honour of being by her side until death did her part. Being a girl who loved to organise her life with a list, she was ecstatic she could organise her own funeral; I managed to talk her down from choosing some very inappropriate songs she thought would be hilarious, and she made me laugh as much as she made me cry. Needless to say, she helped me look at death differently.

While Beck's life was far from ordinary, she still had to deal with what she called 'life admin' right up to the end. I learnt a lot about the day-to-dayness of dying and how most of us mere mortals probably won't even be able to get out of the washing up when it comes time for us to shuffle off.

At its core, *The Very Last List of Vivian Walker* is about keeping your sense of humour at the worst of times. I hope you laughed, cried and fell in love with Vivian Walker as much as I did.

Megan X

Acknowledgements

I acknowledge the Bundjalung people on whose country this book was conceived and written. I am proud to be a Kalkadoon woman and stand with all First Nations people as we continue to strive for excellence and equity.

To my family and friends:

To my talented and patient husband, Marc, for mostly not being Clint even when I have been Viv. You have co-authored my life. Words are not enough. To Jackson for putting up with all the dead people in our house and being the best son a mama could hope for.

To my parents, Jocelyn and Michael, my siblings, Jo, Kris, Patrick and Donna, to my outlaws and my extended family – thanks for always being part of my cheer squad and teaching me how much fun a dysfunctional family can be.

To my hilarious, loving, intelligent, wonderful friends. Thank you for travelling with me on this crazy ride, some of you since kindy! You've watched me go from journo to muso to writer and back again. You've seen me move houses, move country and try to move mountains and you've never once told me I was crazy. There are too many of you to mention by name, but you know who you are – well, most of the time you do! Thanks for loving me so long and always making me laugh. To the Westies, the Gongies, the South Molles, the singing, writing, school, travel and uni buddies, the Wati's and Kungkas, the musos and band families, the journos, the craic-ing Irish, the Ballina-ites, and the community of Kunghur and Uki – thank you for being my rock, keeping me sane and not minding when I'm not. And to my *Deadly Vibe* brothas and sistas and Beck's friends and family, for walking down the hardest paths, yet still showing me how black black humour can get!

For help and advice I cannot thank enough:

My amazing writers group, Bryan, Holly, Jandra, Lisa, Sarah, Steph, Tamara and Tina, in alphabetical order of course. Thank you for your amazing input, advice, and for crying and laughing in all the right places. Not to mention the chai! I literally would never have written this book without you. Special thanks also to Matt for reigniting my passion for words.

This book would not have been possible without:

Fiona Johnson from Beyond Words Literary Agency, thank you for being my friend, agent and trusted advisor, and making Viv and her soundtrack possible.

Rebecka Darling-Darren (nee Delforce), my eternal thanks for your friendship and for not letting a little thing like death get in your way of having a publishing company. Hachette was the perfect choice – two Rebeccas!

The entire team at Hachette Australia and New Zealand. With special thanks to Rebecca Saunders for believing in me from day one – your editing insights have been invaluable. Thank you for not only championing the book but also my music – that meant a lot. Thank you also for leading my stellar team of editors – Rebecca Allen, Celine Kelly and Deonie Fiford, who all did an amazing job of polishing my debut to within an inch of my life. To Lee Moir, the quiet achiever. To Christa Moffitt for your fabulous design – I love my cover! To the entire publicity and marketing team at Hachette for the amazing work you have done promoting *The Very Last List of Vivian Walker*. To Fiona Hazard, it takes an inspired individual to lead such fabulous people. To Pam Dunne and Cindy MacDonald for your accuracy and much appreciated proofreading.

To Amanda from Rubi Creations for my gorgeous website. To Raffaella Dice for taking photos that make me look good.

To the CYA Conference for my first introduction to Hachette, via the lovely Sophie Hamley. I also wish to thank the Australian

Society of Authors for highly commending me for the 2020 Award Mentorship Program for Writers and Illustrators. To the judges of the 2020 Banjo Prize, thank you, it was such an honour to be shortlisted. To the Australian Independent Record Labels Association for supporting the soundtrack through the 2021/2022 Women in Music Mentor Program. To Emma Donovan for being such a deadly music mentor.

While the characters in this book are entirely fictional, thanks must still go to:

Thindy Bombombol, for being partly to blame for Marsha – thanks for your humour and feedback and never conceding defeat in the 'who is the funniest' competition, even after Beck was dead! To Coral for letting me use your nickname – you're funnier than Aunty Sugar – but you'll have to arm wrestle Beck and Thindy for the title. To Catherine for lending me your name. To Jane for the dishwasher advice. To Mili for your spiritual approach to everything, including the Thermomix. To Stephen for waxing your chest for Honduras. To Kaz for your sensible nursing advice and unsensible friendship. To Jackson for consulting on all things Pokémon. To Jackie, Karima and Emilie for being nothing like the therapist in this book.

To everyone behind the scenes:

For typesetting, printing, managing bookstores, selling books, delivering books, putting books into libraries, teaching children to read books and all the little and big things that help make the world a better-read place. Thank you.

To the teachers, coaches and creatives who inspire us all to follow our crazy dreams . . . And yes, that includes Tony Robbins. Particular thanks to Rachel Barnes for turning a real estate dream into a novel – you saw straight through me.

To anyone I have forgotten – thank you. You are still loved and important even if I am the opposite of an elephant and always forget.

hachette
AUSTRALIA

If you would like to find out more about Hachette Australia,
our authors, upcoming events and new releases, you can visit
our website or our social media channels:

hachette.com.au

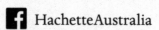 HachetteAustralia

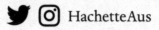 HachetteAus